brothers of paradise

RED HOT Rebel

olivia hayle

Copyright © 2021 Olivia Hayle

All rights reserved. No part of this publication may be distributed or transmitted without the prior consent of the publisher, except in case of brief quotations embodied in articles or reviews.

All characters and events depicted in this book are entirely fictitious. Any similarity to actual events or persons, living or dead, is purely coincidental.

The following story contains mature themes, strong language and explicit scenes, and is intended for mature readers.

Edited by Stephanie Parent
www.oliviahayle.com

EPIGRAPH

"We love because it's the only
true adventure in life."

— *Nikki Giovanni*

1
IVY

I look up at the giant Hamptons mansion with nothing but trepidation. It's the first time my modeling agency has sent me to do a live modeling gig. They're bizarre things. *Stand here and look pretty.* There's a reason I've always turned them down, but when Tina showed me the paycheck for this one, there was no refusing.

Melissa comes up beside me. "We're going home together?"

"Absolutely," I tell her. "Right after our shift is up. I have a portable charger in my bag, too."

"Good call." We'd been stranded at a shoot two months ago, both of our phones dead, with no way to contact an Uber.

We turn at the sound of high heels on the path behind us as the rest of the models join us. Some of them I recognize. Far from all these women share Melissa's and my... well, let's call it *dedication* to staying on the right side of the line. Throw around the word "model" and you'll get invited into a lot of exclusive areas. Places with expensive drinks and even more expensive drugs.

"Two years ago I was the face of a national jeans

campaign," Melissa mutters at my side. "Now I'm posing at a designer's party for all his friends."

I shoot her a smile. "It's three hours, and he's paying well."

"Thank God for that." She pulls her bag up on her shoulder and leads the way into the house, where a woman with a headset and a clipboard is waving us in. "Let's get this over with."

Ten minutes later, I'm smoothing my hand over a dress that barely covers my butt. Short, flimsy and colorful, it's part of the designer's spring and summer collection for this year.

"Time to move!" Clipboard-Lady calls out. One of the newer models from my agency, a girl I don't recognize, is struggling with the tiny clasps of her strappy heels.

I bend to do up the little clip. "Put them on looser than you need to," I advise her. "When you're walking a runway, you want straps like these to be tight. When you're standing or posing at a photoshoot, you want them loose, or they'll cut into your ankles when they get swollen."

She shoots me a shy smile. "Thank you."

"Anytime. I'm Ivy."

"Jordan," she says and falls into step beside me as we walk out of the pool-house-turned-dressing-room.

The house is stunning, with the turquoise water of the pool beckoning in the summer sun, and the open-air bar is fully stocked with liquor. The bartender watches us walk and grins in appreciation.

"Here, here, hurry," Clipboard-Lady says. She's clutching it tight to her chest. "I want the first four of you over here.... You, you, you, and you."

Melissa is in that group, ushered into the house. "You'll flank the entranceway—I'll see you in a second." She turns to the five of us remaining. "There are small x's put around the pool. Find one each."

And those are our only instructions.

I shoot Jordan a chagrined smile, like *the things we have to do,* and walk around the pool in search of an x marked by tape.

The one I find is on the back corner, close to a secluded area of the yard with lounge chairs. I suppose it won't be long until they're filled with guests.

"That's it!" Clipboard-Lady calls. "Stay there, and if you need refreshments or to use the bathroom, you can rotate back to the pool house."

Then she leaves us in a stomp of righteous agitation, off to solve another logistical puzzle to this Hamptons party.

The five of us look around at each other.

"Everyone put on sunblock?" I call.

That earns me a few laughs from the other models.

And then the boredom begins.

That's what I'd always feared with these live modeling gigs, the ones fancy companies, clubs or designers host.

I run my hand through my hair, ensure the dress is in place. And then I go through the parts of the human skeleton I need to memorize for my physical therapy test in two days.

The spine, made up of the cervical, thoracic and lumbar vertebrae, sacrum and coccyx. The sound of tropical beats starts soon thereafter, blasting from artfully placed speakers around the house and yard.

I keep going.

The pelvis, made up of the ilium, pubis and ischium.

The first guests arrive, walking out onto the patio in sunglasses and suits. I stick out a leg, put my hand on my hip, and make my expression carefully, beautifully bored.

I continue with my mental study session. It's something I've perfected over the years. Waiting backstage at shows, standing in line for castings… and all the while, I'd study in my head. First for my online bachelor's degree. It might have taken me five years to complete part-time, but I'd done it, while modeling paid the bills. It didn't hurt that the job had other perks too. The dress I'm wearing fits like it was made for me—and I'd heard it whispered amongst the models that the designer in question often gifted his samples to models.

I wouldn't mind taking this one home.

My gaze drifts over the sea of guests milling around the pool. Colorful drinks are in hand, or food from a catering table located somewhere inside the house. I see mini Beef Wellingtons. Oysters served on ice. Something that looks like chicken sliders.

My stomach rumbles loudly at the sight.

I press a hand to my side, making it look like a pose, and glance over to the guests sitting in the lounge chairs next to me. But they hadn't noticed.

It's a group of men in suits. Well, all except one. The man in the middle wears a linen button-down with the top button undone, a long leg thrown over the other. Worn, expensive boat shoes on his feet.

He's not speaking, but he's being spoken to—the others look to him.

He gazes at the man talking with an expression that's haughty disdain and cool indifference rolled into one. Everything about him screams *impress me*.

Then his gaze shifts to mine. A dark lock of hair falls over a tan forehead, the look in his eyes switching into *what do you want?*

I tear my gaze away.

It's unprofessional to stare. To be anything more than a living statue, a piece of art. I'm displaying the clothes, and that's all.

So I keep my gaze on the milling guests beyond, changing poses, sticking out my hip. And yet all my attention is on the group of men to my side.

If I strain my ears, I can just make out their conversation. I'm not a fly on the wall, I'm a model by the pool, but at events like this, there's really no difference.

"Australia is the right move," a man says. "We should have the place open before the year's end."

"Sydney?" another asks.

"Yes."

A deep humming sound.

"Skeptical, Rhys?" the first voice asks.

I dare a glance over.

The man who watched me is leaning forward now, hands braced on his knees. I'd wager he's about thirty.

"You know I am. You're making it too easy for people."

Another of the men laughs. "Yes, and god forbid anything be easy. Where did you just return from? The Andes?"

"Yes." A wild, taunting grin on his face. "You should try hiking sometime."

"No, thank you. I'll leave that to the customers."

The dark-haired man named Rhys gives a snort of disdain. "As if they'd leave a five-star resort."

"Some do. It's all part of the experience."

"The carefully packaged, curated experience, you mean." He leans back in his chair and turns his gaze back to mine, catching me eavesdropping. Our gazes lock.

Again.

"Can we help you with anything?" His raised voice isn't friendly, an eyebrow cocked in the same expression as earlier. Like he's skeptical of the world at large.

Crap.

"No." I toss my hair back. It's a vain move, but it's part of the role I'm playing tonight. "Sorry."

"Can't fault the woman for getting bored," one of his friends points out. He turns drink-glazed eyes on me, sweeping them up and down my form. It's a perusal I'm used to.

Doesn't make it any less uncomfortable.

"How long do you have to stand up there, sweetheart?"

I keep from gritting my teeth at his tone, at the epitaph. Acting professional is all I have to do.

"Until the end of the party," I say, waving a hand over my dress. "Showcasing the upcoming collection."

Well, that was a mistake.

All four of the men now look down at my minuscule dress, and I don't think it's to admire the intricacy of the pattern. Rhys leans back in the sofa, an arm outstretched along the back of it. He doesn't say a thing, even if he'd been the one to call me out on my staring.

"Are you allowed to drink?" one of his friends asks. "Are you even allowed to talk?"

I give them a polite smile. "There are refreshments for us in the back. They said nothing about talking, but I'm guessing it's not what they had in mind, no."

"I don't know how you do it. I'd be bored after a few minutes."

"You're bored with everything after a few minutes," Rhys drawls at him. "This isn't an exception."

Making my expression apologetic, I turn back to the crowd beyond. The sun is setting, and the pool reflects the glorious colors of the sky. Summer in the Hamptons, and all these rich people are enjoying themselves. I still haven't seen the designer, despite it being his party.

The men's conversation is hard to tune out, though.

"Harsh to hire models and not let them mingle with the guests. What's the point of having them here?"

"To look at, of course." Rhys's voice again. It's sardonic—like he hates the practice, or considers it beneath him.

"Hired eye-candy," another one responds. "Here to tempt us, but not to touch."

Okay.

Disgusting.

I glance over in time to see Rhys give a dismissive flick of his hand. "They're just models."

"Oh?" his friend asks, grinning. "I'm sorry, what was I thinking. They're obviously nothing that'd ever tempt *you*."

"That's right," Rhys confirms, ignoring the sarcasm. "After a lifetime of being around beautiful women, I'm immune."

"Well, I'm not. I like the look of the dark-haired one over there."

I know without looking that he's talking about Jordan on the other side of the pool. I grit my teeth and look back out at the crowd.

Their words shouldn't bother me. They're strangers. Rich, asshole strangers, but strangers nonetheless. And yet their comments slide like splinters beneath my skin.

"Ours is better," the fourth man responds. "Blonde, busty —and look at those legs."

It takes every ounce of self-control not to turn and glare. I'm standing *right here,* and they know I can hear them.

Which means they don't give a damn.

Privilege rises from them in waves, like a too-thick cologne, oozing from the tailored clothing and disdainful voices.

I can't wait until this party ends and I can return to the real world, *my* world, filled with cheap coffee, textbooks and gym sessions.

An edge of steel enters Rhys's voice when he speaks again. "They're just *models*. Air-headed and vain, here to do a job and then to leave."

My head whips around to glare at him. He ignores me, but the surrounding men don't. The two who'd commented on Jordan and me just laugh at my outrage.

"We have better things to discuss," Rhys continues. The tone brokers no future deliberation on the topic.

The men fall silent.

Anger curls in my stomach, sharper than before. Who does he think he is, to comment on our purported intelligence while he knows I can overhear?

A movement to my right. I turn my head in time to watch Jordan fall from her spot by the pool, and break the surface of the water.

She's not moving.

My reaction is borne from instinct. I dive off the edge and

break the surface of the cold water. The pool isn't large and I reach Jordan quickly, wrapping my arms around her.

She's limp in my arms. The flowy fabric of her dress is heavy, pulling her down, and she'd fallen into the deep end. I kick my legs against the weight of the water to keep us both afloat. Stunned guests look at us around the edge of the pool.

Nobody helps.

Strong arms brush against mine beneath the surface, wrapping around Jordan. She's pulled out of my grasp entirely.

Rhys comes into view. The man who'd disparaged me as vain and air-headed, his dark hair now plastered in unruly curls over his forehead. He moves in two strong, skilled strokes and then he's reached the stairs in the pool.

I swim after him, gaze locked on Jordan's face. She lolls against his shoulder.

"Jordan?" I kneel on the steps, half-submerged in water. "Jordan, wake up."

She blinks twice, and then coughs, struggling to sit. Rhys releases her but stays next to us in the water.

"Fainted," she whispers, and then breaks into a coughing fit that racks her body. I put an arm around her shoulders and look over at Rhys. He gazes back with serious intent, none of the snideness I'd seen earlier.

"Help me get her to the pool house," I tell him.

He doesn't respond, simply slides his arms around Jordan and lifts her straight out of the water. The crowd parts around us as he carries her toward the adjoining building.

I rush ahead, shaky from the adrenaline, the dress clinging like a second skin to my body. I pull open the door for him. "Put her on the couch."

Grabbing towels, I drape them over her and smooth her hair back from her forehead. She's starting to shake.

"Jordan? Are you okay?"

She nods, then closes her eyes. "I can't believe I fainted here."

"Lucky you fell into the pool," Rhys says. He's retreated, hands deep in the pockets of his wet chinos. The shirt clings to broad shoulders and forms droplets on the tan skin. "A fall on the stone would have been far worse."

Jordan glances at him, eyes wide. A realization dawns in them. "Tina is going to drop me," she whispers.

"She will do no such thing," I tell her firmly. "The agency wouldn't have sent you here if they didn't like your work."

"This is my first booking," she whispers.

And her fear makes sense, as does my sneaking suspicion that she fainted because she hadn't eaten, hadn't had enough to drink, and standing out there in the sun did her in.

I grit my teeth. "When was the last time you ate?"

The guilty look on her face is enough, even if she doesn't answer me.

"All right," I say, all my physical therapy and anatomy lessons kicking in. "You need to change into warm clothing. There are towels in the bathroom. Think you can do that?"

She nods, and I help her walk to the en suite. "Don't lock the door," I tell her. "I'll stand guard, but if you get the least bit dizzy, call out."

"I will," she whispers, pushing the door closed behind her.

I blow out a frustrated breath and run a hand through my now wet length of hair. Tina won't be happy about this, that much is true. The head of our modeling agency rules it with an iron fist. And every model I talk to who doesn't eat enough reminds me why I dislike this part-time industry of mine.

"You should change too," Rhys points out, nodding tactfully to my second-skin dress. A glance down reveals what I already know—my nipples are hard and visible through the fabric. Thank you, unheated pool.

I cross my arms over my chest. "You dove in after us."

He nods. "Of course."

"Thank you." The words come out through gritted teeth.

His words to his friends still ring in my head. *Vain. Air-headed. They're just models,* as if our profession and our identities are fused. I hate it when people do that.

His mouth quirks at a corner, like he's smiling at a joke only he's heard. "All right," he says. "Do you need anything else?"

Anything else? As if Jordan and I had asked for his help. "No thank you," I tell him. "We're just *models,* after all."

He runs a hand through his wet hair, smile widening on his face. "That's right."

Completely unashamed.

The sight of that smile is so disarming that I take a few steps back, caught off guard. The steady dripping of water from my hair echoes in the room.

"I should change."

"Of course." He turns to leave, but pauses with a hand on the door out of the pool house. "You had quick reflexes earlier."

The words are spoken like it's the greatest of compliments.

"Uh... yes."

A single nod of his head, and then he disappears, the door closing behind him. When Jordan and I emerge later, there's an overflowing plate of food pilfered from the catering table waiting outside. But the man who'd left it is long gone.

2

RHYS

Two weeks later

"It's been a long time since we've made a bet like this," I comment, following Ben down the hallways of his luxury travel agency. He'd been tired of me complaining about how all the commercial stuff was beneath me. *You think you can shoot my next travel campaign better than a marketing agency?*

There had been only one answer to that.

Of course I can.

Ben chuckles. "A decade, perhaps more."

"Remind me to stop going out with you," I tell him, "or I'll keep bargaining weeks of my life away."

"Admit it. You love the challenge."

I don't answer. I look at the framed, glossy pictures that line the walls of his agency instead. Highly edited. Oversaturated. Beautiful beaches and turquoise, mirror-like water. It's easy. Basic.

Anyone can photograph beautiful environments and make them look, well, beautiful. Point and shoot. All you need is an iPhone, for Christ's sake. Where's the art?

"*This* is what you want me to shoot?"

Ben slaps a hand on my shoulder, even if he has to reach up to do it. His shit-eating grin is obnoxious. "Yes. Doubting your talents?"

"No. And my pictures won't look anything like this asinine shit." I point to a picture where a coconut has been placed in white sand, photographed up close with the ocean in the background. "Prepare yourself for a masterpiece."

As much as I don't travel like Ben's clients, I understand them intimately. They're my parents. They're my siblings. They're the people I grew up with, the people I meet through my job.

I know what they want.

"I'm ready," he says. "Just remember that it's a marketing campaign. It's not going to hang in the Louvre."

"Oh, I haven't forgotten."

"You'll receive the same brief as the marketing agency we've hired."

"Sounds fair."

"Your itineraries are planned in reverse, so you'll never be at the same resort together." He shoots me a wide grin. "I've never had two contractors race against one another like this."

"Exciting?"

"I might make it standard practice."

"And the best marketing campaign wins the bet," I confirm.

"Yes. We'll take an internal vote, me, my CFO, my head of PR."

I roll my neck, work out the kinks. "Perfect."

"Our shoot director will email you lists of some specific shots we need, some inspiration, what we're expecting. But for the rest? You have free rein, just like you asked for. We're not sending a stylist or assistant with you."

"I don't want either of them," I comment. The part of me raised by my politer-than-life mother urges me to say thank you. But this is just a bet to the two of us, and money isn't an issue.

And I was never good at following my mother's rules regarding etiquette.

"The representative from the modeling agency is here, too, together with the model we chose." There's smug anticipation in his voice. "Ready to meet your partner in crime?"

"If I must."

He rolls his eyes at me. "Try looking a little less tortured, will you? You're getting to stay at all of my best resorts, and you're traveling with a drop-dead-gorgeous woman."

My grin is crooked. "When you put it that way..."

"Just remember to get the campaign wrapped before you cross any lines."

"I would never."

"Never my ass," he scoffs. "You might consider all of this beneath you, but I know you. You've dated models before. Who was the last one?"

"I don't kiss and tell," I say. In truth, I don't know which one he's referring to—Ben's information can't be up to date. I enjoy women and women enjoy me. It's always consensual, it's always brief, and it's always honest.

"The woman we chose is damn good. Sinfully sweet, you know? High-end look, but still approachable. Fierce, but would help a friend out in a pinch. Could be a good new face of Rieler Travels."

"I thought you wanted the locations to be the face of Rieler Travels."

"Have I ever told you how annoying I find you?"

"Regularly, yes."

We turn down a corridor, passing office after office. Corporate prisons. I'd trade one of those for the beaches in the oversaturated pictures in a heartbeat.

Ben grins, hand on the door to the conference room. "The model? She's someone... how do I put this? She's the kind of person who'd dive straight in to help a friend."

My eyes narrow. "Ben, what did you do?"

He doesn't respond, just pushes the door open to reveal a

conference room, beige walls, colorful art on the walls. A testament to Rieler's luxury clientele. And seated at the table, flanked by two middle-aged women, is his latest practical joke.

It's the blonde model from the Hamptons party, the one who'd looked at me with such disdain. The one who'd shivered after her dip in the pool in that tiny dress.

Fucking hell.

Ben handles the introductions, transformed into the picture of professionalism. If you hadn't seen him drunk at two a.m. in New York clubs, like I have, you'd doubt he's ever anything else.

"This is Rhys Marchand." He introduces me with a flourish, but I can hear the glee in his voice. "He's the photographer hired to shoot this campaign."

"Delighted. I'm Tina." A dark-haired woman extends her hand to me, her hair cut in a no-nonsense bob and a calculating look in her eyes. From Star Model Management, apparently. We shake hands.

I extend my hand to the familiar model next to her. Her blonde hair is pulled back from a face made for the camera, flushed and agitated. The eyes locked on mine are filled with more than simple dismay. Not alarm, exactly. Anger? Distaste?

Then her own professionalism kicks in and she grasps my hand. "Ivy Hart," she says. "It's a pleasure."

I grip her hand tight. "I'm sure it is."

Her eyes flash, but there's nothing she can say, not in front of everyone.

I grab a seat across from her and turn my attention to Ben and the shoot director, giving her absolutely none.

So her name is Ivy.

Ben must have contacted the designer from the party, learned the name of the agency. Hunted her down somehow and hired her to spite me. It's just his sense of humor.

My hand curls into a fist on the table.

I'd expected some vapid girl who'd want to party in every location we'd visit. Someone I'd spend as little time as possible with.

But no. It has to be the honey-blonde knockout I'd insulted in an effort to shut Ben's inane friends up.

"This is your itinerary." The shoot director pulls up a list on a giant screen, his over-styled hair like a helmet on his head. It doesn't move when he turns.

And I'm to take direction from him?

"You'll start in our Caribbean resort and end in our newest hotel in Sydney, Australia, still under construction. That'll be fifteen days solid of traveling and shooting. We know it'll be grueling, so we've put in a few rest days here and there."

Ben winks at me.

I shake my head at him.

"Star Models will provide all the clothes for Ivy. They'll be clearly marked for each day and each shoot for you."

"I've been briefed," Ivy says. She's composed herself into the picture of calm professionalism, but there's a note of annoyance in her voice.

Yeah, I'm not happy about this either.

"Rieler will be in charge of all the logistics. You'll have contact personnel at each location; they'll be the ones to pick you up at the airports, drop-offs, arranging transportation to locations where you might want to shoot. Suggestions will be available at each place for you, Rhys."

I tip my head in a shallow nod. I'll find my own shot locations.

Helmet-Hair swallows and continues. "As you've both been briefed, I'm sure, we're looking for both pictures and moving images. Filming clips that can be used for a travel video. On this note, I was informed that Rhys would handle all that, as well?"

It's unusual as hell, that Ben is giving me this much leeway. "I will," I say.

And despite Ivy's presence, the challenge burns in my veins. I can see the shots I want to film already. One of my drones is packed, set to take aerial shots of locations.

"Excellent. We'll be here all the time if you have any questions. Just a phone call away. You can never ask us enough questions." Helmet-Hair laughs to soften the blow of his words. He's not sure about this at all—nor, I'm guessing, is Rieler's creative team. Hiring *two* marketing teams is unusual.

Even more so when one is the owner's friend.

Ivy is the one who thanks him. "We appreciate that," she says smoothly. "Thank you for your detailed itinerary and all the suggestions on locations, shoots and angles. It's very appreciated, and we'll remain in contact throughout."

Helmet-Hair blinks twice, dazed.

Ivy smiles wider, confident in her ability to dazzle.

My jaw works. I don't need or want her to speak for me.

The rest of the meeting is formalities and paperwork and repetition of the word *collaboration*. This is a collaboration. How many times did it need to be said for them to beat me over the head with it?

Ben is the one who stands, stretching his legs. "I think we've hammered out all the details we can here. How about we leave Rhys and Ivy to get better acquainted and I'll show you some of Rieler's newer projects?"

And just like that, I'm left alone in the now claustrophobic conference room with a model staring daggers at me.

I cross my arms over my chest, leaning against one of the walls of the corporate bastion. "Nice to see you're allowed to talk today."

There. That's a good ice-breaker.

Ivy's eyes narrow. "The travel agency couldn't find a more qualified photographer to hire?"

It's cute she thinks that would hurt me.

So she doesn't know about the bet, nor the two marketing teams… or the fact that we're the B team.

"I suppose they couldn't," I respond. "Just like the modeling agency didn't have someone better to send?"

Her eyes flash. It does nothing to mar her beauty. The woman could be screaming in anger and she'd still be photogenic. It's a nauseating level of perfection. And like the artificially enhanced images on the walls, it feels like a mirage.

"I've already thanked you for diving into the pool to help."

"I know you have."

A muscle works in her jaw, like she wants to say something but knows she shouldn't. "I'm surprised you even accepted this project," she says. "Must be unbearable for you to work with a model for fifteen days, considering your low opinion of the profession."

A spark of amusement at her words. She gives as good as she gets, this woman. "Thanks for the concern," I tell her. "I think I'll manage, though."

She swipes up a hardbound book from the table and clutches it to her chest. Her portfolio? "Good, because I'm committed to holding up my end of this *collaboration.*"

"Good."

"Great."

"*Excellent,*" I say, glancing from her to a picture of a smoothie bowl against a Bali sunset. This is beyond childish.

Her voice is collected again. "We don't have to like each other to do this job. We just have to be professional," she says.

Right. Because photography never includes a measure of trust. I run a hand through my hair, cursing at how easily this woman has managed to goad me.

If I'm going to pull this bet off, I need to find a way to get onto her good side.

"I'll be professional." I grab one of the printed itineraries from the table, reading from the top as I make my way to the door. "I'll see you next week at three thirty at the Diplomatic Hotel in St. Barts."

She narrows her eyes at me. "I'll see you there."

I wake to blinding lights through my windows, New York's sun not the least bit diminished by the construction outside. A pounding headache, too, courtesy of Ben's insistence that we share celebratory drinks last night. As if spending the last weekend in the Hamptons with him hadn't been enough.

I prefer him in small doses, like I do with most everyone. Anyone becomes grating in large quantities, and that includes myself.

I drag myself out of bed and walk through my apartment. Stacks of books line the wall to my office. Manuscripts, potential projects. Brew a cup of coffee as I sort through the emails in my phone. A few from one of my editors, excited about the latest photography book we're publishing. Running a small publishing company isn't as much of a one-man show as my family likes to think.

My hand stops over an email from Ben.

We'd just been out last night.

But my scrolling stops as I read the headline. ***Ivy Hart's contact details.***

And it comes back to me. The conversation we'd had, the anger in her dark-blue eyes. The challenge I'd looked forward to has become something genuinely challenging.

I run a hand over my face and head into the living room. Pause in front of the display cabinet where I keep my cameras.

The gritty, old Canon is at the top. My favorite.

My gaze shifts from the camera that promises gritty authenticity to the shiny one I keep on the shelf below. I'm going to have to use this one to shoot Ben's campaign in all its high-quality glory.

But I reach toward the old Canon DSLR just in case.

I'll have to clear my schedule for the coming two weeks to shoot his campaign, but the alternative is reneging on a bet, and my pride would snap rather than bend. I turn one of my cameras around in my hands. Besides, it's been a while since I was pushed out of my comfort zone. This'll be another adventure.

Meeting people that have real lives and real problems, and not the kind who attend Hamptons parties in the summer. A party where someone hired models just to lounge around. The sheer vanity of such a thing.

What's more, the inaction of all those high-flying guests when a woman had fallen into the pool, when her friend had been struggling to help her... disgusting. They'd all probably been too afraid to ruin their hair and dress and makeup.

Ivy had been so angry at me. It had been there in her eyes as she'd glared at me, first after I'd tried to turn the men's attention away from the models, and then again in the pool house. Facing me like a queen, even as the thin, soaked fabric she wore made her look naked.

I put my camera back in the cabinet and close the doors to protect them from dust. Two weeks traveling and shooting a campaign is just what I need. Dirt on my hands and languages I don't speak.

My phone rings. I debate letting it go to voice mail, but a quick glance at the name changes my mind. "Hi, Lily."

My little sister's voice is cheerful. "Good morning. Did you sleep well?"

"Why do you want to know?"

"Instantly suspicious," she chides me. "I might not be calling because I want something."

"When you ask about my well-being," I point out, "you always want something. I've known you for... twenty-nine years."

A soft gurgling sound, and then a childish chuckle. Lily makes a cooing sound. "There, there. Jamie wants to say hi," she says.

"Hi, bud."

My nephew's happy little voice rings out, more babble

than words. I make out what sounds like *row row row,* and when I point it out, Lily laughs.

"We've been singing a lot of 'Row Your Boat,'" she explains. "Hayden is keen on getting started on Jamie's sailing."

"Good man," I say. He'll have three uncles who'll instill the very same thing.

"Are you coming back to Paradise soon?"

I run a hand through my hair. Summer is the best season for Paradise Shores, and the pull from my hometown is never stronger than now. But I have plenty of practice resisting the siren's call.

"I'm going away for a few weeks, actually."

"You are?"

"Shooting a campaign for a travel company. I can send you the itinerary."

"Please," she begs. "I spend all my time at home or in the gallery, and always with a toddler in my grip."

"You can live vicariously through me."

"Thank you," she says. "You won't miss Dad's seventieth party, will you?"

I close my eyes. "I'll likely be away."

"Rhys…" she says. There's no censure in her voice, just kind concern.

"You know I hate those things. It'll be all status, no substance."

Not to mention it's an event celebrating my dad, who I haven't wanted to exalt in over a decade.

"Don't come for him," she responds. "Come for us. For the family. You know we'd love spending time with you. And hey, Jamie always wants to see his uncle."

"Lily, stop with the guilt."

"Fine," she responds. "I'll just find a different tactic."

"That's what I'm afraid of."

"At least think about it, okay? You know the seaside

cottage is empty. Stay for a week. Stay for a month. Stay forever."

"I'll think about it."

"That's all I ask," she says. "I miss you."

I close my eyes. "Yeah, Lils. I miss you too."

But as we hang up, and as the guilt she'd tried to instill sinks it's claws deeper into me, I already know I'm not going to that party. I have a campaign to shoot, a model to argue with, and adventures to embark on. And solving the drift between my father and me is not one of them.

3

IVY

Penny looks up from the giant, oversized, pre-packed suitcase to me. *"Please,"* she says.

"Absolutely not. The clothes in that one are steamed and prepped and if we take anything out, there's no way it'll fit again."

My little sister runs her fingers over a piece of deep red silk. A dress? A shirt? I have no idea—and I'm not bound to find out until I'm in each location, struggling to find the correct outfit labelled *Singapore, day two.*

"I think I can fit in here," Penny says. "I'm actually pretty sure I can."

Laughing, I grab one of the pairs of jeans I'm packing into my personal suitcase and lob it at her head. She disappears in a huff, stretching out on my fluffy living-room carpet. "There's no way foreign countries would let you in. You're too big of a threat."

She pokes her head up, blonde curls in every direction. *"Me?"*

"Yes. You'd be the one to finally knock over the leaning tower of Pisa. The Sphinx would lose *another* of its appendages if you come near."

Penny sits up with a huff, but she's grinning. "I'm not that clumsy."

"Sure you're not. Everyone breaks as many bones as you do."

She lobs my jeans back at me and I catch them soundly, folding them up into a tight roll. I'm trying to pack for this monster of a trip like a pro. I've watched YouTube videos—I've ordered packing cubes on Amazon—there's no way my suitcase will turn into a writhing heap of fabric by day two.

One can hope, at least.

Penny clears her throat and continues to read from the itinerary. "Paris. Rome. Singapore. Bali. Sydney—Ivy, you're going to *Australia!*"

I look up from my careful roll stacking. "I know. Can you believe it?"

"No! You have to take pictures of everything."

"That's sort of my job." But I grin at her as I say it. "I'll buy you stuff, too. Treats from every destination."

"God, that sounds so *glamorous*. But you know what my favorite thing is?"

I smile. "That you get to live through me?"

"Well, yes, but what else?"

"What?"

"It says you'll be shooting with foreign models, too. In Rome." Her eyes grow to two round saucers. "You know what that means. Some hot, Italian model will be feeding you pasta and wine in a cute little *ristorante*."

"I doubt it'll be like that." And then, because I can't keep up my big sister facade anymore, I squeal with her. "But I know. Imagine if it is! Rome! I can't believe I'm getting to go to all these places. Penny, what am I going to do with myself!"

She grabs my hands and swings me around. Hard to do, in my tiny Manhattan apartment, but it works. "You *have* to get with some of them. With one of them, at least. This is the chance of a lifetime!"

I laugh at her. "That would be beyond unprofessional."

"Unprofessional? You're leaving the country the next day! Besides, you *never* tell me about guys."

My laughter turns a tad strained, and I pop her on the nose. "Not everything is fit for your ears." And, most importantly, I had no stories to tell. None at all, and over the years, that had become embarrassing in and of itself.

Penny rolls her eyes. "Right. As if I don't tell you every embarrassing story about Jason? Pfft." She sinks back down on my couch, fishing out a pair of beautiful shoes from the do-not-touch suitcase sent by my agency.

"Dolce & Gabbana heels," she sighs. "Ivy, why don't I have your life?"

"Because you're infinitely smarter than me."

She stretches out on the couch and closes her eyes, so I resume packing. What do you need to visit seven different countries? I'll be in agency clothes most of the time, but for the rest... Gah. I had never even left the country before.

"I'm going to enjoy staying here while you're gone," she muses. "Jason will come up one weekend, too. He's promised to take me out to Broadway."

"Good." I reach for my sneakers and stuff them in a plastic bag for traveling. "What did Dad say?"

"Oh, you know. That I should be careful in the big city. That I shouldn't get any ideas about following Ivy's career path. The usual."

Penny's voice is cheery, so I try to match that. Dad has never been pleased about my choice to model. I grab the pile of physical therapy textbooks I've sorted out. Three should be enough to occupy me on the long flights, although they weigh the same as a toddler.

"You're really bringing those?" Penny asks. "Ivy, you'll be in the most beautiful, exotic places, with hot foreign models. You can't seriously be trying to study at the same time."

"I have to. There's an exam a few weeks after I get back," I say, fitting book after book into my tightly packed suitcase.

"But don't worry. I plan on enjoying every single moment as well. I've already started writing a list—" Penny groans, but I barrel on, "with all the things I can't miss in every destination. Eat a croissant in France, go to the Colosseum in Rome. Take a picture with the Trevi Fountain."

"Thank God you put that on a list!" Penny says dramatically. "You might have forgotten!"

"*Exactly,*" I say. "Plus, I was imagining myself doing all of these things as I wrote the list. Visualization, you know."

"You have to add being kissed in Paris."

"What?"

"It's the city of love, Ivy!"

I laugh, shaking my head at her. "Who would I even kiss?"

"A mysterious Frenchman?" Penny asks. "And didn't you meet the photographer a few days back? How was he?"

I close my suitcase with a loud, plastic *snap*.

"Ouch. That bad? He's not some old creep, is he?"

"He's not. He's just someone I don't like."

"You like everyone," Penny says. "What's his name? Let me Google."

"He's not that famous," I say. "I don't even know why he was chosen. Had no idea he was a photographer until a few days ago."

"That sounds sketchy."

"Yes, but it doesn't surprise me. He has the kind of arrogance, you know? Photographers nearly always do." Too much, actually. More than their fair share. I frown to myself as I see Rhys in front of me, dark curls, sardonic smile, hard glint in his eyes. Traveling with a cynic who found me airheaded.

Awesome.

"So why do you dislike him, then?" Penny flops over on her stomach and stares longingly at the Dolce & Gabbana heels, now placed on the floor in front of her.

"It's like I dislike him because he dislikes me. From the

first time I saw him, it's like I've rubbed him the wrong way. Like my very presence offends him. He thinks models are vain, by the way." I pause, looking out the window. The summer heat has just begun hitting New York, a tropical assault. "I know exactly how the men he's friends with think. They never have to work for *anything,* you know? They'll spend five hundred dollars on a bottle of champagne and laugh it off with a self-deprecating joke about how they're stimulating the economy. Doing their part. And he dislikes models on principle."

"Mhm," Penny says. "Sounds like you've thought about this a lot."

"I haven't, really."

"And is he attractive?"

"Conventionally speaking, yes, I suppose." Though the word *conventional* could never really be attached to Rhys Marchand. I suspect he would buck under the word, indignant and angry at ever being called something so basic. The thought makes me smile.

"Right," Penny says, "you're in trouble. He's attractive and he's a challenge for you."

I put down my handbag. "I'm *not* in trouble."

"Of course you are. Tell me, when was the last time a guy was ever truly a challenge for you?" My little sister grins like a cat who's just eaten a particularly juicy canary. "When they didn't just barrage you with demands for your phone number? When they outright challenged you?"

I frown at her. "Toothpaste. I've forgotten to pack toothpaste."

Her voice reaches me easily in my small bathroom. Everything in this apartment is small. Square feet is an endangered species in Manhattan. "The last time was never!" she says. "They're always asking you out or judging you on your looks and you *hate* it, Ivy. You also hate when someone is angry at you or doesn't like you. Ipso facto, this photographer is like your specially designed kryptonite. A man who doesn't immediately swoon. You're in trouble."

"You're being ridiculous. Can you imagine how unprofessional that would be?" I force my suitcase open to fit my toothpaste inside. "Not to mention *I* don't like *him*. He's an overgrown trust fund brat. I've seen my fair share of them."

"Mhm."

"Give me a little credit, Penny. Getting with a photographer would be beyond irresponsible."

"But wouldn't it be romantic?"

I shoulder my suitcase over to the door. It's tiny in comparison to the gigantic Samsonite the agency sent over with all of my outfits. "What time is it?"

"A quarter to nine."

"The car should be here in ten minutes." I give my handbag a last check—wallet, passport, keys. "I'm going to miss you."

Penny bounds up off the sofa and wraps me in a hug. Her hair smells like it always has, papaya and coconut. She's used the same shampoo since she was fourteen. "Have the *best* time," she tells me. "This is a once-in-a-lifetime trip."

"I'm going to enjoy every minute," I promise.

"Good. And don't let a spoiled photographer or dear Dad get into your head." She pulls back, grinning. "Or me. I'll be here, protecting your apartment for you."

"That makes me feel so safe." But I'm smiling too, ruffling her hair. She ducks under my hand and grabs a hold of the Megalodon of a suitcase.

"I'll help you bring all this stuff down. And you're really traveling alone? They're not sending someone with you?"

"No, just me and the photographer. But there will be ground staff in each location."

She lifts the giant into the elevator with a huff. "This is a workout, Ivy."

"Workout clothes. Did I pack that?"

"Yes, I saw you roll it up all neatly."

"You're sure?"

"Yes." Penny winks. "But you can work out in other ways. Hot foreign models, hot challenging photographers…"

I shove her and she shoves me back. But she stays on the sidewalk as I step into the black Town Car waiting outside, waving to me as it speeds away toward JFK. Away from Manhattan and the life I've led, from the only country I know.

The photographer might not like me, but I'm not going to let him take away a single minute of enjoyment from this trip.

4
IVY

"Ivy Hart?" The man asking is in a suit, a black cap on his head and an electronic sign in hand. And on it, my name is written in capital letters.

I've only been traveling for six hours, but it's already exceeded all of my expectations. Rieler Travels has gone all out. Business class seating on the plane—I did *not* know you got as much champagne as you wanted—and someone to pick me up? Never had my in-country travel in America been like this, not on any of the shoots I'd attended in Los Angeles.

"That's me."

He reaches for my bags. "Welcome to St. Barts, miss. Or is it Mrs.?"

"No, just miss." I glance over my shoulder for Rhys, as if he might magically appear out of thin air. Wouldn't surprise me if he could, but he's nowhere to be seen. Hadn't been on the flight, either.

"Is this your first time here?" The name on the tag reads Étienne. He speaks with a thick French accent. I'd been reading up on the plane, and now I know absolutely everything there is to know about St. Barts, from its time as a Swedish colony to its incorporation as an overseas territory of France.

"Yes, it is. I'm very excited."

His smile widens. "Why, I get to play tour guide too! My favorite role."

Warm, humid heat hits me the second we step out of the air-conditioned airport, but it's not overwhelming. The parking lot is tiny, just like the airport is tiny. Because this island is tiny.

Étienne drives to the other side of the island, as he says, but it takes no time at all. He tells me stories throughout, of the island's cultural makeup, of the French and Portuguese who inhabit it. My eyes are glued to the passing landscape of green hills and glimpses of blue water. At one point I consider rolling down my car window, but think better of it when I realize I'll be sitting with my head out like a dog.

"Here we are!" Étienne slows to a crawl as we arrive at Rieler Resort. The road is lined with palm trees, and beyond them, a sliver of beautiful turquoise water glistens.

I can't believe I'm here!

Étienne parks outside of a beautiful villa with a straw roof and begins unloading my large suitcases. "Right through there," he says with a nod to the reception. "They've been expecting you."

And so they have. Attentive staff help me with everything, from checking in to rolling in my luggage to showing me the way to my room.

Although I can't really call it a room. It's a poolside *and* oceanside villa, one on either side, with the largest king-size bed I've ever seen. Perhaps this life is normal for really high-end models, but not for most of us. Work is usually shooting in warehouses in Brooklyn or changing backstage for shoots while stylists scream at you for buttoning a shirt wrong. This kind of glamour, on the other hand...

I throw myself on the bed. It's like floating on a cloud.

I let myself float for a solid five minutes before I bounce back off and head to the double doors that open up to my own private patio. The itinerary is clear. We're not to start shooting until one of the local staff knocks on my door for hair and makeup. So I'll stay put. It's not a particularly hard place to be.

I'm taking pictures of the view for my sister when there's an impatient knock on the door to my villa. "Be right there!"

Reaching up to tug my ponytail into place, I pull open the door with a smile.

It dies when I see the person on the other side. Rhys is in a button-down and slacks, a camera in one hand and a scowl on his face. Judging from the tan that dusts his skin, he's been here for a while already. When did he arrive?

"Good," he says. "You're finally here."

I cross my arms over my chest. "I arrived right on schedule."

"Come on, then. Let's go shoot." He takes a step back and nods toward the beach, like I'm to follow him right here and right now. Dressed in jeans. With my hair undone.

"I can't shoot like this," I tell him. "Besides, the itinerary clearly says that we're to start in an hour and a half. I have hair and makeup first."

The bastard actually looks up at the sky, like I'm being impossibly difficult. "The light is excellent right now," he says slowly. "I'd like to shoot now."

"All right. Perhaps you can shoot scenery? But for our shoot together, I'm sticking to the schedule." If there's one thing I've learned in my years of modeling, it's that you don't disobey orders regarding a shoot. "There is no way Rieler Travels wants me photographed like *this*. I'm not even wearing makeup."

Rhys pushes a hand through his dark hair and mutters something that sounds very much like *vain models*. Right, buddy, as if you're a peach.

"It's my job," I grind out. "So I'll see you in… an hour and a half for our scheduled shoot to begin."

"Fine," he says.

"Fine," I repeat.

"I'll be by the beach. Come on down when you feel inclined to work." And on that scathing note he strides off, down from my villa and toward the glittering ocean beyond. I force my fists to relax at my sides and to *not* scream at him that the entire island is a damn beach and how the hell am I supposed to find him?

So he thinks this is beneath him? Doubting my abilities, too, surely.

Well, he'll see about that.

Ninety minutes later I'm done, dressed in the first of several bikinis the agency had packed, a wide straw hat on my head. My hair is washed and blown out in soft, beachy waves. I give myself a quick once-over in the mirror and feel the familiar flares of self-consciousness. There's not a model in the industry that doesn't have the same thoughts, and they're always magnified ten times over when it's a swimwear shoot.

But I've done my damnedest not to fall into the same pit. I look good. I look strong. The bikini fits well—my agency knows my sizes to a T—and the spray tan they'd made me get is natural. I look good and I refuse to let my job make me doubt that.

I repeat it again. *You look good.*

And then I stride down the walkway to the beach in search of a photographer I don't have a shred of trust for. I've been photographed by strangers. By photographers that barely spoke English, that I didn't understand or connect with.

Somehow, though, I have a suspicion that Rhys will be different.

He's staring at the ocean when I spot him. The beach is deserted—I wonder if that's the hotel's doing. Had they cleared it out for our shoot? Looking down, I make sure that my bikini top is still sitting correctly. It is.

And then I clear my throat. "Ready to work?"

Rhys turns, an eyebrow raised and mouth open to deliver

a retort. But none comes out. For a magical second, he falters, his gaze taking me in. It's the briefest of victories, but it's there.

But his face soon snaps back into the usual mask of cynical nonchalance. "Finally," he says. "I want to start with you walking along the water's edge."

"Challenging," I say, putting down my water bottle on a nearby table. "From here to there?"

"Yes. I'll film you walking from behind, panning out to the resort."

And so I walk. Over and over and over again, the water lapping warmly around my ankles. Rhys doesn't say a thing. I've had silent photographers before, but they've never been this silent. It's like he's trying to unnerve me.

"Now walk toward me."

We switch, and go over that a fair number of times. It's not hard—looking out at the horizon, clutching at my hat, kicking at the lapping water. We do it with his drone, we do it with his camera, over and over and over again. Is he a perfectionist?

I pose on one of the lounge chairs, my legs crossed over, lowering the hat so that it covers my face entirely. He dislikes that pose, though, telling me to change after only a few takes. "You look too…" He frowns. "Posed."

I grit my teeth and try to look more natural. Like I'm just sitting here. Ignoring the angles I know I look best in is difficult.

"Look back at me, yes, like that."

I do what he says, but what comes over me then, well… I look straight into the lens—into Rhys's eyes—and lean back on the chair with my arms bent. It's a provocative pose, and he keeps snapping. Slowly, I twist around onto my stomach, my head on my hands.

He'd insulted my dedication earlier.

Well, let him watch me work.

And work we do. It's endless suggestions, poses, *stand*

there and *stand here.* I accept a drink from one of the staff in about a thousand different variations that I never get to taste.

The sun is just beginning to set when he lowers the camera. "Getting tired?"

"No." *Not that I would ever admit that to* you.

His lip curls. "Good. The sun is about to set this sky on fire."

I stand, dusting off a bit of sand from my legs. "Where do you want me?"

"Why don't you show me what you've got?"

I can't raise just one eyebrow like he can, but I do my best to smirk. "Is this a test?"

"No. It's me asking you to do your job."

Asshole. "And I have free rein?"

"Yes."

He wants me to fail. We've already shot practically everything on this beach, from every possible angle. I've done everything there is to do.

Well.

Not everything.

I've long since tossed the straw hat to the side. Walking down the warm, white sand, I step past the waterline. Warm water laps at my feet. It feels like a crime to be on this beautiful beach with the entire Caribbean stretched out in front of us and *not* swim.

I look back at him, standing in knee-deep water with the blazing sky behind me.

Rhys looks back at me. And slowly, almost reluctantly, he lifts up his camera.

These poses come effortlessly. Reaching down to feel the water, turning to beckon to someone on the beach, looking up at the beautiful sky. And with each step I'm deeper in the water. It laps around me like a blanket of warmth.

I dip my head back and wet my hair entirely. It drips down my back as I emerge, grinning, the sky now a marvelous mixture of purples and oranges above me.

Rhys takes another picture.

I swim toward him on the beach, and when I get to the shoreline, I don't get up. I lie on my stomach instead, my head on my hands, and look at him like he's the best thing that's ever happened. The only thing I've ever wanted in life.

Rhys falters, finger on the shutter.

And then he sinks down to his knees and keeps shooting. I close my eyes and lie like that for a moment. The photographer dislikes me, and yet this is the best shoot I've ever done. I'm on a beach in the Caribbean. Nothing else comes close.

When I open my eyes, Rhys has moved back, still snapping pictures. He lowers the camera when he sees me watching him again.

For a long moment, neither of us speaks.

"The sun is almost gone," he says finally. "No more light."

I don't want to get out of this water. I don't want to leave this island. "Okay."

He looks down at his camera and puts the lens cover back on. There's no way he's going to admit that I *did* bring it, but the nonchalant way he says the next words still feels like victory. "I suppose we should eat something."

I get up reluctantly, the warmth of the water dripping away into a slight chill. Dismissing him like he's been dismissing me feels fantastic. "I have plans," I say, thinking about the pool outside my patio, room service and the FaceTime call I promised my sister. "But thank you."

And then I march straight past him.

5

IVY

Rhys is waiting in the lobby the next day, arms across his chest. Admiring him is difficult, because it has to be when he's not looking, which means I now have the perfect opportunity. He's tall. A lot of men are, but when you're as tall as me, the number who make you look up are vanishingly small. He's one of them.

And he moves like the world is one big personal insult. Or perhaps like *he's* the insult, constantly saying screw you to anything that might come his way, smiling ironically the entire time. Even the way he stands now, shoulders wide and arms crossed, like he's daring the world.

I square my shoulders and head his way. Rhys sweeps his gaze over my flowing, floor-length dress. The red silk is cool in the heat, and the long split up my leg keeps the fabric moving with every step.

"You're wearing *that?*"

"Yes."

"We're going into Gustavia, on a tour of the old town." He's speaking like I'm a toddler. "Not the Met gala."

"Are you sure?" I ask sweetly. "I thought this was a ball." And then I twirl in front of him for good measure, the red silk billowing out around me.

A muscle jerks in his jaw. "Ivy."

"It had a note pinned in the label. *St Barts, day two, town shoot.* Would you like to see it? I think it's still in my room."

"No. Let's just get going."

"Thought you'd never ask."

To my delight, the man waiting by the car is one I recognize. "Étienne!"

"Miss Hart." He tips his hat. "You look beautiful today."

"Thank you. Will you be our tour guide today?"

"*Bien sûr,* I even volunteered for the job!" He looks to Rhys, whose scowl is growing deeper by the second. "And who is this? Your boyfriend?"

"Oh, he's my photographer," I say, barely keeping the smile out of my voice. I don't dare look at Rhys, either, but he feels like a black cloud at my side. "Shall we?"

Étienne holds the door open for me. "After you."

Rhys slams his and I have to turn my face toward the beautiful surroundings outside the window to hide my grin. Perhaps I could make annoying Rhys a game during the trip. If it's always this easy, not to mention fun, I'll be having a ball.

Étienne drives us in a loop around the island, pointing out beaches and coves he thinks we should see, often sprinkling them with anecdotes from his own experiences. Some are less appropriate than others—one beach is, apparently, especially good for lovemaking. Rhys snorts at that.

When we drive into Gustavia, he starts extolling the town's virtues.

"Gustavia is unique in the world, because it has no… what's the word… *restauration rapide.*"

"Fast food," Rhys comments.

"Yes, exactly! There is none of that here. But we have a lot of fine dining. Many Michelin chefs." Étienne turns onto a minuscule street in Gustavia, barreling down toward the sailboats in the harbor. I hold on to the door handle and look at Rhys.

"You speak French?"

He shrugs.

Right. What an answer.

"I will leave you here," Étienne says, parking next to the central harbor in Gustavia. He hands us a business card. "You call me when you're done and I will come."

"The hotel is not that far, is it?"

"No. But the lady is in… *talons hauts.*"

Rhys frowns, glancing down at my feet. "High heels. Yes, that she is."

I look down at the shoes in question. They're fairly low heels, and they're wedges, too. I want to kiss the agency stylist who thought of that little detail.

"Thank you, Étienne. We'll see you later."

"Good luck!"

Rhys doesn't look at me when we're the only two left in the calm harbor. Gustavia's colorful houses and small streets beckon just yards away, and a palm tree next to us waves in the breeze.

"I'm ready," I say, shaking out my hair. The hair stylist this morning had styled it straight, and it hangs in a golden waterfall down my back.

Rhys turns his camera over in his hands, looking over the settings. "Good for you."

"Thank you. That means a lot, coming from you." There's liquid sugar dripping from my voice. "All I've ever wanted in life is your approval."

He shakes his head. "You're a nuisance."

"More compliments! What have I done to deserve this?"

He starts to walk away, but I keep up easily, even in my *talons hauts.* "The call sheet says we're to shoot me walking on these streets. Interacting with local culture. Eating lunch."

"I've read the call sheet too."

"Awesome, you're literate. See, I can give out compliments too. But you're heading in the wrong direction."

"Am I?" If my voice had been sugary-sweet, Rhys's is desert-dry. "I hadn't noticed."

"Yes, you see, blue is ocean."

"How are you so energetic? Did you eat an all-sugar breakfast?"

"No. I got up early and exercised."

He stops by the edge of the dock, back to me, and takes a few pictures of the harbor. "This is good. I want you to stand here."

I walk past him to the very edge of the dock. "For you to push me in?"

"Don't tempt me." But he backs away, camera raised. I take a deep breath. Showtime.

Posing isn't always difficult, but sometimes it is. When there aren't clear elements to work with. When I'm unsure of the direction the shoot is going. When I know the photographer isn't pleased.

"This isn't working," he says, putting down the camera a few minutes later. "Try sitting."

"On the edge?"

"Yes."

I pause, half-crouched. "You're definitely planning on pushing me in."

He sighs. "You flatter yourself."

I sink down on the edge of the dock and swing my legs over the edge, the turquoise water glittering below. Being pushed in wouldn't even be that bad. The dress would be ruined, but as long as I could blame it on Rhys it would be cool.

Leaning back on my hands, I shake my hair over my shoulders and look at the horizon. "Are you taking pictures?"

A testy voice behind me. "Yes."

And then a hand on my shoulder and a sudden exertion of force. I grip onto the edge of the dock and push back, and the pressure vanishes immediately. Behind me, Rhys laughs.

"You asshole!"

"I couldn't resist. Don't worry, I wouldn't have gone through with it."

"I don't believe you." Standing up, I brush off the dress. It falls like a cloud of red silk around me.

"Come on," Rhys tells me, looking out over the distance. A dark curl has fallen over his forehead. It's very, very easy to see how the roles could be reversed. *Give me your camera and I'll photograph* you. "The all-mighty call sheet has dictated that I'm to shoot you walking in the streets."

He strides down the dock, shoulders wide, camera gripped in one hand, like a soldier at war. Perhaps that's what he'd rather be shooting—nature or people or wartime atrocities. Not me.

We spend the rest of the afternoon walking around Gustavia. I do all kinds of mundane things, posing all the while. Sipping a glass of wine at an outdoor café. Buying fruit from a vendor. Walking down cobblestone streets. Twirling under a giant, blooming bougainvillea.

"Good," Rhys says finally, looking through images in his camera. "We're done for today."

But I'm not. Because somewhere in the distance, music is playing. "Do you hear that?"

He frowns down at me. "Hear what?"

"That's a live band playing." I walk down an alley, following the tune of a saxophone. It's definitely live. A few turns later and I emerge in a small square. Nestled against colorful houses, a band is indeed playing, and people are dancing salsa in front of it.

I clutch my bag to my chest. "Oh."

Rhys snorts by my side—I hadn't been sure he was following. "You were right."

"This is perfect."

"For what? For shooting?"

"For... experiencing." I head to one of the small tables by the side and sit down, grabbing my phone. I have to take a picture of this for Penny.

Rhys sprawls in the chair next to me, placing his camera on the table with a sigh. "Filming for your online followers?"

"And so what if I am?"

"I thought you wanted to *experience* this." He raises his hand for a waiter. *"Une biere, s'il vous plait,"* he orders. "Ivy?"

"Just water for me, please."

"Bien sûr," the waiter says, retreating through the dancing couples. I watch them move, the beat intoxicating.

"So you do speak French," I say.

"Guilty."

"Are the French?"

"Usually." His small grin tells me he's somewhere else, thinking of other experiences. And perhaps that's more infuriating than anything he's done so far—because he's intriguing.

I want to ask how. Why. But it'll no doubt yield nothing at all, so I watch the dancers instead. Breathe in the scent of the town, the beat of the live band, the feeling of being someplace new. It's addicting. Beside me, Rhys fiddles with his camera, the picture of bored elegance.

A middle-aged man in a French boater hat breaks away from the group dancing to stop in front of our table. He looks straight at me, holding out his hand.

"Mademoiselle?"

There's only one answer to that.

I put my hand in his. He pulls me out amongst the other dancers. The man leads me into a hesitant salsa, but grins when he sees that I know the steps.

"I used to dance," I tell him. He nods, still smiling, and turns me around. The music flows through me, the beats strong and seductive, and I let go. It's been years since I've danced like this. No routine, no plan, no timer. Just pure uninhibited dance.

He spins me once, twice, the skirt billowing out around me. The second I'm still again, he grins. *"Trés bien,"* he tells me. I don't know how long we dance for, as one song bleeds into the next. And perhaps I put a bit extra sway in my hips, knowing that Rhys is sitting a table away and watching.

Sweat is running down my back, beneath the beautiful silk dress, when the man I'm dancing with nods toward the beach and asks me something.

"Oh, I'm sorry. I don't speak French," I say.

He chuckles, like I've made a joke, and his grip on my waist tightens. He repeats the question, smile widening.

I pull back. "I'm sorry, but I think I'm done dancing."

Raised eyebrows and yet another question spoken in the same incomprehensible language. I shake my head and take a step back. "Sorry."

A tall figure appears by my side, a hand resting lightly on my lower back. Rhys says something in French that I don't need to interpret to understand. It's a polite but decisive *fuck off*.

Straw hat guy grins again and steps back, hands raised. And when the music picks up again, well... Rhys and I are the ones left dancing.

His hands are light on me, barely touching, like he doesn't know if he has touching rights. I don't know if I have them either, but his shoulder is firm under my hand.

"I can role-play as a boyfriend when I have to," he says darkly.

"How chivalrous."

"You okay? He wasn't too forward?"

"Well, I couldn't understand what he was saying, so I'll give him the benefit of the doubt." Around us, dancers are moving in tune with the beat. And nothing, not the sweat on my skin, not even Rhys's perpetually bad attitude, can take me down off the high I'm on. I smile up at him. "This place is fantastic."

Rhys is quiet for a beat. He leads me slower than the beat, perhaps not as used to dancing, but he makes up for it with his physicality. "Where did you learn to dance like that?"

"I danced growing up." Pulling at his arm, I spin underneath it, returning to his side in the next second. "It was my first passion."

He doesn't respond. I look up at his jaw, still tense. Is it always tense? "What?" I tease. "Surprised I have some form of marketable skill?"

He snorts. "Truthfully, yes."

"You don't pull any punches, do you?"

Another beat of silence. "I prefer honesty," he says. We sway softly side to side, not really dancing, not really standing still.

"Even if it's brutal?"

"Especially if it's brutal."

Nodding, I spin again, unable to entirely resist. "Let me ask you something then."

Wariness. "All right."

"I get the feeling that you'd rather photograph endangered species or bombing sites or perhaps just anyone who isn't me. Is that true? I just want to know what I'm dealing with here."

"I don't prefer shooting models, no."

"Then how come you accepted this job?" It's an honest, serious question.

We sway to a complete standstill. "I prefer brutal honesty," he says. "But that doesn't mean I'm an open book."

"I'd never confuse you for that," I murmur.

A twitch of his lips before they stretch into his sardonic smile. "Well," he says. "How about we just agree that we don't like each other very much and leave it at that?"

It must be clear that I don't like that, because he chuckles. "You were the one who said that, in New York. All we have to do is stay professional."

"You're right." My hands slip from his, dropping to my side. "And great collaborations have been built on worse."

6

RHYS

Flying is a bitch.

It's just not logical. Our species didn't evolve wings for a reason, and nowhere is that fact more obvious to me than when I'm halfway up in the heavens and surrounded by clouds. It's unnatural. Worse, it's *deranged*. And yet the collective world has somehow agreed that this is now the preferred mode of travel and woe to anyone who'd have preferred a good old steamship.

I look down at my watch. A minute has passed since I last looked, and we've only been weightless for an hour. What joy. I push my chair back and close my eyes, breathing through my nose. The beginning of a flight is always the hardest. Thank God for the extra space in first class.

"These peanuts are very salty," Ivy comments at my side. "Did you know they always add far more salt and spices to airplane food than normal? Apparently human tastebuds are desensitized at these altitudes."

First class isn't quite spacious enough, though, because we've ended up next to each other. I suspect that I'll find the same pattern emerge when I look at all of our future travels. No doubt Ben thought he was doing me a favor.

I don't open my eyes, and I definitely don't open my mouth.

"Oh," Ivy says. "Sorry. Are you busy brooding?"

"I don't brood."

"You're the textbook definition of a brooder."

"I am? Show me the textbook, then."

"See? That's exactly what a textbook brooder would say, while pondering the questions of life and it's endless miseries."

"I don't ponder life's endless miseries." A small part of my brain registers just how petulant my response sounds, but the other is too busy being annoyed by Ivy Hart. I'm not brooding. I'm busy surviving our five-hundred-miles-per-hour hurtle through the Earth's lower stratosphere.

"Its pointlessness, then? Its inequalities? How unfair it is that you're forced to fly to Europe together with someone you find marginally annoying so you can shoot a campaign worth several thousands of dollars?"

"You're wrong."

"About which part?"

"I find you far more than just *marginally* annoying. Especially right now." But my grip on the armchair has loosened, somewhat. At least her inane babble gives me something to focus on.

"You can't argue and brood at the same time. Which one do you want to do the most?"

"Brood," I say. And then, "Damn it, I'm *not* a brooder, Ivy."

"If you say so." Her voice brightens and I open my eyes, too curious not to see. She's scrolling through the movies on her screen. She stops at one that's awful. I'm talking would-make-Shakespeare-spin-in-his-grave-at-the-fate-of-the-entertaintment-industry-kind of awful. "This one is my favorite," she says, and apparently there's something worse than argumentative Ivy. It's chirpy Ivy.

"All right, now you're the one picking a fight," I say.

"How am I doing that?"

I raise an eyebrow. "*That* movie? It's pure shit, filled to the brim with clichés. I bet I could predict every single plot point."

"So you haven't seen it?"

"I don't need to. It writes itself."

"How do you know it's terrible if you haven't seen it?"

I reach for the small case with toiletries we've been given. There has to be an eye mask in here. Fishing it out triumphantly, I put it on. "Some things you just know."

"You're impossible."

I lift up the eye mask a while later to see Ivy snuggled up in her seat, her hair a thick, blonde braid down her side and a pair of beige sweats on. Her headphones are in and her eyes are glued to the screen.

She catches me watching and takes out an earpiece. "See? You couldn't resist watching either!"

I demonstrably pull down my eye mask. Lovely blackness beckons. "Wake me when we land in Italy."

She mutters something that sounds like *such a bore*. To my surprise, though, I actually manage to fall asleep, and I'm woken by the announcement in the speakers hours later. Beside me, Ivy has already packed together her things.

She's glued to the window.

I shouldn't ask. I shouldn't be intrigued. But I do it anyway. "First time in Rome?"

She doesn't turn from the view. "Yes."

"Good thing we're shooting all around the city." I pull out the itinerary from the inside pocket of my jacket. The small, innocuous piece of paper, a list of places they wanted me to shoot Ivy in front of, besides, behind or with. But traveling isn't a checklist. It's an adventure.

"I can't wait," she says, and there's a dreaminess to her voice. No pretense. No guard up, either. It's… disconcerting. I look at her as she looks at the rapidly approaching ground, and find that it's almost a surprise when the airplane's wheels touch the tarmac. My hands aren't gripping the armrests.

Ivy is quiet beside me the entire way through passport control, as we get into the car to the hotel, even as she disappears down to her hotel room.

"We start shooting in an hour!" I call.

She just nods, lost in some sort of daze. Shaking my head, I head into my own opulent room. Ben had truly pulled out all the stops for this trip, showing us the best his hotels and travel agency had to offer. Luxury trips for luxury clients, a tailor-made package for all needs.

And I'm supposed to shoot this dream.

Grabbing the old Canon from my suitcase, the one that's only fit for my own photography, I open the windows of my hotel room wide. The hot Roman air greets me, along with a view that is almost impossible to beat. Terracotta roofs and beige, stone-colored walls beneath a blue, cloudless sky. A city landscape of cobblestone streets and trattorias. I snap a picture of the tranquility. Perhaps I'd have time later to shoot around the city just for me, not with Ivy or my expensive digital camera. It sometimes captured life in too sharp of an image.

Life can be a dream, and dreams are best a bit blurry.

Ivy is the one who knocks on my door an hour later. "Come on," she announces. "The eternal city is waiting, and we don't have many hours of sunlight left."

I run my eyes over her form. Gone is the surprisingly gentle vision of her on the plane, in sweats and without makeup. Back is the woman with sharp eyes, even sharper eyeliner, and perfectly blow-dried hair. She's wearing another silky dress, but it's a burgundy color today. A straw bag hangs at her side.

She looks like the elegant poster child of Italian dreams.

"Yes, yes," she says impatiently. "This is what they put me in. I know I'm wearing heels, but I stuffed a pair of flats into my bag. I won't slow you down this time."

I could say that she hadn't last time. Or that she looks stunning. But neither are appropriate, nor relevant, so I just nod.

"Good. Let's get going."

"When are we meeting Paolo?"

"Paolo?"

"We're shooting with a model tonight. Another model, besides me, I mean." Am I imagining it or is there genuine excitement in her voice? She flicks her thick hair behind her shoulder, and with her heels, she's *almost* the same height as me. It's a very rare thing. It *almost* throws me off my balance.

"At seven," I say. "Haven't you been studying your itinerary?"

She rolls her eyes. "All right, all right, I'm the schedule queen," she says. "Are we starting in this neighborhood."

"Yes." I grab the camera and undo the lens, following her out into the Roman afternoon. The air is beautifully warm, the building behind her a soft sienna color. Ivy stops in the street and looks around. For a moment, she doesn't do anything, just breathes in the air.

I raise my camera and take a picture. It's impossible not to capture that moment of first contact, of blissful intoxication on her face. It's not fake, either.

For the coming hour, I don't direct her at all. I let her walk down whatever streets she fancies, and what she does seems to come so naturally. It's barely posing at all, the way she interacts with the city. I've taken well over four hundred photos before the hour is up.

For being a model, well… she's damn good at her job.

Not to mention it's getting harder and harder to dismiss her as *just* a model. Some people do stop when they see her, or when they see *me* photographing her with a professional camera, but she handles it in stride. Like she's used to it, because she likely is.

No doubt she's been gawked at since she was a teenager.

It's mid-evening by the time we stop on Ponte Sant'Angelo. The beautiful statue-lined bridge is not on the list, but there's no way I'm in Rome and *not* photographing it. Ivy leans against the railing and looks out over the Tiber, her hair glittering in the late-day sun.

"This place is magical. I wonder what that building is. Or used to be."

I look up at where she's pointing. "Castel Sant'Angelo. It was once the mausoleum of Emperor Hadrian, but it's been used as a bunch of things since. Pieces have been added and rebuilt and torn down, like everything in Rome."

"It really is the eternal city," she breathes.

"Yes. I think this bridge is around two thousand years old."

"You're not serious." She looks down at her feet, firmly planted in a pair of sky-high heels on the stone bridge, as if it's about to collapse under her.

"It's sturdy, don't worry. The Romans knew what they were doing."

"You've been here before."

"I have, yes."

She narrows her eyes at me, like I've said something wrong, but she doesn't comment. Her gaze sweeps to the side instead, to the setting sun. "We're going to be late," she says.

"No we're not." I nod toward the adjoining district. Little cafés line the street. "I asked Paolo to meet us there."

She strides past me, but I keep up easily. She might be skilled in walking in heels, but my legs are longer.

"I can't believe I'm about to shoot this."

Ivy cocks her head. "Shoot what?"

"You and him. Did you look at the sample pictures they sent over?"

"I did." She doesn't sound the slightest bit agitated. "And so what?"

"It's like I'm shooting a bad perfume commercial." I roll my neck, trying to work out an age-old crick. "A scene from *Lady and the Tramp*."

She chuckles, pausing on the sidewalk. "I always liked that movie."

"Of course you did."

She fishes out a smaller bag from her larger one, a clutch this time, and hangs it over her shoulder. Fixes her hair. Rummages around after something.

"What are you doing?"

"The instructions were clear," she says. "I'm supposed to transition to an evening look." She pulls out a small mirror and a black lipstick tube. Her full lips part as she applies red lipstick, looking at her reflection through half-lidded eyes.

Christ.

I raise my camera and take a picture of her applying her lipstick, her hair a tumble around her shoulders and Rome the backdrop.

She glances past the mirror to me, a challenge in her eyes.

I take a picture of that too.

"I'm not posing right now."

"I'm aware of that."

Ivy closes her mirror with a snap, once again the woman who'd stood up for herself in New York. "Come on," she tells me through newly painted lips. "I have an Italian model to meet."

Right.

Paolo is every stereotype come to life. I hate him immediately, not in the least because he's leaning suit-clad against the corner of a house, a cigarette in hand and the other clasping his phone.

He looks up and sees Ivy, and I see the exact moment the calculation crosses his mind. *She's gorgeous. I wonder…?*

She extends a hand, but he pulls her in for a kiss on the cheek instead. "Paolo," he says, his English softly accented. "Nice to meet you."

"Likewise." Ivy rocks back on her heels and gives him a wide, blinding, thousand-dollar smile. "Want to go for a stroll?"

"I'd love to." He takes her arm and tucks it under his, effortlessly, like this was the agreed-upon direction. The two of them begin to stroll up the trattoria-lined street like they're a real couple just out together.

"Where's the photographer?" he asks her.

Ivy glances over her shoulder. "Oh, he's back there."

All right, Ivy.

Perhaps she's still pissed about the *just a model* comment from weeks ago. Or some of the other things I've said. And perhaps rightly so, but this is in no way a proportional response. I grit my teeth as the Italian runs a hand through his wavy, styled hair and smiles widely down at Ivy.

He looks like every Italian male model ever.

I shoot the two of them walking arm in arm from behind. Turning down little alleys, stopping as Ivy points at a trattoria sign. It's all mindless, thoughtless pictures, meant to look enticing to the high-end clients Rieler attracts.

I hate that it's working. Even just walking around, the two of them attract admiring looks from tourists and locals alike. Maybe it's Paolo's form-fitting suit. Maybe it's the way they complement one another. Or maybe it's Ivy's wide, effortless smile. She's aiming that thing around without a thought to who might get hit.

I gain small, vindictive pleasure from snapping a few shots where Paolo has his eyes closed.

Ivy looks over at me. It's the first time she has given me a second glance since Paolo arrived. "Gelateria?" she asks.

I nod. It's not on the list of shots or locations they want, but it's a solid idea. I regret it five seconds later, though, as I'm forced to photograph Paolo feeding Ivy a scoop of lemon gelato.

Objectively, it's a gorgeous shot. Ivy looks up at him with something akin to amazement, and he's smiling crookedly, a dimple in his cheek.

He knows that's the moneymaker.

People around us stop to watch as Ivy giggles, as they

pose, as Paolo bends his head closer to whisper in her ear. My finger keeps moving over the shutter at a furious pace.

"Excuse me," an accented voice asks at my side. "But are they, like, famous?"

I glance over to see a woman with wide eyes standing at my side, a map of Rome in her hand. A tourist.

"No," I say.

She nods absentmindedly, but she grabs a picture with her smartphone regardless. And I can't really blame her, not as Paolo has his hand on Ivy's waist. They're eating from the same ice cream cone.

"All right!" I call. "We're done at this location."

And the bastards don't look at me! Paolo just laughs and offers Ivy a napkin, and she blots at her red fuck-me lips.

"Vespa now?" Paolo asks me.

"Sure." *Why the fuck not.*

So I shoot the two of them on a Vespa, as Paolo drives up and down the same, carefully chosen street. Ivy keeps her arms wrapped around his waist, her blonde, perfect hair flying in the wind. And just before they dip out of view, she turns and gives me the money-shot.

Gorgeous.

Over and over and over we do it.

I don't know who's more relieved when we're finally by the tiny trattoria specified on the call sheet we'd received. This is where the agency wants the shot of the two of them sharing a romantic, candle-lit dinner.

I busy myself by rearranging the chairs and props, but their conversation is easy to overhear.

"You're only here for a few days?" Paolo asks.

"Yes, we're off to the next location tomorrow."

"That's such a shame," the softly purring Italian says. I consider if he'd look better with a black eye. Now, I'm not a violent person—not usually, anyway. But I grew up with two brothers and one who was basically adopted, so I know my way around fists.

"Have a seat," I tell them. Ivy sinks down onto a chair like it's an art, crossing her legs and letting the silky fabric drape around her. Tanned legs and high heels on display, and I can't fault her for them, not when they make her look like that.

The woman is a walking painting.

Damn it. I was supposed to be immune. I'd once told her I was.

She rests an elbow on the table, her hand softly curving around her cheek. Long hair flows down her back. Okay. So this woman knows her angles, and she knows them damn well.

"Where are you from in Italy?" she asks Paolo in a soft, mellifluous voice that fits the scenario we're shooting perfectly. Intimate. Casual. Elegant.

He leans back in his chair and stretches his long legs out in front of him, proving that he *too* knows his angles. I take a step back and alternate between filming and shooting.

"Napoli," he says.

Ivy leans across the table, an alluring smile on her face. I shoot that too.

"In the south of Italy?"

"You know Napoli?"

"I know of it." Her eyes light up. I zoom in and snap a few shots of her, just like that, perched on a chair in Rome, no Italian in sight. Anyone could imagine they were on the receiving end of that sweet gaze. Anyone.

"You should visit someday," he says. "When you have more time."

"I'd love that—"

"Let's change the seating arrangement." I step forward, motioning for Paolo to move.

He shifts closer to Ivy. "Like the set images we received?"

I think of the images that we'd received from this shoot—an elegantly dressed couple practically making out.

I nod. Forming the words would be too difficult.

Ivy leans her head against his shoulder and takes his

hand. They sit like that for a while, posing while looking very un-posed, letting me snap pictures. Wine arrives, and they hold it, sipping, gazing at each other. And all the while my camera keeps going. *Snap, snap, snap.*

Paolo turns to face her. His mouth crooks up and leaning forward, he pushes her hair back. Ivy's mouth opens softly.

It's a killer shot. Obligingly, I take it.

I don't know if I'm happy or annoyed that they're handling this so well on their own. Do I *want* to be the one to give directions to this? He's touching her, and now she's touching him back.

Her hand is on his shoulder as she bites her lip. There is laughter in her eyes, seduction in her expression.

I photograph them like that, with the quaint Italian trattoria behind them, cobblestones under their feet. We're selling the Italian dream to tourists, the idea that anyone who comes here on vacation can be what they are. Can look like they do. It's an illusion, but it's no less gorgeous for that.

My hands grow tight around my film camera when Paolo leans in to kiss Ivy on the cheek. Her eyes flutter closed and I catch the entire moment, the coy laughter she gives as he pulls away, the way she ducks her head, the way he reaches for his wine and takes a deep sip. He says something I can't catch and she blushes.

And then I call cut.

"We have everything we need." I start to pack down my camera and equipment. Photography used to be my secret, hidden joy. At the moment it feels like a death sentence. "Shoot's over."

Paolo helps Ivy to her feet, steadying her when her heel gets caught in a cobblestone. Fucking death traps, those. It might make her legs look killer, but I prefer them unbroken. Whatever stylist had chosen her outfits was an idiot.

"You were amazing." Paolo's voice is filled with confident swagger. "So talented."

"Oh, thank you. You did good too."

"Let me show you Rome tonight," he offers. "The real Rome, not a set."

I screw one of the lenses on and ignore the conversation. It's very, very difficult to.

Ivy's voice is kinder than it's ever been when it's directed just to me. "Oh, I'd love to, but we actually have a bit more of shooting to do. Just Rhys and I—the agency wants a few night shots."

The agency doesn't want a few night shots. But I look straight at Paolo as I nod. "Sorry, man."

He gives an elegant shrug. "Another time, then. You'll be back to Italy, Ivy. I'm sure of that."

"I can't wait." There's no doubting the sincerity in her voice. Paolo pulls her unnecessarily close to kiss her on the cheek.

"Until next time," he tells her, before he shakes my hand. His grip is firm. I make mine firmer. Petty, perhaps.

But satisfying.

And then he strolls off, down a street where people turn around to watch him. Like Ivy, he must be more than used to that.

She sinks back down on the chair with a sigh, bending to take off her heels. "I am *so* hungry. Do you want to go grab a pizza?"

For a brief second, it's hard to find words. She'd turned down an Italian model for pizza with me? The heady sense of victory that sweeps through me is as unbecoming as it is potent, but it's there. I shoulder my camera bag and hold out my hand to her.

"Make it two, and you have a deal."

7

IVY

My feet feel ten thousand times better once I've switched back to my flats, the beautiful Jimmy Choos back in the bag on my shoulder. I'm starving and tired, but I always am after shoots. It's supposed to be easy, modeling, or at least that's what everyone says—including my father. But it's not. It's exhausting having to remember what you look like at every single angle at every single second.

Rhys leads the way down the quaint, cobbled street, the air the perfect amount of hot, not humid. "How about the place we saw earlier?" he asks.

"The one that smelled amazing?"

"Yeah."

"That's the one." I smile at him, and to my surprise, I get a crooked smile back.

"Surprised you don't want to go to a Michelin star restaurant," he says.

"I could say the same about you."

He puts a hand to his chest. "Me? I'm but a simple man of the people, not a supermodel."

I roll my eyes at the exaggeration, on both counts. Whatever Rhys is, it's not simple, and certainly not a man of the people. "Everyone loves pizza, and if they don't, they're not human."

"No disagreement here," he says, stopping at one of the tables that line the street. "Here?"

"Yes, please." I sink down onto one of the wobbly wooden chairs with a sigh. My whole body aches from the day of walking and shooting, but it's nothing. I'm in Italy. I'm sitting on a busy street, watching as people from all countries walk hand-in-hand or arm-in-arm.

Rhys motions for a waiter with a wan hand. With his dark hair and tanned skin, he looks more Italian than the model I'd shot with. How would the pictures have looked if he'd been the one who had nuzzled my neck instead of Paolo?

How would it have felt?

We order a pizza each. I go for the parmesan and prosciutto, and a glass of white wine. Rhys raises an eyebrow immediately after I've ordered.

"What?" I ask.

"Nothing."

"Just tell me."

"Well, most models I've met wouldn't order a pizza just like that."

I reach for one of the breadsticks and take a decisive bite. "I know."

"But you do? That's impressive."

"It's not impressive. It's indulgent. But," I tell him, waving my breadstick around, "if someone tries to tell me that I'm in Italy for the first time but I'm not allowed to eat pizza or pasta, I might stab them with this."

Something darkly amused sparks in Rhys's eyes.

"I would never be that person," he vows. "I'd be the person handing you more breadsticks as ammunition."

"Good answer." I reach out and grab the olive oil for good measure, pouring a small dollop onto my bread plate. "In truth, of course I shouldn't eat this. I should be watching my every bite. My agency likes to remind me that I only have five more years, and that's a generous estimate."

"They like to do *what*?"

"Oh, it's not very surprising or anything. Models are young. If I'm lucky, one day I won't be." I shrug. It's an obvious thing, and it's one I'm happy my dad made me well-aware of when I went into the profession. It's never been my everything—and I've seen what's happened to the models to whom it *is* everything, who see doom in every new wrinkle and imperfection.

Rhys drinks his wine and a dark lock of his hair falls over his brow. Watching his sprawl on the small chair, long legs stretched out, it's hard to imagine that *I'm* somehow the model here.

But I don't tell him that.

"How did you like shooting Paolo?" I ask him instead. "Considering you don't like shooting people, shooting *two* must have been your own personal inferno. Dante's, perhaps, since we're in Italy."

"You read Dante?"

"No one has actually *read* Dante. People read *about* Dante."

A small, sideways smile. "I don't dislike shooting people. I just don't like shooting uninteresting people."

I make a dramatic show of putting a half-eaten breadstick against my heart. It's not difficult, with the low-plunging neckline of this silky dress.

He snorts. "I don't mean that you're uninteresting."

"Of course you don't. You just think I'm vain and airheaded."

He runs a hand through his hair, a furrow on his brow. Like he's bothered by the words he'd spoken by the pool in the Hamptons. "Well, most models just kinda *are,* in that they're being photographed because they're attractive. I'd want to photograph people to share their story."

"Like for *National Geographic*?"

"Something like that, yes." He raises his wineglass, looking over the rim at me with dark eyes. "And just for the record, I don't find you air-headed or uninteresting."

"What a compliment," I say. "Please, try to control yourself."

His lips twitch. "It's very high praise coming from me."

"So I'm gathering." I flip my hair and gesture with my hand. "Come on, what else. You *don't* find me intolerable? I'm *not* awful? Hit me with it."

Rhys snorts, reaching for one of the breadsticks. "You're not going to monopolize the breadsticks for much longer."

"That's not a compliment."

"I guess I ran out."

My response is cut off by the arrival of two giant, delicious-smelling pizzas. Cheese oozes across the surface. "Buon appetito!" the waiter announces, disappearing back through the throng of tables.

"I'm going to slaughter this pizza," I announce. "Absolutely demolish it. Blast it into space."

"Do you have a violence fetish?" Rhys asks calmly, starting to cut his into triangles.

"With pizza? Sure." I fish up my phone and snap a quick picture of our food.

Rhys groans. "Of course you're the kind of person to photograph your food."

"Of course you're the kind of person to be annoyed by that," I deadpan. "The way I see it, I can only eat it once, but I can look at it forever."

"Brilliant logic." Rhys lifts up a slice to his mouth, taking a bite. For a second, he just closes his eyes and chews. "Yes, this is what it's supposed to taste like."

I follow suit and an explosion of marinara sauce, mozzarella and flavorful meat takes place in my mouth. It's like I've died and gone to food heaven. I'd been absolutely right to ignore the little voice in my heads that warns we're shooting tomorrow too in order to indulge in this. So what if I have to drink a gallon of water to combat the sodium.

You only live once.

"Besides," I tell Rhys when I've regained the ability to speak, "I'm photographing this to send to my little sister."

"She appreciates unsolicited food pics?"

I shake my head at him. "I can't believe you went there."

He shrugs, not looking the least bit contrite. "It was ripe for the taking."

"And to answer your question, yes, she does want unsolicited food pics. I'm under strict orders to photograph anything of interest to send it back to her. She wants to live vicariously." Perhaps I've revealed a bit more than I meant to, there. It's clear from my comments that we're not a family who travels a lot, and he's, well… a Marchand. A simple Google search the other day had revealed that his older brother is building New York's new opera house, and that his little sister runs a renowned art gallery.

And that's not even accounting for his father.

But Rhys doesn't comment. He just nods. "Cute."

My mouth babbles on. The filter must have become disconnected somewhere around the second slice of pizza, tiredness starting to set in. "She'll have my head, though, when I tell her I didn't see the town with a genuine Italian."

"Paolo," Rhys says. "Did he have to have such a generic name? I wonder if it's a *nom de plume*."

It takes me a second to sort through hazy memories from English Lit class. "Like a stage name? Why on earth would he have that?"

He shrugs. "To sound more authentically Italian. Imagine if he was actually called Mark."

"You mean Marco."

"Why did you turn him down? He was devastated," Rhys says, cutting up another slice of his pizza.

"He was not."

60

He raises an eyebrow. "Sure he was. I think he was offering more than just a simple *tour* of Rome, too."

"You're being ridiculous."

"If you can't see that, then you're the one who's ridiculous," Rhys says. "Surely you must be used to men asking you out all the time."

Ah, the age-old assumption, the stereotype, the truth-verging-on-untruth. I take another bite of my pizza and think as I'm chewing. I'm finding that with Rhys, I don't want to give flippant answers, either.

"I am," I say truthfully. But it's only part of the truth. It's often like Paolo had just done it, offhand, confidently, expectantly. By men who know they're good-looking.

By men who have expectations of how I'll act and behave.

And their expectations always kill mine.

Rhys nods, like I've confirmed something he knew all along. "Can't be astonishing when that pattern carries over to Europe too."

I shake my head. This is not what I want to talk about, not what I want to get into. My lack of romantic experience—and the reasons for that... I can't go there. I can't even tell my own baby sister that I'm still a virgin.

"As if you're not ogled everywhere," I tell him. Turning the tables—a surefire tactic.

Rhys scoffs, but he doesn't protest. I don't know if that's conceited or insightful, or perhaps both, a combo only he could carry off. He reaches for his wine and drinks, holding the glass between his fingers afterwards with the ease of someone who knows vintages. "Tell me something."

"Tell you something? So I'm not just *not* uninteresting, but now I'm interesting too?"

"Don't gloat," he says.

"I'll try to. Make it interesting."

"Tough crowd," he says. "Very well. Tell me why you chose modeling when you could've been anything else."

It's not a question I've ever been asked—not by anyone that isn't my father. Everyone else, from high school, from my town, who I meet in the industry, sees this career as a lottery ticket.

The answer is a foregone conclusion. It's self-evident.

I lean back in the chair and grip my own glass of white wine by the stem, trying to adopt at least a portion of his controlled composure. "I could have chosen anything else?"

Rhys snorts. "That's fairly obvious, yeah."

"And here I thought I was *just* a vain model."

He glances past me toward the piazza beyond, and is it just me or is there a hint of contrition on his usually unforgiving features?

"I just told you you weren't uninteresting. And anyone who spends five minutes talking to you can see that you could've been anything."

I sigh, looking down at his glass. "I don't know."

"You don't know?"

"It's the honest answer. I was scouted a few years back and toyed around with the idea of calling the scout back. And once I did, things started to snowball. It's not an easy industry, not by any means, and I've worked hard at it, but I've never had my entire heart in it."

"Which is why you're also a student."

Now it's my turn to look up. "You know that?"

"I saw the textbooks on the plane."

"I thought you were asleep," I murmur.

"Not the entire time."

I shift in the seat and stretch my legs out beside me, crossing them. It's odd, being around men that are considerably taller than me. Both Rhys and Paolo had been today. "I'm studying part time," I say. "Like I said, I know I won't be a model forever. We have a rather finite shelf-life."

His lip curls slightly, and it's not in a smile.

"What?"

"I don't like that description."

"It's common in the industry. It's the truth."

"Which I'm normally a fan of, but this expression…" He shakes his head and motions to the waiter for another glass of wine. I shake my head for a no. If there's one thing I know, it's that I can't spend a whole day posing in tight outfits with a hangover. Learned that one the hard way.

"Right," I say. "The more brutal the honesty, the better."

He smirks, looking past me to the people milling about again. I wish I had a camera at hand to photograph him doing just that—there's something intriguing in his expression… "You remember."

"Of course. A pretty violent metaphor, by the way."

"I guess we're both fans of violence," he says.

"Or exaggeration."

"Let's go with that one."

I find myself just looking at him, my mouth curving into a smile. He looks back at me calmly, but there's something swirling in the depths of those eyes, too. "You know what," I say. "I don't find you uninteresting either."

His eyes spark. "Well, perhaps this trip will be tolerable after all."

8
—
IVY

We touch down in the City of Love midday. I feel like a kid in a candy store. This had once been a distant dream, and here I am, about to walk streets I've only fantasized about.

"You never told me why you speak French," I say to Rhys as we follow the bell boy upstairs to our rooms. The Rieler hotel in Paris is magical. The ride to the hotel had been magical. I think that might be the lead word for this stop—*magical*.

"No, I didn't," he says, like that's a reply. I roll my eyes at his broad back. Predictably unpredictable, that's Rhys.

The bellboy opens the door to a room that is splendor personified. Gilded bedframe. Painted ceilings. It looks like a pared-down version of Versailles. He informs me in near-flawless English that the hotel has a gym on the fourth floor, that breakfast is served from seven, that the staff are at my beck and call. I can barely focus on the words, my eyes locked on the balcony doors.

I open them the second I'm alone, and the view... the Eiffel Tower stretches up into the blue, Parisian sky in the distance, a giant amidst the mid-rise silhouettes. I can clearly make out the sliver thread of the glittering Seine.

It's a balcony to loudly proclaim *Let them eat cake!* from, minus, you know, the subsequent beheading. I grip the railing tight and just breathe it all in.

You're a lucky, lucky bastard, I tell myself. And then I take pictures and send them to Penny, complete with a small video of myself freaking out on the balcony.

A knock on the door and it's time for makeup and hair, done by a very talented French woman who gives reluctant smiles at my enthusiasm. Forty minutes later I'm all done, dressed up in the first of the four outfits the agency has packed for me to wear in Paris.

So when Rhys knocks on my door, I answer it with the widest of grins. "We're in Paris," I tell him.

He blinks at me. "Yes, we are."

"I've never been here before." And for good measure, I twirl, my skirt floating around me. "And I have the best hotel room in the world, courtesy of Rieler."

Rhys looks past me, eyes zooming in on the balcony immediately. "We should shoot there, perhaps around sunset."

"Yes, good idea."

"After all," he says dryly, "we're selling the hotel, too."

"Yes we are." Not even his trademark cynicism will dampen my mood. Paris beckons outside the hotel doors like a flirtatious lover, all its secrets and streets available to us. Rome, yesterday. Paris, today.

Rhys snorts by my side. "Excited, are we?"

"Just a tad. Where do we begin?"

He eyes the bag of clothes I'm carrying. "You're planning on changing a lot?"

"I was told they wanted shots of all these outfits."

"Then we'll grab taxis. I think we'll start at…" He looks at the shoot list and shakes his head in disgust. "Whoever wrote this has never been to Paris."

"Wasn't it put together by Rieler?"

"Yes. But there's no logic in this. Montmartre first, then St.

Germain, then up to Le Marais? We'll be crossing the Seine the whole day. Idiots."

I bite my lip to keep from smiling. "But *you* know Paris."

He lifts his camera high and snaps a picture of me like that, looking at him on the sidewalk. The sound of the trigger goes off like ammunition. "Yes," he says, "luckily for us, I do."

Rhys talks to the cab driver completely unhindered, his French fluent. I try not to let it show on my face how deeply impressive I find that, but perhaps I fail, because he turns to me with a raised eyebrow.

"What?" he asks me, like he doesn't already know, the arrogant man.

We shoot along the winding, tourist-filled streets of Montmartre, both with Paris as our backdrop and Sacre Coeur as the majestic church above us. Rhys swears more than once about the absolute mass of tourists.

"And I thought we'd bypass them by being here early," he mutters, reaching out impatiently to put a hand on my low back. I can't walk fast in these heels, but I'm trying to keep up.

"We could return tomorrow morning."

"We could." He shakes his head again. "Fucking tourists."

"Isn't that what we are?"

"No, we're here to work."

"You speak like a local." He lowers his hand and I slow my pace, grateful. Perhaps I should switch into the flats I'd brought—depending on how far we're walking…

Rhys is quiet for a beat. "I was, for a while."

"A local?"

"Yes."

I pause, sinking down on one of the low stoops. "Changing shoes," I inform him. "You've lived in Paris?"

"For two years, yeah."

I want to roll my eyes and gape at the same time. It doesn't seem the least bit surprising, in many ways, that he would do something like that. Was there any part of the world that wasn't your oyster when you were a Marchand?

"So that's why you speak French?"

His smile is a slow curve. "No."

"Do you thrive on being a mystery?"

"I can't answer that."

"Why not?"

"Because then I'd stop being mysterious."

I roll my eyes at him, but I'm smiling. "And you accuse models of being vain."

"Never said I wasn't." Out of his back pocket, he fishes out the shoot list. He studies it for a second before returning it, crumpled up on his pocket. "They want you walking by the Louvre and along the Seine next. We'll do those back-to-back, including Tuilières."

"Sounds good," I say. "But I think I should change."

He hands me the bag of outfits that he'd insisted on carrying. "Where?"

"Here?"

He glances from left to right. "You can't change out here."

"Then where else?" I head into one of the more quiet alleys and hear him following me. There are no tourists here. "This is the life of a model."

"Changing out in the open?"

"Yes. If you've ever been backstage at a fashion show, you know there's no such thing as modesty." My words are confident, strong, but my heart is beating fast. It is *normal*, that's true. But not with him here.

I find the garment bag labelled *Louvre*, stuffed in the bag. Short skirt, blazer, camisole—and I get to wear the flat loafers. Victory.

Rhys scoffs as soon as he sees the blazer. "They're dressing you up like the stereotypical Parisian."

"I'm selling the dream," I tell him, glancing past his shoulder toward the main street. A few people are passing by in the distance, but none really look into this alley.

So I reach down to the hem of my dress and start pulling it off, only to discover that Rhys has acted just as quickly. He's holding up the blazer like some sort of shield.

It's tiny, it covers almost nothing, and I'm still in my underwear—practically like I'm wearing a bikini. But Rhys is looking away with his features locked in iron, the face of a man completing a herculean task.

I laugh, and he glances at me at once. "What?"

"Nothing, nothing." But I'm chuckling as I reach for the skirt, tugging it up my legs. "I don't think that blazer covers anything."

He glances down and frowns, coming to the same realization. "Worth a shot."

I put on the camisole, and then, because the list of outfits had dictated it, I take off my bra. I do it underneath the shirt, the way every woman who's ever lived knows how to.

Rhys raises an eyebrow but doesn't look away. "They want you to go without underwear?"

"The straps," I say, tapping my shoulder. "They'll show whenever we photograph sans blazer."

He mutters something that sounds like *Jesus Christ*. Perhaps it's that, or perhaps it's the warm Parisian air, but it gives me courage. "What?" I ask him. "I thought you said you were unaffected by models. What was the word you used? Immune."

He looks up at the sky as if it might give him strength.

"You did say that," I point out.

"I say a lot of things."

I grin.

Above us, out through one of the many open windows, someone calls something in French. I don't catch a word of it, not that I would have understood it if I did. Rhys does, however, and he looks up to yell something back. Whatever it was sounded decidedly un-nice.

"Someone commenting on me changing?" I grab the blazer he holds out to me and shrug into it.

"Someone who didn't know their manners." Rhys grabs the bag and shoulders it for me again. "Shall we?"

"Sure." I run a hand over my hair. "I'm actually a little bit surprised that they just let out us out like this."

"What do you mean?"

"Rieler Travels is a big company, right? I was told this campaign was really important to them. That it would make or break the coming year for them, and that we'd be given help on each location. And, I mean, we have been—but not as much I would have expected." I hurry to keep up with his sudden very long strides. "I don't *mind* changing on the street, but I just didn't think I would be."

"Yeah," Rhys says, raising a hand to flag down a cab. "Well, I guess they decided we could handle it."

"I suppose so." I shrug and follow him into the cab. It didn't change the fact that it was an amazing opportunity for me, both personally and professionally. The biggest campaign I'd ever booked.

And any thoughts of that evaporate as the cab rolls down the cobbled streets of Montmartre toward the center of Paris, toward the Louvre and art and culture and life and everything I've ever wanted to see.

We spend the rest of the day working. Rhys is relentless, but so am I, and we try every angle, every possible idea he has. He listens to mine, too, when I suggest that he film me running through the maze labyrinth in the Tulières Garden or sitting on a balustrade by the Seine, my blazer around my shoulders. Getting material to be used in the editing room.

The sun is beginning a slow descent when Rhys puts down the camera and leans against the bridge railing beside me. His linen shirt clings softly to his chest, his shoulders, and his hair is tousled by the wind and the long day's work.

It's not the first time my fingers itch to photograph *him* instead.

I don't think it will be the last, either.

"Back in your old hometown," I say. "Have you missed it?"

"Yes and no." He looks out over the gilded bridge, the statues that line it, the Place de la Concorde to our left. "Remember Paolo?"

"We met him yesterday, so yes, I remember him."

"I don't want to sound like him," Rhys says, "but I'm afraid I might."

"Oh?"

"I'm having dinner with my cousin tonight. Care to join?"

I can't help it. I laugh. "What part of that sounded like Paolo?"

"I could try it in an Italian accent." But Rhys's lips are curved.

"I'd pay good money to hear that, actually."

"My cousin is insufferable sometimes, but harmless. Join us."

We're not friends. And yet...

"Are you sure? I won't be able to speak French. And perhaps you want to talk about family business." Why am I talking him out of this?

He snorts. "He speaks English, and if you're there it'll save me from the latter."

"Ah." I push off from the railing and walk backwards, away from him. "So I'm supposed to be your buffer."

"Was it that obvious?"

"Yes. You could have just come out and said it."

"But then I'd appear weak," Rhys says, but there's nothing weak about him at all as he follows me, tall and dark and with a sly look in his eyes. "We should head back to the hotel to get the shot of you on the balcony."

"Right." And I tell myself it's only Paris that's responsible for the sudden intrusion of butterflies in my stomach, but it sounds like a lie, even to my own ears.

———

"Will you give me some hint as to what I'm walking into?"

"You'll do great as you are."

"But what am I acting as a buffer against?"

"Annoying questions," Rhys drawls, reaching up to run a hand through his still-damp hair. He had showered at the hotel, and now he smells like soap and fresh linen and man, dressed in a pair of slacks and a button-down. I'd seen the thick, branded watch on his wrist, too. It's the only casual display of wealth I'd seen on him so far.

So modest, Rhys Marchand.

"How descriptive," I say. "Please try to rein in your flowery language."

His lips twitch. "I think I like you best when you're being sarcastic."

"Because that's your native tongue?"

A full-fledged smile now, the crooked, glorious thing that it is. "Yes. Thank you for recognizing that."

I smooth a hand down my dress. It's one of my own, and couldn't I have packed nicer things? The black, scalloped dress is certainly nice, but it's a far cry from the red silk I'd worn on the streets of St. Barts. I'd just assumed I'd be in the agency clothes most of the time.

Rhys stops outside an innocuous-looking facade, and swears under his breath. "Of course he wanted to meet here."

"What's wrong with this place?" It looks nice. Inviting. I glance down at the menu, but I don't understand a single thing listed apart from the prices.

And I nearly have a heart-attack. 120 euros for… whatever *magret de canard* is?

I can't afford that. I mean, I can, but I shouldn't. I save everything I can and it's not to spend it on this. But then Rhys's hand settles on my lower back and he whispers in my ear that *he'll translate the menu for me* and I focus on smiling.

Buffer. Dinner. Cousin. Focus on money later.

And for 120 euros for dinner, you bet your ass I'm going to photograph the hell out of that meal.

"What was wrong with this place?" I whisper as Rhys leads me through a darkened corridor. A hostess dressed in, well, wow, that was revealing, leads us down a pair of stairs and out onto a secluded courtyard. Lanterns hang from the branches of a giant olive tree and the chairs are filled with throw pillows.

"It's very trendy," Rhys murmurs back, distaste dripping from the last word. Something's working in his jaw. Damn, but he really does need me here as a buffer.

"The horror," I whisper back. *Smile for me.*

He doesn't, but the glance he shoots me is approving. Note to self—keep deploying sarcasm against Rhys Marchand.

A young man rises from a nearby table, curly brown hair and intelligent eyes looking us over. I get the impression that he sees far more than simply our forms. "Rhys!

His voice rolls over the *r* and drags out the middle *ees*.

Rhys clasps his cousin on the shoulder. "Baptiste."

A flurry of French, too quick for me to follow, ensues. And then I'm introduced. "This is my co-worker, Ivy."

Co-worker. I almost want to elbow Rhys for that one, but I don't, extending my hand to Baptiste. He ignores it and leans in to kiss me on both cheeks, smelling faintly of rosewater. "It's a pleasure," he tells me, "to meet a friend of Rhys's."

"Likewise."

Baptiste looks at Rhys with a wide smile. "Traveling the world with a beautiful model, *hein*? Not a bad job to have."

Rhys reaches for the menu. "I've had worse."

"When Rhys told me you were joining us, I had a look at your social media," Baptiste tells me. "The amount of followers, whew. It must be challenging?"

"It can be, yes. I mean, it is. I'm still not entirely comfortable with it, especially not considering so many of my followers are young."

Young, an impressionable. I know exactly what striving

for unrealistic beauty standards feels like, and the idea that I might be contributing that myself...

"Fascinating," Baptiste says. "And using that kind of thing for marketing, too? You must be swamped with people wanting you to, ah, promote things?"

"Oh yes, I get a ton of messages. I turn it all down, though." I order the cheapest thing on the menu, but it's still eighty-seven euros. *Live now, think about money later,* I tell myself. The waitress is more than attentive to us, going so far as to bring us an extra bread basket.

It feels like unusually good service in a city Rhys had just earlier derided for its lack of hospitality.

"Ah, yes," Baptiste says at some point, waving his hand at Rhys. "I'm glad you're here, Ivy. Perhaps you can settle a dispute between us."

"Not this again," Rhys groans.

"Yes, yes. You see, my American cousin believes that Paris is overrated. Over-hyped. I keep telling him it isn't—no Parisian could ever say that. Rhys disagrees. You, our beautiful guest, will have to decide."

I take a sip of my wine. "I've only been here for a day."

"Oh, but that's even better! You've seen it all with virgin eyes."

My wine gets stuck in my throat and I have to cough once, twice. Rhys puts a hand on my back. "You okay?"

"Yes, thanks, I'm fine."

Baptiste looks between the two of us. "Or perhaps you're not impartial, ah? You're biased?"

"Baptiste." There's a warning in Rhys's voice.

"It's just a question." His smile turns teasing, raising a glass to me. "We're becoming friends, aren't we, Ivy?"

"Sure." I raise my glass to his. "And I'm not biased."

"You're not?"

"No."

He glances toward Rhys, smile widening. "Good to know."

The dinner is nearly over when I finally start picking up on the reason I'm supposed to be a buffer. Baptiste's voice turns casual, nonchalant. "And of the family, Rhys? What's become of my other cousins?"

Rhys pushes his glass of wine away. "They're good."

"Henry?"

"He's doing well. Busy, but, when is he not?"

"That's Henry," Baptiste agrees. "I remember. Lily?"

An entirely private smile plays on Rhys's lips. "She's doing well. Her son is almost a year, now."

Baptiste sighs. "Little Lily, a mother."

"Mhm, I know. It was a mindfuck for me, too."

"She's your sister?" I ask, and they both nod. I'm getting to hear about his family. Piece after piece, more of the real Rhys Marchand is falling in line.

"Parker is good too," Rhys says. How many siblings does he have? "He's thinking of buying the yacht club, actually."

"In Paradise?"

"Yeah."

Parker Marchand, the one sibling that hadn't come up when I'd googled his name. My curiosity feels like a burning thing inside me, one that I can't really contain. I force it down with another sip of wine.

"And my aunt and uncle?" Baptiste asks, draping his arm around the back of the chair next to him. "They never come to France anymore."

Rhys gives a sharp nod. "It's rare."

"My mother misses Eloise." Baptiste gives an elegant shrug, reaching for his glass. "It's a shame, really, that siblings should drift apart like that."

"It really is," Rhys agrees, reaching for his own.

There is so much subtext here, and I don't know any of it.

"But," Rhys drawls, "the good thing is that flights go both ways."

Baptiste's lips quirk, but not with any real humor. "So they do, cousin. So they do."

Both of them pause to drink wine.

I stare at one of the waitresses moving between the tables and try to think of a way to undercut this tension, to turn this thing around. I come up empty.

"D'accord," Baptiste murmurs. And then, in a voice that makes it clear we're turning the page, he asks me, "and what are your plans for your one night in Paris?"

"My plans?"

"Yes. Where is Rhys taking you after this?"

I glance toward Rhys, but his face is the same inscrutable mask he always wears. "I think we're going back to the hotel?" I ask him.

"Of course you're not." Baptiste waves for the check. "You're coming out with me."

"We are?"

Rhys sighs. "We can't be out late."

"Oh, I know, I know… but there's a great bar just around the corner. It's not even midnight, no way you're leaving yet." He grins at me. "Let us show you the real Paris."

And unlike with Paolo, I find myself nodding. "Okay. Yeah, let's."

He gets up and stretches, smiling at us both. "Restroom break, like you say."

Rhys shakes his heads and reaches into his back pocket for his wallet. "We don't have to go," he says quietly.

"Do you not want to?"

Another beat of silence. And then, "I do want to see you dance again."

We could be anywhere, surrounded by anyone, and I wouldn't be able to look away from his eyes. They're dark and unfathomable and tentative. Like he's offering a tiny bit of truth, and it's not cloaked in sarcasm or wit.

I swallow. "Okay, yeah. We'll do that."

Rhys pays the entire bill. When I try to stop him, he just shakes his head. "I invited you out," he says, returning the black credit card to his wallet. "It's only fair."

But his eyes aren't entirely clear, and I don't know if it's because of me or because of Baptiste's convenient restroom excuse after asking for the bill.

There's more here than meets the eye, but hasn't that always been the case with Rhys Marchand?

9

RHYS

Baptiste monopolizes Ivy during the short walk to the nearby bar. It's not surprising—I'm starting to understand the impulse—but I have to clench my teeth together to keep from interrupting him as he asks what it's really like to *be* a model.

Like it's a mode of being and not a profession.

I shouldn't have accepted his text to go out to dinner. The possibility of an evening alone in Paris, perhaps showing Ivy around, drawing out the magic that Paris possesses but is so good at hiding... yeah, that would have been better. But the opportunity has passed.

I force my clenched fist to relax at my side as Baptiste loops back around to me. Nearly as tall as me, we'd once been thick as thieves growing up. Summers spent in the French countryside had seen us racing on bikes down to the ocean. He'd been someone to discuss French history with that my siblings weren't interested in. If it wasn't a painter, Lily wouldn't listen—if it wasn't an architect, Henry wouldn't. Parker didn't care about history at all.

But things had changed sometime in our teens, and irrevocably when I left Paris all those years ago.

"A model," he whispers to me in French, clasping my shoulder. "You're really living in the fast lane, Rhys!"

"She's a person."

"Of course, of course. And you're not together?"

I consider lying. "No."

"Excellent." Baptiste's smile is wide. "A model," he repeats to himself before returning to Ivy's side. Her hair flows softly down her back, and the dress she's wearing fits her better than anything she's worn so far on the trip. It's more... her. Understated. Gorgeous.

Natural.

She gives us both a wide, blinding smile when we stop outside the bar. Music blasts through the open door. "Is this the place?"

"Yes. It's not too loud, is it?"

"Not at all!"

I step past Baptiste as we enter and put a hand on her low back, bending to whisper.

"We can leave whenever you want," I tell her. "Just let me know."

She turns her face up, distractingly close. "All right. Dance with me?"

She smells like woman and warm skin and whatever sweet, floral shampoo she's used. And there's only one response. "If you want to."

Her smile is a mischievous thing, reminding me that she's more than I'd first thought she was. She disappears into the bar, nodding for us to continue. I shrug to Baptiste and follow her inside, with him on my heels.

Ivy weaves her way to the middle of the dance floor. I follow her less gracefully, using elbows and half-shouted *pardons.*

She finds the rhythm instantly, as if she'd been waiting to since she heard the song. Baptiste asks her what she'd like to drink, and shoots me an obnoxious smile as he heads to the bar to get it for her.

So he can pay for her drink but not his own dinner?

It's such a small thing, but knowing what he would have asked me if Ivy wasn't there, it grates.

She beckons me closer, holding on to my shoulders to reach my ear. "This place is amazing," she tells me.

"It's like every other bar back in New York," I half-shout back.

Her smile then is breathtaking. She's truly enjoying this, seedy and cramped though it is. "Yes," she shouts back, "but it's *not* in New York!"

I grin back at her at that. She's embracing the adventure, and for fuck's sake, so should I. It's my brand, after all.

Baptiste returns soon enough, handing her a tall cocktail and me a beer. Ivy manages that careful, oddly feminine thing of dancing while she's sipping her drink, her body fluid. Having seen her dance salsa in St. Barts, I know she's talented, but somehow she can carry that over to the mindless beating drums of contemporary pop. It's spectacular to watch.

I want to photograph her dancing.

A well-lit studio and Ivy twirling to a song that only she hears. The image strikes me suddenly, the angles, how I could try to capture movement with a still image.

Baptiste's attempts to engage her in conversation are skillfully deflected. She smiles and dances, tossing her hair, a moving flurry under the beating lights. He doesn't seem to mind, which is his style, but I'm irrationally pleased nonetheless.

It's not my business if she chooses to spend time with Paolo or Baptiste.

And yet, I'm glad she's not taking their bait. And why should she? I have no doubt this is a commonplace occurrence for her.

The music shifts into a deep, throbbing beat that I feel in my bones. Ivy tosses her hair and twists her hips a little, subtle but irresistible, and glances my way. There's a smile on her lips.

Maybe it's her. Maybe it's the alcohol.

But I can't look away, and through it all, it feels like she's dancing for me, because I asked her to.

A woman stops at my side, putting a hand on my elbow. She says something in low French that I don't hear.

I bend my head. *"Pardon?"*

She repeats her question, a variant of *do you come here often?* I'm a bit harsher in my response than I usually am, but I thank her for her interest and tell her I'm here with someone. Not technically a lie, not technically the truth. I'm skirting the line.

I'm starting to skirt a lot of lines.

When I glance back, Ivy's not where I'd left her. She's dancing with Baptiste and he has his arm around her shoulders. The emotion that courses through me isn't something I'll be proud of later.

I push my way through the throng of people, and perhaps I've gone completely mad, but I see relief in Ivy's eyes. She slips under Baptiste's arm and comes to my side, still moving, as if she's never stopped dancing. As if it's all part of the routine.

Baptiste gives me a shrug, the universal sign of *I had to try,* and nods toward the bar. He disappears a few seconds later.

Ivy looks up at me with a smile. "I think your cousin was interested in me," she says, but because of the loud music, she has to stand on her tiptoes. Her hand curls around my bicep for support and God help me, but I flex.

"I know he was," I say in her ear, pushing her hair out of the way. "First Paolo, now Baptiste? Must be tough being this wanted."

Her hand tightens on my arm, and her voice… "They don't actually want *me*," she says. "They want the idea of me."

But before I can ask her to elaborate, she pulls away from me with a smile and turns. Her dress flows around her, long legs on display.

"One last song," she mouths, beckoning me forward. So I do. I dance to music I despise, in a club I've never heard of, in a city I have complicated feelings for, all for a sarcastic girl with golden hair and boundless positivity.

I tell Baptiste we're leaving as soon as he returns. He makes the usual arguments, but I silence them with *we have to work tomorrow.*

He pulls me in for a half-hug. "Take care. Come back soon, and bring some of your siblings. We'll go down to the countryside."

"I'll do my best to convince them," I say, already knowing it's a battle I'll lose. Not offering an invitation to New York.

Ivy surprises me by grabbing my hand, pulling me toward the exit. We emerge into the still-warm air of Paris past midnight. It feels like a legendary night in the making.

Ivy is beaming. "Let's walk back to the hotel."

"We could," I agree, shoving my hands in my pockets. "But it's a rather long walk."

"Give me the stats."

"A mile?"

"In minutes."

"About twenty. Think your feet can handle it?"

"Absolutely." She glances down at her flat shoes. "I got to choose my own today, and I want to see Paris at night."

I nod toward an adjoining street, leading us down to the Seine. "It's best at night. The tourists are all gone."

"You really don't like tourists, do you?"

"No, I really don't," I say. Her voice has a floaty, airy quality, and her cheeks are rosy. The wine must be affecting her, too. "Tell me what you meant, earlier."

"About what?" She balances along a low ledge, hair falling forward to hide her face. The street we're following is deserted, a stark contrast to the cacophony of cars that traffic it during the day. That's one of the things that's a pro in Paris's book as opposed to New York's—despite being a major world capital, Paris most definitely sleeps.

The French never miss their beauty sleep.

"You said that men want the *idea* of you."

She jumps down from the ledge with a soft bend of her knees. "I say a lot of things."

"Are you deflecting?"

"Maybe. Is it working?"

"Not particularly."

She pushes back a strand of hair, notching it behind her ear. "You really want to hear a model complain about how tough it is to be a model? It's usually a tough sell."

She's joking, but I wonder…

"Everyone has problems. You're part of everyone, aren't you?"

"Yes." She glances at me out the side of her eye, like she's judging how sincere I am. Is she worried I'll make fun of it? A faint pang of guilt hits me at the first words she'd heard me speak.

"Fine. People hear the word model and it dazzles them. It's like a neon sign goes off in their heads. I can see it in some men's eyes, especially. It's like I become a label or an item on a checklist. Something to tick off."

"I apologize for my cousin," I say.

She laughs, trailing a hand along the stone fence that guards off pedestrians from the murky waters of the Seine below. "He's not your responsibility."

"Still, my apologies."

"Thank you. I wasn't sure you'd understand, you know, considering you're immune to models and all…"

I groan. "I'm always going to be reminded of my comments, aren't I?"

"Yes. At least until I stop being annoyed by them."

"And when will that be?"

"Don't hold your breath," she says. "Or do, actually. Perhaps you'll set a world record. Something new to add to your shelf of trophies."

"You think I'm a collector of trophies?"

She gives me a winning smile. "Yes. You wouldn't call them anything that mundane, though."

Our gazes lock. Challenge dances in her eyes, lit by the moonlight. Her words are teasing but true, striking through a calculated exterior. She digs her teeth into her lower lip. "Will you tell me why you needed a buffer with your cousin?"

I run a hand through my hair. "Is it too much to ask that you drop that?"

"Not likely. I'm good at deflecting deflections too, you know."

"So I've noticed."

"Besides, I've just told you my deepest darkest secret."

I raise an eyebrow. "That men sometimes think you're nothing but a pretty face? That can't be your darkest secret."

Ivy's smile is cheeky. "You're right. It's that I can't raise just one eyebrow like that, like you can. How do you do it and can you teach me?"

"Deflecting."

"No, you're deflecting." She gives me a shove and I step out onto the empty road, hands in my pockets. "I asked you first about my job as a buffer."

"No comment," I say.

"This isn't an interview," she says. "I'm not a journalist. You don't get to say that."

I groan. "You're worse than any journalist I've ever encountered."

"And have you encountered many?"

"My fair share," I say darkly, thinking about the multiple family portraits my father liked the press to do when I was younger. All of us kids interviewed and made to recite pre-prepared answers.

"Fine, I'll lay off," she says. "He seemed nice though. You guys had a lot of stories from your childhood."

"It had its highlights."

She bumps me again. "Come on, spending your summers in the south of France? Do you know how you sound?"

"As privileged as a model complaining about being pretty?" I raise an eyebrow. "How about we both concede that we're privileged, and we won't use that against one another."

"A privilege truce," she repeats. "I can agree to that."

And then she extends her hand to me, a wide smile on her face. She gives them away so freely, those smiles, the ones that make me feel like I've somehow become one of her favorite people in the whole world. It's as undeserved as it is addicting.

I shake her hand. It's soft and warm in mine, and even though there's no loud music to blame this on, I pull her closer as I reply. "Truce."

"Truce," she murmurs. My eyes drop toward her lips and then the expanse of skin down her arms, and through my hazy, wine-addled mind, I recognize something. She's cold.

"You didn't bring a jacket."

"No," she murmurs, her hand slipping from mine.

I shrug out of my thin leather jacket and hand it to her. She accepts, fingers curving over mine. "Thank you."

"Yeah. Don't mention it."

We turn onto a bridge spanning the river, wooden beams beneath our feet and lights glittering across the water. My jacket hangs over her shoulders.

I clear my throat. "This bridge used to be where couples put love locks."

"Really?"

"Yeah."

"Used to be?"

I nod, pointing to a panel of plexiglass. "It got too heavy. The mayor decided to cut them all down."

Ivy's smile turns wistful. "That's a shame. Well, perhaps *you* don't think that. You probably think it was touristy."

"I don't like that I'm so predictable to you."

She laughs, slowing to a halt on the bridge. "Only sometimes. You didn't think it was romantic at all?"

"Mmm. Perhaps a bit." I step closer, unable to resist.

"Although, I suspect most who did it were only doing so because it was a *thing* to do."

She nods. "So it would only have been romantic if you'd have been the first to do it."

"You're impossible."

"Admit it," she murmurs. "You like it when I challenge you." Behind her, the Seine glitters with reflecting lights, as age-old bridges and riverbanks are illuminated. It's a beautiful sight. It's Paris.

But I can't tear my gaze away from Ivy, from the smile on her face. It's innocent and teasing at the same time, like she's offering me something that she knows she shouldn't be.

A mistake we need to make.

"It's growing on me," I admit.

She sways closer, a strand of blonde hair curving over her cheek. My hand aches to smooth it back. "Thank you for showing me Paris today."

"Do you feel like you've had the full experience?" I reach up to smooth the piece of hair back. My finger doesn't stop, though, running down the soft skin of her cheek.

Her eyes are wide, but not afraid. "Almost. I suppose there's one thing I technically haven't done that was on the list."

"It was on a list?"

"Yes. You see, my sister made me add…"

"Add what?"

A blush creeps up her cheeks. "Well, they call it the city of love."

"Do they? I hadn't heard." I rest my fingers on her neck, using my thumb to turn her head up toward me. She's the perfect height for me.

"It's one of those tourist things," she breathes.

"Explains why I don't know it." I run my thumb over her full bottom lip. Disconnect the part of my brain that tells me this is a bad idea. "Let me guess, then."

"Okay."

"You want to be kissed in Paris." I can hear the roughness in my voice. Does she, too?

"To gain the full experience, yes." Her hands come up to rest on my chest. Can she feel how my heart is beating?

My other hand finds her waist, curling around it. "I can help with that."

"Good," she murmurs.

Her eyes flutter closed as I close the distance between us, the most beautiful image I'll never be able to capture on camera. It'll have to be stored in my mind instead, but stored it will be, because I don't think I'll ever be able to forget how Ivy Hart looks under the Parisian moonlight, standing on a bridge with her face turned up for me to kiss.

I ghost my lips over hers gently, once, twice, almost *not* kissing. Drawing out the anticipation. Her fingers curl into fists in the fabric of my shirt.

I put us both out of our misery and kiss her fully.

I'd planned on maintaining self-control, on this being a soft, tentative kiss, one to remember. *Kissed in Paris,* the memory.

But this kiss has a mind of its own, or perhaps my lips do, because soft and tentative are the last two words applicable here.

I flick my tongue along her lips and she opens to me, tasting warm and sweet and just faintly like whatever drink she'd just had. My grip on her tightens, as if this sensation might float away if I don't hold on.

And Ivy, dear God... her arms twine around my neck in a surrender that feels complete, and so trusting. My left hand knots itself in her hair. It's just as soft as I'd imagined.

And I don't want to let go.

It scares me just how much I don't want to lift my head from hers. How completely her sweetness floods my system and hijacks my thinking. It feels like it takes ten years of my life, like it costs me half my hair to grayness, but I press my lips softly to hers one last time. The space between us fills with the sound of our breathing.

"Okay," she whispers. "That was… yeah. Okay."

I untangle my hand from her hair and slide it down, gripping her waist with both of mine. She looks like she could use the steadying.

"Just okay?"

Her eyes flutter open and she smiles at me. Is it just me or does she look dazed? "Better than okay."

I raise an eyebrow. "My ego smarts, but I'll take it."

"As if I could bruise your ego." She slips her hands down from around my neck, my skin tingling through the shirt where she touches. "Kissed in Paris. Thank you."

"Happy to oblige." I let go of her, force my hands to drop to my sides. My entire body still curves toward her, and I swear, if she were to turn up her face and ask for a second round…

But she doesn't. She nods to the other side of the river, a fierce blush on her cheeks. "Let's get back to the hotel."

10

IVY

I'm packed and my hair and makeup is done early the next morning. We only have a half day left to shoot in Paris, and most of that will be filming me walking around little streets and alleys. We've yet to shoot by the Eiffel Tower, too, which is an absolute must.

Beneath the fluffy hotel robe, I'm wearing the flowy summer dress the agency put me in. It clings to my shape perfectly, which means I'll have to think about not hunching over. Combined with the hat they want me to wear and the flats, it does feel a bit... French countryside-ish, not that I have any frame of reference outside of movies.

Sitting on the giant gilded bed, the covers neatly made, my heart feels like it's in my throat. Rhys will be here any minute, knocking on that door with his camera in hand, like he has for the past few days.

We said goodbye last night right outside that door, his kiss still lingering on my lips.

It's only been five days since we left New York, and in that short amount of time I've managed to kiss him. My sister would pass out if I told her, but not before she yelled *I told you so!*

My lips still tingle at the memory.

I haven't been kissed often. I've rarely let men get that close, and every time it's happened, I haven't been able to get out of my own head. But with Rhys, staying in my own head hadn't been an option.

For the first time ever, it didn't feel like I was on the outside looking in. I was fully *there* with him, my lips moving with his.

It was the kind of kiss that makes you understand why people love kissing so much. It was the kind of kiss that makes you want another.

There's a knock on the door.

And he's there when I open it, a stray lock falling down across his forehead. A dark eyebrow is already raised. "Good morning."

"Good morning." I rock back on my heels, unable to keep from smiling. Why am I nervous? "Did you sleep well?"

"I did. Did you?"

"Yes."

He looks down at me. "Did you forget to get dressed?"

"What?"

"The robe?" He narrows his eyes. "You're not terribly hungover, are you?"

"No, not at all. I was actually going to ask you for a favor. Come on, come inside."

Rhys steps into my hotel room, and it shrinks. Perhaps that's one of the undiscovered laws of physics or he's just bending them entirely, but there's *a lot* less space with him standing in here.

"Another favor?"

Another? Does he mean the kiss yesterday?

"Yes. Not... yes. Here." I hand him my phone and struggle to find my way back to a joke, to our camaraderie. "I know you hate photographing with smartphones, so I'm asking you to go against your own principles here."

He groans. "You want me to take a picture of you?"

"Please." I open the double doors to my balcony,

welcoming the already-warm air of the city. The sky is a beautiful pale blue, strewn with wispy clouds, and the Eiffel Tower beckons in the distance.

Nothing could break my happiness today, not even Rhys Marchand's withering comments.

"While I'm standing here. Is that okay?"

He looks from my phone to me. "That depends. My fee is pretty steep."

"Shoot. Do you accept favors? I bet you'll need my help with something during this trip."

He snorts. "I already have—and you helped me with that yesterday."

For a mind-numbing second, I think he's referring to the kiss. But no, it's Baptiste, the dinner, and my role as buffer.

"Right. Well then, take pictures of me here, and then we're even."

"Is this for your social media accounts?" he asks.

My fingers clutch around the balcony railing. "It might be."

He grumbles behind me.

"I know you hate that," I add.

"Yes. But it's the game I hate, not the player." He holds up my phone. "Let me attempt a bit of pointing and shooting, then."

I pose against the balcony railing, my robe wrapped tightly around me. Rhys backs up a little, changes his angles as I transition between poses. We've only been shooting together for a few days, and most of those had been fraught with tension.

Now it's starting to feel... natural. I know what angles he'll ask me for before he does. He knows what poses I look best in before I shift into them.

I've never shot with the same photographer for this long.

"This is a good idea," he says, brow furrowed, the way it always is when he photographs. Concentration makes his features sharpen in intensity. "You're selling the hotel this way, too."

"Rieler might want one of these shots too."

"Hmm. Maybe."

I nod towards the double doors. "What do you call French doors in France?"

He snorts. "Just doors, I suppose."

"It's a riddle." I turn around, tossing my hair down my back, and lean out over the railing. The Eiffel Tower is gorgeous in the distance. "I don't think I'll ever tire of this view," I tell him.

"To the left."

"Look?"

"Yes."

I do as he says, and when I glimpse back, he's shooting with his big camera. "For Rieler?"

"Yes. You… well, you had a good idea."

My lips curve. "Bound to happen every now and then."

"I suppose," he says, but there's a smirk there, too.

"So what do you have against social media?" I ask him, turning around to look at him. He keeps shooting, so I keep posing, even as I wait for his reply. Closing my eyes and tilting my head back. Gripping the waistband of my robe.

Rhys finally lowers the camera. "I recognize that it can be great," he says, words measured. Like he's being careful. "For keeping in touch with people, for getting news. But more and more, people seem to be turning to social media for human connection rather than to, you know, *actual* humans. Not to mention that the beauty standards on social media are sending kids' self-esteem to record lows."

His words are a bucket of ice water.

I tug my robe off, revealing the dress I'd worn beneath, and head back into the hotel room. He follows silently. He doesn't speak when I pull on my shoes either, and he helps me roll one of my giant suitcases down the corridor. We don't speak until we've checked our bags in with the concierge for the day, not until we're out on the bright streets of Paris.

"Hey, I know that was harsh," he says.

I don't reply for a moment, because I don't feel like I can.

"Ivy…"

"You prefer brutal honesty." I look up at the sky, because I can't look at him. The sharp sting of his early judgement is back, but it's so much more cutting this time, because it's reaching a wound that's already hurting. "You touched on one of my biggest fears," I admit.

Rhys doesn't reply, but there's permission in the silence. My words find their way out. "I know this industry is shallow, and models are just… *just models*. Paid to look pretty. I mean, part of that is what you said just two weeks ago."

"I could have phrased it better."

"You know, when the average woman sees a picture of me that's in an ad or a magazine, it's gone through so many rounds of editing. And I'm talking before it ever became digital—this is my *job*." I pause, pointing to my hair. "Professional highlights. My skin? The agency pays for a dermatologist that I see every month. I'm never in the sun. This tan is fake, courtesy of the agency. I work out pretty much every day, and I've worked with both personal trainers and dietitians. My *job* is to look the best I possibly can. Who else can say that? And when images of me, or of other models, end up on social media… There are additional filters. Retouching. And knowing that teenagers compare themselves to… I know, Rhys," I grind out. "I *know*. And yet social media and beauty is the currency of my industry. I don't know how to escape it."

"Shut down your accounts," he says quietly. "I'm not saying you have to, but if this is eating at you, that's one solution."

I look away from him. "I suggested it to my agency. Mentioned it in passing, actually. That I was tiring of the whole thing."

"And?"

"I was informed in no uncertain terms that if I did that, I could find myself another agency."

"You're joking."

"I wish I was."

His hand closes around my arm. "They actually said that?"

"Yes. Don't tell people that, though."

"Of course I won't. But Ivy…"

"That's the industry." I shrug. "How many followers girls have on social media determines what gigs they book, what opportunities come their way, their income… It's everything. That was why I was so happy when I got this job, apart from the obvious—all the traveling. I'm not the model with the highest follower count or the most experience at the agency, but I still booked this one."

Rhys's expression is impossible to decipher, like so much of his personality. Is he judging me? Pitying me? It could be either and everything in between.

"I've tried," I say, but it sounds weak to my own ears. "I never edit the pictures I post. I try to be more real, to show behind-the-scenes photos too."

No sign of his emotions in his eyes. Does it sound as pathetic a compromise to him as it does to me?

But then he sighs. "You're stuck in between a rock and a hard place."

"Yeah."

But what he'd said so succinctly, summed up and neat, had felt like salt in a pre-existing wound. One I've pondered how best to heal, with every solution coming up short. I don't want to be part of the reason why people feel bad. I don't want to be someone people compare themselves to, not appearance wise.

Rhys slides his hand in his back pocket and hands me my phone, which I'd forgotten about at the hotel. It looks small in his grip. Innocent. Like it's not the home of all of these problems.

"You'll figure it out," he tells me. "The fact that you're already thinking about this makes it clear you will. There are tons of public profiles who use their platforms for good."

My smile is a bit forced. The ones who do aren't models, but then again, I'm not planning on being one forever. "You're right."

"You know what else I'm right about?"

"What?"

"We don't have to spend the entire day shooting. After we're done by the Eiffel Tower, I want to show you a few places around town. We have enough time before we have to head to the airport."

"Places you visited when you lived here?"

"The very ones."

"I'm going to get a tour through Rhys Marchand's Paris? Does that make me a tourist?"

Rhys shakes his head and looks away, but he's smiling. "Don't go there."

"Will you be carrying a little sign, so I don't get lost? Are headphones included?"

"Another joke out of you and the tour is cancelled," he says, nodding ahead. "Let's go. The faster we take pictures of you, the quicker we can look at the city."

I pretend to lock up my lips and follow him toward the Eiffel Tower in the distance. We work quickly, gathering the shots necessary for the agency. Rhys adds a few extra ideas, having me stop to buy a croissant, sitting along the Seine, buying art from one of the street vendors. I actually go through with it, too, buying a small painting of the French skyline.

It'll hang in my tiny New York apartment. I already know the spot.

"Tourist," Rhys tells me.

"Cynic," I tell him, and I win, because his lips curve into a half-smile.

We film a lot by the Eiffel Tower—me walking down the steps of Trocadero, with Paris in the foreground. Me sitting on the steps and sipping on a cup of coffee. The clips will be put to good use when he edits together the travel film.

"All right," he finally declares, screwing on the lens of his camera. He's staunchly ignoring the tittering of a few teenage girls who have stopped to watch us as we work. The attention makes me uncomfortable in a way it rarely does. I don't want those girls to compare themselves to me.

I stand, brushing off a few leaves from my dress. "You got what you needed?"

"Yes." He hands me my bag without question. "Time to switch your footwear."

I hold on to his arm as I slide out of my strappy, heeled sandals and into my comfortable loafers.

Goodbye pinched feet, hello freedom.

"That's something I wouldn't be sad if humanity had never invented," I say. "Heels."

Rhys glances back at the people watching us. A few have snapped pictures, probably thinking that his equipment and my posing meant we might "be" someone. They'll be disappointed when they realize we're not.

"Smartphones," he mutters.

I snort. "You're very predictable sometimes."

He looks at me like I've just insulted him gravely, and I can't help it, I burst out laughing.

A reluctant smile tugs on his lips. "Predictable," he mutters. "My family would have a collective aneurysm if they heard me described that way."

"It hasn't been your MO in the past?" I shoulder my bag and wave a little goodbye to the few people still watching us. Two of the girls wave back and turn around, giggling to one another.

"Not exactly. Wait…" He keeps a hand on my arm, the

other reaching up to gently untangle a leaf from my hair. "I shouldn't have made you lie down along that hedge."

"It made for a good shot." I say, speaking more to his Adam's apple than him. The first few buttons in his shirt are undone, showing a slice of tanned skin.

It had been easy to forget the kiss while we worked. Well, *forget* might be too strong of a word. Push it to the side—keep myself from thinking about it, when all I had to do was focus on posing or looking at his camera, not at him.

But it's just the two of us now, and no lens in between us.

He takes a step back. "Come on," he says. "We have places to see, and Paris waits for no one."

We grab a cab half of the way, and spend the rest of the time walking around the small streets in St. Germain. He takes me to a bookstore by Notre Dame, complete with two stories and a cat sleeping in one of the chairs.

"The best English bookstore in Paris," he says. "It's become a bit touristy these days, though."

I look over at where he's standing, having to duck his head to fit under a low beam. The shirt stretches over wide shoulders as he reaches for a book on a top shelf.

My mouth is dry when I speak, and I find myself having to clear my throat. "I saw you reading on the plane the other day."

"Mhm."

"Do you read a lot?"

"Well, I do run a small publishing house," he says absent-mindedly, turning the paperback he's holding over to read the back. "So yes. I've finished that one, though."

I follow him, smiling, as he pays for his book and we head out. He shoves it in his back pocket. "Something for the flight later," he says.

"It's a long one."

He nods, face shuttering. "I know."

I don't want him shutting down, though. "Have you ever been to Kenya?"

"Yes, but it's been a while."

"Have you been to every place we're going to?"

The bastard actually needs to take a moment to think about it. "No," he says, "but nearly."

"This trip must be so boring for you."

"Unbearably so," he says, but he doesn't look the least bit bored. "Tell me about your dancing."

"My dancing?"

"You said the other day that you danced when you were younger. I want to hear about that."

"You find that interesting?"

He raises an eyebrow in that enviable, maddening way only he seems to be able to. "Yes."

We pass Notre Dame, the church closed for visitors, and I stop to take a picture. The reconstruction will go on for years. Somewhere to my left, people are speaking in a language I can't place. Rhys might not like tourists, but I do.

They're a reminder of all the places I've yet to see and can't wait to go.

"I danced for nearly ten years," I say. "From the age of six to sixteen. It was my passion—everything I did was centered on that. Getting as many hours in the studio as I could."

"It shows," he says. "When you dance."

Perhaps it's stupid for that to mean anything, but it does. Something in my chest lurches dangerously. The memory of his lips on mine resurfaces again. Before, under the bright Parisian sun, the kiss we'd shared at midnight felt like an age ago. Belonging to a different time and to different people.

But now... what would it be like to kiss him right here on the street, without the excuse of alcohol or ambiance?

"Ivy?"

I blink. "Thank you."

"Did you ever try to make it into a career?"

The old wound barely hurts anymore, and my bitterness... well, it stings, but it doesn't linger. "I hurt my knee."

"Oh."

"It wasn't too bad, in the sense that I'm fine today. I can do practically anything on it, except a job that means jumping or twirling on it for hours on end." I push my hair behind my ear and shrug. "It's a common enough story for dancers."

"Doesn't make it any easier." His voice is not distant at all, and not the least bit sardonic. It's deep and true.

It's the same voice who asked me last night if I wanted to be kissed.

"No, but the years have passed. I'll always miss it, but... I think it's been a strength."

"How do you mean?"

I bite my lip. This means putting things into words that I never have before. "That's to say... I know other models who make this their identity. They're terrified of the day they have to find another job. But I've already had that, in a way. Dancing was my true dream, not modeling." I shake my head. "I know this is falling in the category of privileged problems."

"Hey, we called a truce on that," he says. "I honor all of my truces."

A smile tugs at my lips. "I do too. So I take it back."

"Good." He pulls us to a pause in the shade of a large tree, right by the Seine. "We have an hour left. You decide what we do. I have suggestions, but..."

"I'm not sure we have time... could we go to the Louvre?" I ask. It had been highest on the list of what I wanted to see here, but I'd no idea we'd actually be able to do it. The schedule was tight enough as it was.

Something pleased flicks through Rhys's eyes, giving me an inordinate amount of satisfaction, like I've given the right answer.

It makes me want to do it again.

"We have time," he says. "And Ivy..."

"Yes?"

"About yesterday. I'm sorry for my cousin."

I shake my head. "Don't be. He was nice."

The faint furrow in Rhys's forehead doesn't disappear. It makes me want to move closer, to rise up and press my lips to his cheek. It's an impulse I've never had with anyone before. The memory of his arms around me comes crashing into me like a tidal wave.

Rhys's lip curls. "Sure he was. I'm also debating whether I should apologize for what happened on the way home."

My heart explodes into a stampede in my chest. "Why would you?"

"Just figured you might be regretting it."

I wet my lips. "I'm not regretting it."

Quite the opposite.

Rhys gives a crooked smile. "Good," he says. "Then I'm not, either."

"Good," I murmur. My mind is trying to find something else to add, something clever, but it's like fighting my way through fog. His face is the only thing I can see. "Thanks for doing me a favor."

"I've been known to be helpful every now and then," Rhys murmurs. "Like right now. Let's see the Louvre before we have to go to the airport."

I force myself to nod. We start walking again, and while it's in no way awkward, I feel like I missed an opportunity somehow. That whatever happened last night... well, the odds of it happening again have grown slimmer.

11

RHYS

I'm short with the hotel attendant. I'm short with Ivy, too, but she's used to it after nearly twelve hours of traveling. The flight to Kenya had been a ride from hell. Like the Devil's private roller coaster.

Turbulence after turbulence.

Ivy hadn't seemed fazed, and I knew there was a possibility that my mind was over-exaggerating things… but fuck, I'm finished with flying after this trip. Done. Trains and boats for me from here on out, thank you very much.

I know my resolution won't last. The urge to travel will win out.

It always does.

Ivy is talking excitedly with our attendant, named Joy. The drive out to the Rieler's lodges is near an hour, the landscape changing dramatically as we make our way into nature. The view of endless grasslands and trees is nearly enough to bring me out of my bad mood. It's been years since I was last in Africa, and Kenya had been… well, near on fifteen years.

It had been a family trip, us kids obsessed with the idea of going on a safari. My little sister had created bingo sheets for all of us with hand-drawn images of the animals for us to spot. It hadn't really worked out—we all saw the animals *together*, after all, so we all got bingo at the exact same time. But it was cute.

Joy pulls the Jeep to a stop outside a beautiful lodge. I have to give it to Ben, his company has sourced some of the most beautiful places in the world. Dark wood, the lodge is nestled into the surrounding landscape, located on a hillscape.

The roof is thatched and thick, and wooden double doors beckon. "Welcome to your lodge," Joy says, jumping out of the driver's seat.

"This place is… wow. It's beautiful," Ivy says.

I lift her heavy bag out of the back of the truck. It's still insane that the agency sent her with this amount of clothes, but… it's starting to annoy me less.

Everything about her that once irritated me is starting to do so less.

"It's the best lodge we have," Joy says. "It's top-tier. Come on, come on, let me show you…"

We follow her into the lodge, and what greets us is nothing less than the best Rieler has to offer. A giant bed is in the center, flanked by windows on either side that open up to the landscape beyond. Private, but right in the middle of nature.

I look into the other areas of the lodge. A living room, a giant bathroom… but only one bed. Ivy registers it at the same time as I do.

"Is there another bedroom?"

Joy falters, but only slightly. "No, sir. We were told to set you up in one lodge. Will that be a problem?"

"No, not at all." I'll grab the couch. Won't be the worst thing I've slept on—not by a long shot.

Joy's smile is back. "All right, then. I'll leave you to get settled. There's a golf cart outside your lodge, which you can take to go to the main house for breakfast and dinner. We're just a call away if you need anything at all."

"And our scheduled safari starts in two hours?"

"Yes, that's right, sir."

I sink down into the giant sofa. It's amazing—it doesn't hurl through the sky at ungodly speeds. Perhaps I could finally get a bit of shut-eye before we have to shoot. "Thank you."

Ivy talks to Joy on the way out. It's a long while until she finally makes her way back into the lodge, and when she does, I have to force my eyes open.

"Are you doing better?" she asks.

I close my eyes again. Something about her noticing that I disliked flying rankles me. It shouldn't, but it does. Almost as much as the fact that she'd thanked me for doing her a *favor* by kissing her.

"I'm fine," I say.

I'm not. The idea of sleeping just a few feet away from her in this lodge creeps through my system like a disease. It meets with the memory of her lips against mine, heat exploding beneath my skin.

Endless possibilities.

It'll be tempting to try to get close again, I know myself well enough for that. What's more—it'll be tempting to get to know her better. She's surprised me every step of this trip.

She'd called me predictable. *Me*, while she is quickly turning out to be the most unpredictable person I've ever met.

She's broken ever box I tried to fit her into.

I put a hand over my forehead and keep my eyes closed against the bright Kenyan light. "I'll sleep on the couch," I say. "It's comfortable enough."

Ivy gives a soft laugh. "Don't be silly. Your feet are hanging off it. You don't fit, Rhys."

I open my eyes to respond but fall silent. No words come out. She's standing over by her open suitcase. And she's not wearing a shirt.

Oh, she's in a bra, and perhaps she thinks that shouldn't matter to me—I've seen her in it before, not to mention shot her in a swimsuit—but it does. Because now it's just her and me. Because there's a locked door between us and the outside world.

And because I know how sweet her lips taste.

"What are you doing?"

"Getting ready." She rummages through the suitcase. I watch as she grabs what looks like a ridiculously sized toiletry bag. No human in existence has ever needed a toiletry bag that big.

"We have two hours to go."

"Yes, but there's no hair or makeup artist here." She tucks the bag under her arm and scoops out *another one*, like she's carrying all of the world's products in there. "I'm doing it myself. The agency sent a list of instructions, so I'll just follow those."

I swallow. "This is unusual for you, right?"

"Sharing a room with a photographer?" She's smiling as she says it, but it still hits me in my gut. It takes me a second before I can answer.

"That too, but handling… all of *that* yourself."

"Yes. I'm still not really sure why they didn't send a stylist with us…" she muses, rummaging for something. How much stuff does she need? "Considering how much they're spending on us, and how important this campaign is, I can't quite understand it."

I put a hand under my head. A brief pang of guilt hits me, but I shove it away. Telling her I'm the reason we travelled like this—that the bet with Ben had specified no crew and no assistants—would accomplish what, exactly?

Besides, she'll get paid regardless of the outcome. It doesn't matter which campaign is chosen as the winning one. It only matters for my pride.

I close my eyes again with that knowledge. "So you need two hours to get ready?"

"Scoff all you like," she says, "but I don't just walk around looking like I did in Paris or Rome. You're welcome to view part of the prep work later. I could teach you the difference between a foundation and a concealer."

"I'll pass."

"Your loss," she says brightly. "It does wonders to cover up dark circles under your eyes." The bathroom door closes, and soon thereafter, the shower runs.

Tiredness is fighting to bring me down, but I force myself to check one final thing. I open the camera on my phone and inspect my face. Whatever she says, I don't have dark circles under my eyes.

There's a message waiting for me from my younger sister.

Lily: Hope you're having fun in Kenya! Just checked your itinerary. Sorry I didn't have time to make you a bingo sheet this time. I also saw that you'll be back in the States right before Dad's party. Please, Rhys? Looking forward to seeing the photos you take!

I put my phone away with a groan, resolving to reply later, even if it won't be what she wants to hear. I have no plans to attend a party in our father's honor.

The sun is high in the sky when I brave the near-sweltering heat on our patio, overlooking the surrounding landscape. It's not quiet here. No, nature is loud. There are cicadas and birds and somewhere in the distance something much larger, much *angrier* makes a sound I can't identify. The sky is a light blue, the ground nearly beige with dried grass.

I lean against the railing and just look. *This* is what life is about—this is what life should be like. Traveling. New experiences. Not a stuffy two-story house in the same town where I was raised, not weekends spent at the Yacht Club, not days in an office. My siblings' choices were theirs, but this... this is mine.

Ivy comes to stand beside me, so quiet on bare feet that I barely hear her. The scent of soap and shampoo hits me, subtle but powerful. I glance over.

They've put her in a pair of white chinos and a khaki-colored linen shirt, complete with laced-up boots and a leather belt. It's magazine safari clothing.

And God help me, but yes, I can tell that she's put in prep work, whatever that means. Her eyes are darker, and somehow they look deeper. Magic. Sorcery. Unnecessary, as if she needed to be more striking.

"Well?" she asks. "Will this do?"

"It'll do," I say.

She leans on the railing next to me. "I know you'd rather be photographing wildebeest than me."

My lips twitch. "Infinitely preferable in every way but one," I say. "They don't handle directions as well as you."

Ivy's lips curve, but it's not her wide smile. This one is... well. It reminds me of the one on the bridge in Paris. The one that's somehow a bit shy, which is the last word I'd ever expected to use to describe Ivy Hart.

"What a compliment," she murmurs.

A million possible responses race through my head. A million more that I discard immediately.

The loud sound of a car horn breaks our eye contact. Someone's outside our lodge, and they're impatient. I grab my camera equipment and follow Ivy outside to the oversized Jeep, complete with the Rieler logo on the side.

Joy is standing beside it, a massive grin on her face.

"Ready for your private safari?"

Ivy's excitement is obvious, and it's infectious, even as I listen to the two of them talk. She asks endless questions. *So this is a national park? Are there rangers? When was the last time you saw cheetahs? Lions? Leopards?*

I shoot from the side of the car. It's not difficult to, not with these landscapes. A horde of gazelles. A giant vulture on the side of a carcass. My entire being itches with the desire to camp out here for a night, to photograph animals up close. To lie in wait with my camera the only tool.

Joy leads us to a group of elephants, and for nearly half an hour we sit in silence and watch the graceful giants move. The only sound is the clicking of my camera.

We finally park on a large patch of grassy area, with the savannah behind us. The light is excellent—so we start shooting. Ivy is grinning as she climbs onto the hood of the Jeep. "You want me like this?"

"Yes," I say, pointing back. "On your elbow… like that." I back up to photograph her, watching through my camera as she adopts her posing face. The one that's casual and relaxed, but displaying all the right angles.

She breaks in five minutes. "Look at me," she says, "just reclining on my Jeep. Come travel with Rieler and you can recline on a Jeep, too!"

I lower my camera. "Ivy," I say, but there's no real annoyance in my voice.

She grins at me. "Sorry, I can't help it. Joy?"

"Yes?" our guide calls back, standing to the side with a book in her hand.

"Is this how most of the guests go on safari?"

Joy laughs. "This has to be a first."

Ivy looks down at her pants. "White has to be the most commonly worn color, too, when in nature."

I snort. "That's on the agency, not on me."

"Oh, absolutely. The same agency that thought it was important I wore a push-up bra for this." Ivy leans back on both of her elbows and arches her back, her hair spilling down. She might be joking around, but this is a great shot. I grab it, the Jeep in the foreground, the wide-open savannah in the background. Perhaps I'll be able to edit the horde of elephants into the back…

Ivy turns to look straight at me. "Should I act more like a wildebeest?"

I'm grinning now. "No."

"You sure? Perhaps a giraffe, then?" She makes a show of sticking her head up high, as high as she can, looking at me from the corner of her eye.

I put my camera down. "You're jet-lagged."

"Yes. I don't know what time it is. Not a clue." She looks up at the sky and closes her eyes, and I take a picture of that too, because... Ivy. "But I'm in a place I've always wanted to see and that's enough, even if I want to see lions and not sit on a Jeep. But then again, you want to photograph said lions and not me, so perhaps we're even."

"You'll do," I say, grinning. "The Jeep's not comfortable?"

She puts a hand down on the metal. "Oh, this is the comfortablest Jeep hood there ever was."

I roll my eyes. "Get off there, you idiot."

She jumps off and puts a hand to her forehead, like the clown she's acting. It's a far cry from the determined, fierce model I'd seen on the beach in St. Barts, despite her dedication for the rest of the shoot. She poses next to the Jeep, under a gigantic tree, walking through the bush. I grab a beautiful picture of her standing in the Jeep, watching the landscape through a pair of binoculars.

I film us driving through the landscape. My drone is a whirl above the Jeep, and I'm so focused on getting all the material I need that I barely notice when Ivy sits down next to me in the car.

"You okay over there?"

"Yes," I say, my eyes on the camera. The drone is capturing the surrounding landscape. I need to get the lodge, too... perhaps in the morning?

"I was thinking," she says, "that we can shoot on the balcony too. In our house? Same as we did in Paris."

"Good idea."

"You two work so well together," Joy comments from the driver's seat. "I always thought it would be difficult to work with your partner, but you have proved me wrong. Me? I could never work together with my husband." She laughs at that. "I'd demand a divorce by noon!"

My thumb stops flicking through images I've taken.

Perhaps it's the devil on my shoulder, or the way Ivy had

laughed on that Jeep, but I want to mess with her. See how far I can push. "It's surprised us too," I tell Joy. "We had the same fear. Didn't we, Ives?"

Her smile is locked in place, but the look she shoots me is deadly. "Sure did, honey."

I give her a wide smile back.

"Well, the two of you make a beautiful couple," Joy says, pulling onto the dusty road leading to the Rieler resort. "I should be the one photographing the two of you!"

"So we're a couple?"

I bite my tongue to keep from grinning, grateful that the camera is shielding my face. Ivy reclines against the terrace railing, the sunset behind her draping the Kenyan landscape in a golden hue. "I couldn't help myself."

"Thought you didn't like lying."

"I make exceptions for comedy."

She reaches up to notch a strand of golden hair behind her ear. "Well, that's good to know."

"Something to bear in mind?"

"Exactly." She smiles at me, looking straight at the camera. And there's not a trace of disapproval or dislike on her features. I snap a shot of her like that, looking at me, rather than posing for the camera.

"That's it," I say. "I think we've got all the shots we need out here."

"Awesome."

"I'll just get some of the landscape."

"That means I can finally remove my face," she says, heading into the lodge.

"Your *face?*"

"The makeup!" she calls back.

Shaking my head, I set about capturing the landscape. It's not long until I have everything I need, which is good, because the sun doesn't stay. It's dark when I pull the door to the balcony door firmly shut behind me. With the AC on and the onslaught of insects outdoors, we want to keep one in and the other out.

I head to my suitcase. "I'll grab the sofa."

"If you insist," Ivy responds. She's taken a cross-legged seat on the sofa in question, her hair in a low ponytail. "But it's not that late yet?"

"Aren't you exhausted?"

"My crazy little jet-lag episode is over."

"It was very amusing, so I didn't mind." I sit down on the opposite side of the couch, my eyes roving the shelves. Is there a minibar somewhere here?

"I can imagine," she says, turning something over in her hands. "I don't know if you'd be interested, but I bought this at the airport in Paris before we left."

"What is it?"

"Cards. Just some simple, effective fun." Ivy shrugs, looking at me. "But perhaps it's too mundane for you."

I snort, holding out my hand. She gives me the deck. "I'll play."

"Awesome." She's removed her makeup, and I'm struck with the desire to take a picture of her right here, right now. Sitting cross-legged and relaxed, with her face bare.

"What are we playing for?"

"The honor?"

I shuffle them smoothly. "We can think of something more interesting than that."

"We can?" Ivy frowns, her gaze traveling across the lodge. Stopping on the giant bed. "We could play for who gets to sleep in the master."

My lips twitch. "You're sure? I've already ceded that, so you don't have to put it back on the table."

"Well, what else is there?" She nods at the cards. "Gin rummy?"

I haven't played that in years, but I know the rules well

enough. With three siblings, every type of game was played growing up.

"We'll play for information," I say.

"Information? You sound like a mafia boss," she says, but she's grinning. "I'm not sure if I have information that is worth enough to be a prize."

"I'm absolutely positive that you do," I say, dealing the cards. "The victor gets to ask a question."

Her teeth dig into her lower lip. "And no deflecting? We're both good at that."

I hesitate only for a moment. "No deflecting."

She rubs her hands together in anticipation, but there's a furrow in her brow. So she has things she doesn't want to talk about either. "I'm ready."

Ivy wins the first round, but it's close. She leans against the back of the couch and puts her head in her hand. "I keep thinking of what you said the other night with Baptiste. The real reason you wanted me there as a buffer... but I'm not sure if that's a good starting question."

I raise an eyebrow. "Are you considering giving me a softball?"

"I can be kind." She looks down at the cards in her hands. "All right. Here's my question—why did you decide to become a photographer? You already run a publishing company, right?"

"I've always wanted to write books, and to publish others. That part was a natural career choice. As for photography..." I glance past her to the wide-open lodge behind, the beautifully designed space. "A photo is like capturing a sliver of time. Of history, for all to remember. It's telling a story. It's... you can't lie with a good photograph. I'm discounting all the editing and fake shit here, what I mean is just a good, pure photograph. The greatest pictures ever taken, the ones that have affected countries and nations, they were honest snapshots."

"That's beautiful."

"And it's mine, photography. No one in my family does it. I have very few friends who do, either. It's a solitary thing." Not to mention it's a disappointing career choice in the eyes of my father. I'd once picked it up as a hobby for that very reason.

But it had stuck.

I shuffle the cards, my movements stiffer than usual. Ivy notices, because she cocks her head. "I thought that would be an easy question."

"It was." I deal the cards. Damn it, why is it difficult to talk about real things with her? I've done it plenty of times before, with all kinds of strangers in my travels. "Your turn to start."

She does, and when the game is nearly over, she puts down her final card with a flourish. "I win *again*, Rhys. What is this? Are you deliberately throwing the game?"

I put a dramatic arm over my face. "Yes. I love being tortured with personal questions."

"It's your cry for help," she says cheerily, reaching for her cards. "You know what question I'll ask."

"No, I really don't. Come on. Hit me with it."

"Why did you want me to be a buffer at dinner with your cousin?"

12

IVY

"You're really asking me that?" His voice is offended, but it's clear he's faking. "How painful."

Rhys keeps his arm over his head, stretched out against the back of the couch. His shirt has ridden up, and there's a sliver of tanned, taut stomach on display. A bit of dark hair that disappears into his pants.

I look away. I've never forgotten that Rhys is an attractive man. That's an impossible thing to do, with how large his presence is. And yet the knowledge slams back into me with the force of a tidal wave.

I reach out with the cards and smack them against his knee. "You said no deflections."

"And now you're resorting to physical violence. It's sad, really," he says. "I can picture the headlines already. Charming photographer clobbered to death by jet-lagged model—vultures feasted on his body."

"Vultures? Try hyenas."

"Even worse." He tucks his arm behind his head. "So you really want to know?"

"Yes."

Rhys raises an eyebrow. "If you hadn't been there, he would have asked me for money."

I put my cards down. "Really?"

"Yes." He looks up at the ceiling, a hand buried in his dark curls. Comfortable, sprawling, elegant. "Do you know anything about my family?"

I clear my throat. "I might have searched you on the internet before we set off together."

"Right. And what did you find?" His voice makes it clear that he already knows the answer. I humor him anyway.

"Well, there was a lot. You have really… impressive family members, for one. Very successful ones."

Rhys snorts. "Yes, and the French side of the family, my mother's family, have tried to capitalize on that for decades."

More questions rise up, and perhaps he sees that in my eyes, because Rhys looks away. "It's not like we wouldn't have helped them out in a pinch. But it's become… greedy. My mother barely speaks to her sister, and my siblings don't have much time for our cousins for that very reason."

A few of Baptiste's comments come back to me, now in an entirely new light. Rhys's face when he paid the bill. His tone when he commented about the choice of restaurant. It makes sense, now.

"Even rich people have family problems."

"Oh, we're very good at them. We make it an art form." Rhys nods lazily at the cards, a lock of hair falling down over his forehead. "Your turn to deal, Ives."

I glare at him briefly before I begin to shuffle. There's a lot more I want to ask.

"I'll win this one," Rhys says. "I'm done being the interviewee."

And damn him, but he does. He wins with a flourish and raises an eyebrow at me. "So, you told me that men rarely see you, they just see your beauty."

I wet my lips. "I didn't phrase it exactly like that."

"But that's what you meant?"

"Yes."

Rhys leans in closer. "Tell me about the last man who *saw* you."

Oh no.

I glance down at my cards and try to find the convenient lie, the one I've told before when people have asked about my exes. *I've dated around a bit.* Or my favorite one, *I work too much for anything to get, you know, properly serious.* Those answers imply experience. They're vague.

They're also lies.

"Ivy?" Rhys asks, and something in his tone sends my lies out the window. I doubt he'd buy it, anyway. So I look at the giant photographs of wildlife on the wall. A leopard in a tree is easier to face than him.

"I'm not sure anyone really has."

He gives a thoughtful hum. "Well, damn. Perhaps I should apologize for my gender."

"You're not responsible for other men's actions." I reach for the cards, but Rhys isn't done.

"So you've only had relationships with men who don't see you?"

I shuffle the cards, keeping my eye on them. There's an illustrated image of the Eiffel Tower on the back. "I've never had a proper relationship with a man."

Rhys blows out a breath, his gaze piercing. "How is that possible? Men must have tried."

"Have you seen the men who usually hang around models? The men *you* hung out with at the Hamptons party?" I shake my head. "They ask me out, sure, but I know what that entails. It's not me they want, it's a model. It's the status. And I know the part I'm expected to play in return for a fancy dinner—and I have no interest in that."

His lip curves. "Ivy," he says, "I hope you take this as a compliment, but you're interesting enough for men to talk to beyond that. They might want *that*, sure, but I doubt it's the only thing all of them want."

I deal the cards. "You've gotten a lot of mileage out of your question."

"It was an interesting answer. One that's spawned more questions." He raises a finger to me. "So don't worry, I'll win again."

I groan and get up from the sofa, heading toward the shelves. "In that case, I think we need reinforcements."

"Excellent thinking." He reaches for the hotel phone on the side table at the same time as I open the hidden minibar I'd found earlier. There's still nothing in it but a few sodas and miniature bottles of alcohol.

"Mix our own?" I suggest.

He shakes his head. "I'll order drinks. What do you want?"

"A glass of wine."

"We'll get a bottle. Red okay?"

"Excellent."

I drift off to my giant suitcase and listen to Rhys as he orders a bottle of wine, discussing vintages with the person on the other end in a confident, competent tone. He has his back to me, so I shrug out of my pants and shirt with a pounding heart. Pull on my silken pajama shorts and the matching top.

He gives me a once-over when I return. "Getting comfortable?"

"If we're to play games and drink, I don't want to be in pants I've laid on a Jeep in."

"But it was such a winning pose."

The wine arrives a few minutes later, and he pours it into two glasses, one for each of us. "Your turn to start," he says, nodding toward the cards.

He wins this time again, and not by a little, either. Rhys runs a hand through his hair. "You might need more wine for this question."

"It's that bad?"

"Yes. And perhaps I shouldn't ask, but I want to know."

I clasp my hands together in my lap, and his eyes track the movement. "Go on," I murmur.

"Before Paris, how long had it been since you'd kissed someone?"

Oh God.

My cheeks heat up, but I don't look away from his dark gaze. Not when I'm standing on the edge of admitting something that has been buried deep, deep inside me for as long as I can remember.

"I see," he says softly, and I wonder if perhaps he might.

If he might be the only one who's ever seen.

I look down at my hands. Nude, short nails. No rings. "It's been at least a year," I confess. "Perhaps a year and a half."

"Hmm."

"What are you thinking?"

His long hands sort the cards with elegant competence. "I'm thinking that's a shame, since kissing can be so much fun."

"Was ours?"

"Fun?" He glances at me, an eyebrow raised. "I think you already know the answer to that."

I bite my lip to keep from smiling. "Yes, perhaps I do."

He hands me the cards, and I watch him do it, staring at the broad, tanned backs of his hands. "Aren't you going to ask me the final question?"

"The final question?"

"About sex," I say, the word like acid on my tongue. I can't believe I'm inviting in his opinion like this.

But here, with him, a thousand miles from the largest city and with only the sounds of the savannah as our companion… it feels different. Like my worries about this were all childish.

"I'm not that much of an asshole," Rhys says.

I take another sip of my wine, wondering if it's giving me courage or making me foolish. Perhaps it's only ever a mixture of both. "But you want to know?"

"Of course I do. And by the way you're goading me, I wonder if perhaps you want me to ask you."

"And why would I want that?"

"You tell me." His hand stops next to mine as he finishes dealing out the cards. The space of couch between us has shrunk in the past hour. We're closer than when we started. "Perhaps you don't talk about this to a lot of people."

"Oh, I don't."

"Tell me, then," he murmurs. "If you want to. If it'll make you feel better."

I look down at his hand. Wonder if I can take it, and then admonish myself for the thought. Whatever Rhys and I are, we're not *that*. Kissing on bridges in Paris had given me ideas.

"I've never had sex," I admit. "It's just… never happened."

Rhys is quiet for so long that I have to look up to see what's happened. Has he had a stroke? But no, he's watching me, his eyes inscrutable. I meet them and can barely hear his words over the furious beating of my heart.

Rhys blows out a long breath. "Well, that's not what I was expecting."

"No?"

"I thought you'd say it'd been a while. That you'd had a less than satisfactory experience. That… well. Not that." He raises an eyebrow. "You know I have even more questions now."

I bury my head against the back of the couch, and he laughs, breaking the tension. Something pokes my bare knee and it's him, using the deck of cards the same way I'd done to him earlier. "Come on. Doesn't it help to talk things out? I feel like I've been told that once or twice myself in the past."

"And you're a therapist?"

"I can be, for the evening." There's no judgement on his face, which was what I'd been afraid of. What I'm always afraid of—that people will draw all kinds of false conclusions.

"Well, we're on a couch," I say, taking another sip of my wine.

"You know what I'm going to ask. You already know I'm thinking it," he says.

"Yeah, I can guess."

He runs a hand through his hair again. "You're a virgin," he says. "I'm sorry, but how the hell can that be true?"

"I don't really know."

"You don't know?"

I blow out a frustrated breath. "It's like, somehow, everyone around me in high school started getting boyfriends, got used to having sex, and then it was all casual hook-ups all the time, everywhere, like everyone was on some express train to Sexville but I'd still not gotten a ticket." I throw up my hands, half-smiling out of awkwardness. "I go to college online. I'm working most of the time, and the men who ask me out all expect it to happen on the second or third date. There are expectations, and that's what I hate, those damn *expectations*. Because I don't know if I can deliver on them."

Rhys frowns. "And you don't think they'd understand? If you told them?"

"They might." I wrap my arms around myself. "But I've never met anyone I felt comfortable telling. It's all so… Look, I regularly delete comments on my social media. I don't read my direct messages anymore. It's all a flood of things, of men who only want one thing. And I guess I'm afraid that if I were to admit to this, I would be…" I can't bring myself to complete the sentence.

"They'd see you as even more of a trophy?"

"Yes. And that's the last thing I want."

He nods slowly, like he's trying to sort through a puzzle. I hope he'll share the solution with me, if he finds one, because I could use some clarity. "So what do you want?"

"What do I want?"

"Yes? Do you want to have sex, ever?"

My cheeks heat up. "Yes, of course I do."

"Right. And what would your ideal situation be like?"

"Rhys, I—"

"No, I mean it. Is there one?"

I close my eyes. "Yes, I suppose. I'm not... it doesn't have to be serious. I'm not walking around and waiting for *the one*, not that there's anything wrong with that. But I don't need that level of commitment. I just want to... God, Rhys." I push my hair back. "I just want there to be trust. To go slow. To laugh. And to be seen."

He nods slowly, the cards abandoned between us. "I get that."

"You do?"

"Yeah. You don't like the pressure."

I breathe out a sigh of relief. "Exactly."

"I also think you might be too kind for your own best interest."

"What do you mean?"

He leans back against the couch, arms over his chest. "You can tell a man you don't want to sleep with him. You can tell him mid-sex that you want to stop. You can make him wait ten, fifteen, twenty dates. You don't owe anybody anything, and fuck them and their expectations if that makes them annoyed. You don't have to please them in any way."

It's like he's put his finger on my pulse and calculated it expertly, all in a matter of minutes. And from the expression on his face, he knows it.

"It's one thing to know that intellectually," I say, "and another to do it. I clam up at the idea of it, of having to explain this to someone I've just met."

"Of course you do. It's scary, but I know you're brave enough."

"You do?"

He snorts. "Yes. You agreed to this crazy trip with no one else to accompany you but me, didn't you? And you'd never left the country before?"

I wet my lips. "No, I hadn't."

"So yes, Ivy, you're brave enough."

I glance toward the giant, linen-clad bed in the lodge. Think about all the different things I want to know, to see, to experience. The comfortable sense of exploration I've sought.

"Can I ask you something?"

"Without winning a round? I don't know. Seems greedy." But Rhys is smiling crookedly, so I go ahead.

"How was your first time?"

He barks a laugh. "Not what I was expecting."

"Too personal?"

"I think we've already strayed deep into personal territory tonight. What's another step, right?" He loosens a long breath. "I'm not sure you'll enjoy my answer."

"Why not?"

"Well, for the first thing, it was spectacularly unromantic." He raises an eyebrow. "It wasn't what you described at all. It was more... how did you put it? Like getting my ticket to Sexville. Very poetic, by the way."

I groan. "Don't tell anyone I said that."

"I'll try my very best not to," Rhys says seriously, "but it might end up in my memoir, when I inevitably write one."

"You think those words are worth preserving for posterity?"

He grimaces, but his words are sage. "That's for posterity to decide."

"How noble."

"That's me."

I rest my head on my hand. "So it wasn't spectacular?"

"No. It was at a party in my hometown. She was two grades above me, more experienced. We didn't talk much before, during or after."

"That sound fantastic," I deadpan.

He rolls his eyes at me. "It was all right, but I reckon we've both had far better since then."

"That reminds me, I'm curious. When was your last kiss

before me?"

Rhys shakes his head. "We're supposed to be talking about you."

"Well, I'm switching things around. It's only fair after all the things I've said."

He seems to consider it, whether he should answer or not, but when he does it's unquestionably honest. "Two and a half weeks ago."

"Wow." I look away, comparing his response to mine. We really are different people, at least in this way. It makes my cheeks heat up again, and this time, it's true embarrassment. And I'd been hoping that the kiss had been as powerful for him as it had for me.

"Ivy? Hey, look at me."

I do. His gaze softens, deep and dark and enthralling. "Not only do I have more experience than you, but I'm what, seven years older? Stop comparing yourself to everyone who managed to get a ticket, all right?"

"To Sexville?"

"Yes," he says, lips curving, "to Sexville."

I smile too. "Will I get a share of the royalties?"

"What?"

"Of your memoir, if you end up using that phrase?"

Rhys nods. "Of course. I'd never cheat a fellow artist out of their due."

"Thank you." I look down at his hand, resting close to mine along the back of the couch. I really, really, really want to find out what it would feel like. Nothing else, nothing more, just... learn his body the way I'm starting to learn *him.*

Rhys clears his throat. "Perhaps we should go to sleep soon."

"We have to work tomorrow," I agree.

Neither of us moves, though.

"I don't think it's fair that I get to sleep in the bed. This couch isn't long enough for you. Won't your feet hang off the end?"

His smile is crooked. "Nothing I'm not used to. It's fine, Ivy."

But it's not, despite his protestations, and I can't decide why. Why my heart is pounding quicker again, as if this entire evening hasn't been nerve-wracking enough. As if my body doesn't feel like it's been locked in fight-or-flight mode.

I stand from the couch, pulling at my pajama shorts. "Come on," I tell him. "It's big enough for two. Besides... we're friends now, right?"

Rhys rakes a hand through his hair again. "Yes, I suppose."

"Even if I am *just* a model."

He runs a hand over his face. "You know I just said that to get the other guys to shut up and stop objectifying you."

"You chose a backhanded tactic."

He snorts, rising from the couch. Glancing toward the bed. "I could've handled it better."

"Yes. Now come on. No doubt we'll be out like a light anyway," I say, heading to the bathroom to brush my teeth. "Jet lag and all. Not to mention long flights, and a long day at work. And the wine."

Shut up, Ivy, I think as I brush my teeth. My heart still hasn't entirely settled down, and it certainly doesn't when I slide under the cover. It's thick and downy and this bed is heaven. How is it that hotel beds always feel better than your bed at home?

Rhys pauses by his side of the bed in nothing but a pair of boxers and a T-shirt. "You're sure?"

"We're just sleeping, Rhys."

He snorts and reaches for the hem of his shirt. "I know that," he mutters. Pulls the shirt over his head. I look away, but not before I've glimpsed the wide expanse of his chest, the dips and grooves of his stomach, the smattering of hair, the tanned skin.

I stare up at the beams in the ceiling wide-eyed.

Rhys slides into bed beside me and reaches for the light. A

click and it's out, the lodge submerged in darkness, the both of us quietly breathing next to each other. There's still a veritable ocean of bed between us.

"You know what this means," I say, because I can't figure out when to shut up, and my brain has become scrambled eggs after seeing his abs.

"What?" His voice is everywhere in the darkness, and why hadn't I noticed it was that deep before?

"I'll have more questions for you."

"Well, I'm sure I'll be able to match that," he says. "You haven't exactly become uninteresting, now, either."

"Right. Thank you."

"You're welcome."

"You might regret opening this door, though. Because I might abuse it."

"In what way?"

"I've never had a male friend I could ask questions about sex."

Rhys sighs in the darkness. "Never thought I'd live to see the day."

"No? I thought you'd thrive in the role of instructor. You could quote books and sound superior and ask people to call you sensei."

He laughs. "Now that you mention it, that does appeal to me."

"Good, because I have a lot of questions." Things I've wondered but never been able to ask. Things guys have done or said that never made sense. "I've googled practically everything I want to know, but there are more intimate things. Guy things."

A long breath. "All right. I'll do my best to help you buy a ticket to Sexville."

"Good." I turn on my side, trying to stay the beating of my heart. In the darkness, he could be anywhere. "I'll think of a few questions for the coming days."

"God help me," he murmurs.

13

IVY

"Are you sure this is a good idea?"

Rhys looks over at me from the driver's seat, and the look on his face is withering. I hold up my hands.

"Fine, fine, I'll stop asking."

"I've done this before," he says, also for the hundredth time. So I settle back into the passenger seat and turn my face to our surroundings, because... *wow*.

We're at the entrance to Kenya's Nyiri Desert, on the outskirts of the national park where Rieler's resort is located. Joy had told us earlier that day that it's not particularly large, and laughed when I asked her what it was like compared to the Sahara.

"Like you next to a blue whale," she'd said.

But that didn't mean it wasn't gorgeous. Beautiful red dunes beckon, sloping and rising in all kinds of formations, the wind rearranging them day by day.

It's a foreign landscape, something out of a painting.

And I'm here—in a four-wheeler currently racing up the side of a slope, driven by someone who had been *very* determined that we didn't need a guide. He'd made the two-hour drive out here himself. We have a few hours to shoot here before the sun sets, which means driving in the darkness later. That, too, seemed like nothing at all to him.

"They emailed me just the other week about these pictures," Rhys says from my side. "They might use them for their Kenya promotion or when they open their new hotel in Dubai."

"So I might be in Kenya or I might be in the Middle East in these pictures?"

"Yes." Rhys shakes his head once. "Marketing," he says, spitting out the word like it's a curse.

I grin at him, and he sees it. "What?"

"It just struck me that you sometimes have the attitude of a grumpy, curmudgeonly old man, and you're not even thirty."

"I'm thirty-two."

"Well, the rest of my point stands."

He snorts. "Curmudgeonly. You'd really destroy my reputation if you got a chance, wouldn't you? Suddenly I'm predictable and grumpy."

I bite my lip to keep from grinning and look out at the dunes. I can't wait to send pictures of this place to my sister.

Rhys pulls the car to a stop on the top of a sloping dune.

"Here?"

"Here," he agrees, putting the car in park and grabbing both his camera and his drone.

I climb out of the car and put my bare feet gently down on the sand. It's warm at first, but the longer my soles are against the desert sand, the hotter it grows. Yep, flats on.

When I make it out of the car, I stop, just staring. We're surrounded by red dunes in nearly every direction, with the exception of where we'd come from. The gravel road is still visible at the base of our high dune.

"Okay," I say loudly, "you can pinch me now."

"Pinch you?"

"Yes. I don't really think I'm here. I must still be in my cramped New York apartment, and I'm just *dreaming* of traveling the world." I close my eyes and hold up my bare arm. "Come on, Rhys. I'm ready."

I hear a camera click and open my eyes. "Hey!"

"You looked good." His voice is unrepentant behind the camera. "Despite the monstrosity they've put you in."

I twirl, which isn't an easy feat when you're standing on sand. The silk chiffon swirls behind me. It might be the most beautiful dress I've ever worn, the blue contrasting starkly with the red sand.

"Tell me it won't look good in pictures, though."

"It will," Rhys says darkly. "It's the only reason I'm willing to let it slide."

"Where do we start?"

He lifts up the drone. "Run," he tells me, a crooked smile on his face. So I do, running along the dune, down the dune, up the dune, making sure the dress flows and spreads out around me like the petals of a flower. The only sound is that the of drone softly humming above us.

I finally halt with my hands on my knees. "We done?"

"Running out of breath?"

"Yes," I say, "you could say that."

"Almost." He grabs his camera from the car and looks off in the distance. Calculating, thinking. A burst of wind grabs hold of the locks of his hair and tugs at his linen button-down, as he stands there on the top of the slope. His jaw works as he thinks.

I should photograph him.

And perhaps it's our conversation yesterday, or the fact that we'd woken up in the same bed, but I tell him that. I even grab my phone from the car.

"Ivy," he complains, but I shake my head.

"No, you look... impressive right there. Like a modern-day explorer."

He sighs and looks at me, resigned, masculine, chaotic. "I refuse to recline on the hood of the car."

My lips twitch. "What a shame. You would have been the cover model for this month's Hot Men with Jeep Calendar."

He shakes his head and looks across the dunes, a smile tugging at his lips. I click, grabbing the perfect picture. "There. Thank you. Wasn't so hard, was it?"

"It was excruciating," he says, but his voice is light.

"We really should flip this. Me, the photographer. You, the model."

"We really shouldn't," Rhys says, lifting his large camera to his face. I rearrange myself, standing on the dune, posing. Looking off into the distance. Sitting down with my skirts flowing behind me.

"Perfect," Rhys murmurs, and the word sends shivers up my arms. Everything means more when it comes from him, I'm learning, even though I'm scared to discover quite *why* I feel that way. "Look at me, Ivy."

I do, turning to the camera. Smiling. "You snore," I say.

"I do not," Rhys says behind the camera.

"Very faintly."

"That's libel."

"Libel is written defamation. You're thinking of slander."

He lowers his camera, his eyes meeting mine. I shrug. "Sorry."

"Don't be. Now I know what to put when I take you to court."

"You're welcome to try," I say sweetly, "but the act occurred outside the continental US."

"Damn it. I'm at the mercy of you entirely, aren't I?"

"Seems like it, yes."

He nods to the car. "The sun is about to set. I want more photos over there."

"Okay." I smooth a hand over my skirt. "Sure you're able to drive out of here in the dark?"

"You know the difference between libel and slander, and I know cars."

The following half an hour is probably the best shoot I've ever had. I thought that in Paris. I thought that in Rome. I definitely thought it in St. Barts. But no, this, sitting on warm sand under the sinking golden sun, the air clear and thick, and red dunes spreading out around us ablaze with the sun's rays...

"I could live like this," I murmur.

"You could?" Rhys keeps shooting—I hear the clicking, but I'm closing my eyes and breathing in this experience. "Always traveling?"

"I didn't think I could, but it's very, very appealing at the moment." I reach down and grab a handful of sand, watch it run through my fingers like water. "I might start making really cheesy remarks soon, like *carpe diem* or *hakuna matata*."

"As long as you don't start singing 'The Circle of Life,' we're good," Rhys says. There's a smile in his voice, but I don't turn to see him. I lean back on my elbows instead and watch the last of the sun sink behind the dunes in the far distance.

"Shouldn't we get going?" I ask. "Not that I want to, but..."

"Yes, we should." Rhys offers me a hand and I take it, letting him pull me to my feet. It's warm and softly calloused against mine. "Unfortunately."

"At least we have a nice lodge to return to. It's not this, but it's something."

He lets go of my hand, but not before his thumb smooths gently over mine. "Not to mention a comfortable bed."

"Very comfortable."

Rhys raises an eyebrow. "So what's the review?"

"The review?"

"You slept with a man for the first time last night, right?"

I can't help it—I laugh. He chuckles too, his right hand in his pocket. "I suppose I did," I say, bumping him with my elbow. "I was a bit nervous at first, but he made it really great for me."

"What a relief to hear. I would've had to kick his ass otherwise."

"You would've?"

Rhys nods. "As a gentleman, it's my duty."

"Didn't know you were one."

"I keep it under wraps," he says. "Don't tell anyone."

"It would ruin your reputation?"

"Completely, I'm afraid."

I pause with my hand on the passenger door. "Your secret is safe with me."

His eyes darken, and I don't know what's in there. If we're still joking. What we're even talking about. "Good to hear," he says.

I climb into the car while Rhys chucks his equipment into the back. But when he turns the key to the ignition, the car doesn't budge. Not even an inch.

He tries again. Restart. Restart. The engine of the four-wheeler roars, but we're not moving more than a few millimeters. If anything, we're digging ourselves in deeper.

"Fucking hell," he mutters, climbing out of the car. I follow suit and grimace at what I see. Both tires on my side are at least half-buried in the dune.

"Rhys," I say softly. He doesn't respond—he's too busy walking around and inspecting the catastrophe. "I think we might need to be pulled out by another car."

He crosses his arms over his chest. "This car is supposed to handle this. It's made for this."

"Perhaps not for being parked on a dune," I say gently.

Rhys swears again, but then he sighs. "You're right. The weight has made it sink, and it's dug in. Fuck."

"Can we contact the lodge?"

"Yes." He reaches for his sat phone, but he's frowning. "Little chance of them making it out to us tonight, though. It'll be pitch dark before they arrive."

I swallow. Run my hands over my dress. Then I hitch up

the hem and walk around to the trunk. "All right," I say. "Call them and let them know. I'll make us a bed back here."

Rhys is completely quiet for a second. Another second. I open the trunk to the Jeep, each back door. We should be able to fold the back seats.

Rhys's voice reaches me. "You'd really *sleep* out here?"

"Well, if you don't think they can reach us in the darkness, what other option is there?"

He's quiet again for a beat. "None. But I thought you'd sound a bit more displeased about it."

I snort. "My father took my sister and me camping every summer. I've slept in far worse than this monster of a Jeep. We'll be fine."

But even so, there's a thread of uneasy excitement running through me. It'll just be the two of us in the middle of nowhere for the ten hours or so it'll take until dawn. The sun is setting fast, and after that it's just Rhys and me, a pair of flashlights and the wide-open Kenyan landscape.

What had my sister said before I left?

Make sure you have a grand adventure.

Well, Penny, watch me now, I think. *You wouldn't believe your eyes!*

I fold the seats and listen to Rhys's conversation. He's testy, but accepts that he made a mistake in parking. I grin at that. Curmudgeon perhaps, but not above accepting his mistakes.

Whoever's on the other line probably agrees with him, although Rhys sighs. "Yes, we can manage. Thank you. I'll send our exact coordinates."

I reach for the duffel bag I'd thrown into the Jeep this morning. It has one thick sweater and a few snacks, but nothing more than that. Perhaps it'll do as a pillow.

Rhys snaps the phone shut and comes to inspect my handiwork. It's getting difficult to make out his features in the near darkness.

"Cozy," he comments.

"It's not our white heaven bed, but it'll do."

He sighs, glancing down at the heavy watch at his wrist. "As much as I'd rather stay outside, bugs will make their way into the car if we keep the flashlights off."

"And lions."

He chuckles. "And lions."

I shut the lights off, throwing the whole car into darkness. "Come inside. We can make do, right? I have... two apples, one for each of us, and a chocolate bar. And tons of water."

"A feast." But Rhys has a seat next to me on the back of the car, both of our feet in the sand. Mine, barefoot. His, in boots.

The landscape is quickly falling into darkness around us. "I'm sorry," Rhys says. "I know you probably want to say 'I told you so' right about now."

My lips tug, but I keep myself from smiling. "I would never."

"You're a better person than me," he says, accepting the apple I hand him. "I would rub my own nose in it by now."

I tug one leg up and tuck it beneath me. "You don't give yourself a lot of credit."

"No, I know myself," he says. "So your father took you camping, huh?"

"Yes. He's ex-Marine, very big on nature and survival." I break the chocolate bar in half and hand one to Rhys. "Our vacations were the three of us in a car, heading to some faraway national park."

We eat our bars in silence, listening to the sounds of nature. Of faraway crickets, of the beautiful and absolute serenity that only being alone in the wilderness can produce. I've missed it.

"Your mother?" Rhys asks.

"She left us, very early on." It doesn't hurt to say. Her face is one I know only from images in photo albums and scrapbooks, and my grandmother's muttering about *that woman*.

Apparently *that woman* decided children and a husband were too much for her to handle.

Rhys hums. "I'm sorry to hear that."

"I'm not," I say, "so don't be for me." I jump out of the Jeep and look up at the sky above. With the sun setting, the stars are starting to appear. "I think we're in for a treat tonight."

Rhys stands next to me, his arm brushing mine. The solid presence of him is oddly reassuring. "I think so too. The night skies down here are beyond."

"Did you bring a camera for that?"

He shakes his head. "You need special lenses. As this was an entirely accidental overnight trip, I didn't bring them."

"Guess you'll have to take mental pictures."

He groans. "That's terrible, Ivy."

"My terrible jokes are part of my charm," I say.

"God help us all if that's the case." But he doesn't sound like he means it, his voice a deep, soft hum.

One after one, the stars in the sky start to come alight, until it's shimmering above us, the Milky Way on full display. It's breathtaking. Unlike anything I've ever seen before. "It's because we're in the Southern Hemisphere," Rhys says. "The constellations are different."

"Wow." This is one of those experiences I can tell Penny about, but she won't really believe or understand the true magic of. Standing on a dune in the middle of nowhere, under the wide-open heavens, with Rhys by my side.

I shiver. The air turns cool quickly out here when the sun's abandoned us. Deserts are mercurial that way.

Rhys notices, and nods to the Jeep. "Feel like reclining?"

"On the hood?" I climb into the open space I've made, pulling at the silken dress. "I think I'll take the inside of the car this time."

"How traditional," he says. "I thought you were more adventurous than that." But he follows me inside, closing the trunk behind me. I tug the door on my side shut too, locking us in.

"No lions."

He laughs as he cracks the front windows for air. "They can't get in through this."

"Good." I rummage through the duffel bag for the sweater and pull it on over my silk dress. The Jeep might be large but it's still a tight fit, what with the two of us.

"Cold?"

"A tad," I admit. "I wasn't exactly dressed for this."

Rhys reaches for something, and then I'm handed a soft jacket. "Put this over you too."

"You'll get cold, too," I protest. "The night's just getting started."

"Well, in that case I'll steal it back," he says. "Come on, I'm not the one who's wearing a silk shift."

I accept the weight of the jacket and turn on my side, facing him, head on the duffel bag. He rearranges himself too, stretching out.

"Do you have enough space?"

"It'll do."

"Your legs can't fit."

He snorts. "Not really, but I'll manage."

I try not to say what I do next, but I can't help it, not really. "So I'm sleeping with a guy two nights in a row."

Rhys laughs. "Once you start, you're really committed, I'll give you that."

"Who knew?"

"Not me, that's for one." He turns onto his back, his shoulder now only inches from my face. There's not enough space here to sleep like we had last night, an ocean of linen apart. The thought sends a shiver of something unidentifiable through me. Anticipation. Excitement. Nerves.

"I'm still waiting, you know," he says.

"For what?"

"For you to ask me the first of whatever sex-related questions had you so flustered last night."

I groan into the duffel bag. "There's no good way to start."

"The best way to start is just to do it."

"That sounds like a motivational poster."

"Damn it," Rhys says, "you're right. Give me another try, and I'll find some quote by Hemingway."

"The moment's passed."

He shakes his head in the darkness. "You're tough. I respect it."

"Thank you."

"I can start, then, because you bet I have questions for you."

I fold my hands under my head and try to think past the excited ball of nerves in my chest, in my stomach. "Okay."

"Have you ever *wanted* to sleep with a man? If you disregard the fact that you haven't met someone who wasn't a creep, or felt brave enough to try."

"Yes."

"Yes?" He tucks a hand under his head. "Meaning you've been turned on by a man before?"

"Yes, I have." I bite my lip, and then power on. If I'm ever going to get the ticket to Sexville… "I mean, I have seen sexy scenes in movies, read books, seen guys that I found attractive on the street."

"Ever watched porn?"

"Christ, Rhys."

I can't see it, but it's easy to hear the wolfish grin on his face when he speaks. "What? Perfectly normal thing to ask someone you work with."

I'm glad I can't see his face, because I don't think that would make this any easier. "I have, yes."

"Hmm," he says, the sound of a man deep in thought. "And you have no trouble getting off to that?"

"Rhys!"

He chuckles into the darkness. "All right, all right. Maybe

you need to ask me questions first before you feel comfortable answering a few of my own."

I rack my brain for questions to ask, but all the ones I most want to know feel almost too crude to speak. Does he watch porn? What does he like women to do in bed? Would he be turned off by someone's inexperience?

I tug his jacket tighter around myself, tucking my arms close to my body to keep from the cold. It smells like him, and the memory of the bridge resurfaces, as it has so often these past days.

"The kiss in Paris," I say, because there's no thinking now, apparently. It just slips out. "What did it mean for you?"

14

IVY

Rhys releases a quiet breath, the tension rising between us. I shouldn't have asked. "You asked me for a favor, Ives. I did it."

"That's true," I murmur. "But what I mean is, what did it feel like for *you?*"

"No, you asked what it *meant* for me. There's no need to overanalyze that. It means I find you attractive."

My breath catches in my throat. "Right."

"I figure it felt pretty much the same way it felt for you," he continues. "Which is to say, awesome."

I reach over to push against his shoulder, and it's meant to be playful, but I don't take my hand away. It rests there, against the solid curve of him. "I never said it was awesome."

"It was clear on your face."

"You can read me that well, huh?"

"I'm starting to, yeah." Rhys's voice lowers. "I'm a very good reader."

I open my mouth to speak when another shiver rocks through me. It's not really that cold, but my legs are completely bare, and have been for hours.

"Shit. Come here," Rhys says, his arm moving. I shift

closer and he tucks it beneath me, his other coming up to rest around my waist.

He's warm. That's the first impression, that's he's warm and big and everywhere against me. I rest my cheek against his chest and wonder at how natural this feels, when it should be sending my breathing into overdrive. But I'm not nervous.

His hand strokes up and down my back quickly, trying to get my body heat up. "I owe you one after making you spend the night out here like this, dressed in nothing but this ridiculous thing."

"You said it was pretty earlier."

"I said it would photograph well," he corrects.

I smile against his chest. "What is it with you and frivolity?"

"I guess I'm just a grumpy old man who'd prefer the world to read books over social media posts and women to wear shoes they can walk in as opposed to death traps."

"You're confusing."

"I am?"

"Yes. I thought you were this... high-flying, rich, good-for-nothing guy who goes to summer parties in the Hamptons. Who's seen so much beauty that he's immune to it."

He snorts. "I wish I could have those words erased from your mind."

"But you're not that," I say, and then grin. "Well, not *only* that."

His hand settles around the curve of my waist, fingers digging in just slightly. "Well, considering I thought you were vapid and materialistic, I think we're pretty even now."

"I've changed your mind?"

"Try not to sound so gloating about it."

I chuckle, daring to reach out an arm and wrap it around him, too. His body is hard to the touch. An image of him last night, pulling off his shirt, comes back to me. That's what I'm touching right now, that rigid set of muscles covered by tan skin.

"So you want to have sex," he says. "It's not a question of a lack of want."

"Right," I say. "Are you continuing to play therapist?"

"Perhaps. Is it working?"

"Yes, but I wonder if you're going on a sort of power trip."

"You can tell me to shut up if I do. I won't be offended."

I snort again, my fingers curling gently into the fabric of his shirt. He really is very warm. "Do you know," I say, "I've never really enjoyed kissing before. Before Paris, I mean. Most of the time, it was with men who were… rushing, somehow. Like they thought they only had a short window of opportunity to kiss me and they had to go in there like a rocket, all force and all tongue."

"Rockets use tongue?"

I chuckle. "You know what I mean."

"I guess I do. So you're telling me that being kissed by me was the first time you've enjoyed kisses, period?" I feel him run a hand through his hair. "Fuck, Ivy, but you're doing wonders for my ego over here."

"You're welcome."

"You're also not doing great for my self-control."

"How so?"

He groans, his hand tightening on my waist. "Look, I just told you I was attracted to you, right? And you've told me over and over that you're very used to that from men. In fact, you kinda wish they were *less* attracted to you."

I blink. Twice. "That's… yeah."

"You've also demanded that I answer any sex-related question you might have, and I agreed."

"*Demanded* is perhaps a bit too strong of a word."

He snorts. "Regardless of the word choice, you do realize what all this is leading me toward? And I'd be a damn bit more subtle and smooth about it if it wasn't for the fact that you're tired of men putting the moves on you."

I wet my lips, my heart a sudden pounding beat in my chest. Being around him is giving me heart palpitations, and that can't be healthy. "I thought you were immune to beautiful women."

"I'm not. Not to you, anyway."

I have to swallow twice before I speak. "I realize what it's leading you toward. It's leading me to the same place, I think."

He groans. "We're discussing this so calmly. Fuck, but it's bizarre."

"I'm sorry."

"Don't apologize."

"Okay, then I won't."

His hand comes up to rest on the side of my neck, a thumb stroking across my skin. In the near dark, it's difficult to see, but it's not impossible. And I see well enough when he turns his head to mine.

"You want someone to explore with."

"Yes," I murmur.

"And you enjoyed kissing me."

"Mhm."

He rests his forehead against mine, and my hand on his shirt grows into a fist. "Let's explore, then."

I don't know if he's the one who closes the gap between us or if it's me, but then his lips are against mine, warm and soft. Expert, but leashed.

He's thinking about the comment I made about men and tongues and rockets. It almost makes me smile, but I can't, my lips pre-occupied.

He breaks apart for a second, lips a hairsbreadth from mine.

"Still good?" he murmurs.

I don't answer—I kiss him instead, catching his lower lip with my own. He groans softly in the back of his throat, deepening the kiss. His tongue sweeps softly over my lower lip before slipping in, and it's delicious, sending heat dancing down my spine.

He lifts his head again.

"I could get used to that," I whisper, and even I can hear the dreamy quality to my voice.

"Keep going," he whispers back. "My ego isn't big enough."

I chuckle, but it dies the second he presses his lips back to mine. This time, I slide my hand up his neck and into the thickness of his hair. His curls are like coarse silk through my fingers.

Rhys rises up on an elbow, moving until he's half-above me, his lips never lifting from mine. It makes it easier to wrap both arms around him, and I use the newfound liberty to explore. His hair, his shoulders, his neck. Down to the solid strength of his chest.

I don't know how long we kiss for, because kissing time seems to run on its own clock, but I'm breathless when he lifts his head again. "This is good," he murmurs. "You're practicing."

"Mhm," I agree. "Great practice. Great exploring."

"Definitely." What are we even saying?

Slowly, he tips my head back and presses his lips to my neck. Oh.

Oh.

"I didn't know that would feel like... *this.*"

Rhys keeps kissing my neck. The jacket he'd given me is tossed to the side, so there's nothing stopping him from continuing further down. He doesn't, though.

I look up at the dark ceiling of the Jeep and try to form thoughts. To find the apprehension I *should* be feeling. But there isn't any.

I bend a knee, and he fits more naturally against me.

"Neck kisses are great," I say. "Why didn't I know that before?"

"A shame," Rhys murmurs, "but I'm happy to rectify it."

I run a hand down his arm, the one he's bracing himself on. His bicep is like a rock to the touch, and I wrap my fingers around it, unable to circle more than a third.

"Rhys?"

"Hmm?" His lips pause at my collarbone.

I find his other hand, the one that's still curved over my waist, and slide it upwards. "Perhaps I should get used to being touched, too."

He laughs against my skin. "You're more than welcome to give me orders."

"Just a suggestion."

His lips begin to move again, his right thumb grazing the underside of my breast. I shiver, but it's not from the cold now. My body feels like it's gathering electricity with every touch, every kiss.

His hand slides up to cup my breast entirely. My nipple is hard and he must feel it through the thin silk, because he curses softly. "Ivy…"

"Yes?"

"You're going to have to talk to me."

"Okay." I arch my back a little, because the pressure of his hand on my aching nipple is magical.

"You're not feeling buried under expectations right now, are you?"

"No. In fact…" I reach up and push the thin shoulder strap down. He slips his hand underneath and then there's nothing but skin against skin.

Rhys presses his lips to mine as he gently worries my nipple between his fingers. I'm caught between the two sensations and the third one, the one that's growing between my legs.

And I don't feel scared.

I reach down to his shirt, tugging at the buttons. His skin is hot to the touch beneath.

Rhys rests his forehead against mine again. "You can tell me to stop whenever," he says. "We're just exploring."

"I know."

And then he's gone, bending his head to my chest. His lips close around my nipple and dear God I did *not* know that would feel like it does. It's sensitive and sensual and I make quick work of my other shoulder strap, tugging it down too.

Rhys takes my cue and switches, tending to them both, and I keep my hand buried in his hair. How did we end up here? How did I get to experience this?

And how do I make sure it doesn't stop?

Rhys rakes his teeth over the underside of my breast before lightly biting down on a nipple. I gasp, and he chuckles. "Good?"

"Good," I agree. "Rhys, I want you."

He closes his eyes, and even in the near darkness, I can see how his jaw works. "You don't mean that, not in the way it's usually said."

I reach for his shoulders, for the half-unbuttoned shirt still hanging off him. "Yes, I do. And I've never meant it before. We could try, can't we?"

He shakes his head. "I'm not sleeping with you in here."

I make my voice light. "You might have to, unless you plan to sleep outside."

"Ivy."

"Rhys."

His hand smooths down my chest, my stomach. "Your skin feels like silk," he murmurs. "Are you really saying you want to try to have sex? With me?"

I don't trust words, so I go with the tried-and-tested—sounds. "Mhm."

"Damn."

"If it's not too much to ask."

He laughs, and it brings out my own. "Too much to ask? No. I'll help you get your ticket to Sexville, but not in a Jeep, and not tonight." Then he snorts. "Christ, I can't believe I'm using that stupid expression now."

"It's catchy. And what's wrong with this Jeep? It's sturdy. Has a good hood."

He settles next to me, his arm still moving over my body.

Stroking across my stomach, cupping a breast, down to my exposed legs. I shiver as his fingers trail up my thigh. "Not here," he repeats. "We need to make the proper preparations."

"Preparations?"

"Yes. Tell me, how high are your expectations, exactly? Conditioned by years of waiting, of hearing others, of reading about sex and watching porn." He kisses me after asking that, which makes it hard to think, but I manage.

"Are you saying you're not up to the task?" I'm teasing, but my voice turns shaky as his hand returns to stroke my thigh. Moving from outer to inner.

"Oh, I most certainly am, which is why I know I'm not going to do my best work in this cramped space."

"Coward," I say, but it's all bluster. My muscles relax at his words, at the realization that as nice as this is, it's not going to happen tonight. But there will be other nights with him.

"I've never liked being demeaned in bed before, but this is kind of working for me. By all means, go on."

I laugh, turning my face against his arm. He smooths a hand over my shoulder. "Besides," he murmurs, "there's no reason to rush. If we're going to do this, we'll do it right. Build up to it."

His hand returns to my breast, a warm, teasing presence. "I like that," I whisper.

I can't see his smile, but I can feel it. "I noticed," he says. "You like teeth, too."

"Mhm."

"I wonder..." His hand skims lower, across my abdomen. My poor, beautiful silk dress is bunched around my stomach, but I'm not cold now. His fingers skim the lace edge of my underwear and it sends shivers dancing across my skin. "You touch yourself on occasion, right?"

"Rhys," I murmur, closing my eyes as his fingers continue stroking the lace edge.

"Too personal?" He kisses me again, lips teasing. "I thought we were past that."

I nod against his shoulder and thank the darkness in this Jeep that he can't see my furious blush. It feels like crossing a threshold, this, not exactly uncomfortable... but unfamiliar. Saying the words, performing the actions.

His hand is so tantalizingly close to the waistband. My body has none of my mental hang-ups and twists toward him without shame, my legs widening.

Rhys hums low in his throat. He bends to kiss my neck at the same time as his fingers slip under my waistband. "You'll have to show me how, Ivy."

But I can't, because I can't breathe, not as his fingers inch downwards. Giving me time to back out. But I don't. The fire he's stoked is burning at a fever pitch, and I might be nervous, but I'm not scared.

His fingers reach *that* spot, right at the apex between my legs. "Here?" he murmurs, his fingers gently circling.

My breath is shaky. "That's where I usually focus, yes."

"I bet." Rhys bends to take one of my nipples in his mouth again, sucking at the same tempo as his fingers move. And he's doing things with his fingers that I don't. Circling, pressing, pinching and stroking. My breath grows embarrassingly loud and I reach out to fist a hand in his shirt again, wanting him close.

"I wish I could see you," he mutters, his fingers delving further down. "Jesus Christ, Ivy."

"What?"

Is he breathless, too? "You're wet."

I bite my lip and wish I could make out the expression on his face. "That's the desired effect, no?"

"Oh yes." He grabs a hold of the lace of my panties. I lift my hips as he tugs, pulling them down my legs and tossing them aside in the darkness. And thank God for the darkness, I think, my heart pounding in my chest.

He chuckles, as if to some private joke. "What's funny?"

I feel him shake his head, but he answers anyway. "I've fantasized about sliding your panties down your legs before, but I've never been able to settle on what they look like. What kind of underwear you wear. And now that I have, I can't fucking see them."

I laugh at that, even as desire clutches at my stomach. He's fantasized about this? About me? I want to ask about that, but he's stretched out beside me again and his hands are spreading my legs wide.

"All right," he murmurs. I shiver at the return of his touch, skilled and strong and *not my own.* And then we both groan as he slides a long finger inside of me, knuckle by knuckle. "Tell me if it's too much."

But it's not. It's deliciously *just enough,* and I turn my face toward his chest, my skin against his. The few buttons I'd managed to undo come in handy.

"Have you used toys?" he asks, the heel of his hand pushing down on the aching spot above. He slides his finger out, and just as gingerly back in. It feels better than it ever has when I've done that myself, because it's *him.*

"I have, yeah." My sister had gotten me one for my birthday a few years ago, which might have been the most Penny thing ever, and it had... well. It had been well-loved.

"A vibrator?"

"Yes."

His fingers continue moving. "And you've used it inside of you, as well?"

"Yes, but not as often."

"Okay, that's good to know." His voice is hoarse, the drawl he so often uses absent. He sounds like he did on the bridge in Paris, when he'd asked me if I wanted to be kissed beneath the moonlight.

He rises up on a shoulder and kisses me, his tongue moving in the same tempo as his fingers. Teasing me, moving in and out, shifting back up to circle. When he presses three fingers down and rubs, I have to break apart from the kiss to gasp. Electricity blazes down my thighs, up my stomach.

"Like that?"

I can't reply, but he gets it, because he gives a low growl of satisfaction and keeps going. And keeps going. Beyond the point where I'd have slowed down myself, pushing me ever closer to the edge. And then I have to turn my face into his chest, because I can't possibly watch him as this is happening.

He pushes me over the edge and I'm falling, my legs open, his hand working. His heartbeat is strong under my cheek as I shatter, but it's got nothing on how mine races.

I bite my tongue but a moan slips out.

The pleasure has a hold of me far longer than the orgasm itself, lingering in every limb. Rhys continues touching me, but slows down, softens, strokes my inner thighs.

"That," he murmurs, "was excellent, Ivy."

My breath is shaky, but his words and the obvious satisfaction in his voice drives away any embarrassment.

I'd just come in his arms.

"I thought so too."

He continues to touch me, but softly now. "And you're not cold anymore?"

"No, not at all."

"Mission accomplished, then," he says, and if there was light in here I would have sworn he winked. "Do you think you'll be able to get some sleep?"

"I think we'd better try." But I don't move from my place against his chest, and he doesn't push me away, either. His hand gently pushes my legs closed and settles around my waist. I swallow my fears and shift closer, until my hip is next to his.

"What about you?" I ask, wondering if I dare move my hand south. "You haven't... you know."

"I'm not the important factor in this equation, nor is my... *you know*."

"I'd say you're pretty vital to this plan."

Rhys chuckles. "Only tangentially, and I'm not in a rush. This was a good first step."

"I've approached the ticket office?"

"You've approached the ticket office," he agrees. "Sexville is the next stop."

I settle against him and his right arm returns under my shoulders, holding me close. Sneakily, as if he wouldn't notice, I slide my hand inside his half-unbuttoned shirt and rest it against the warm skin of his chest.

"Don't get me wrong," he murmurs, "because I have absolutely no problem holding you while you're practically naked. But won't you be cold?"

"The silk didn't cover much to begin with."

Fabric rustles, and then he drapes his jacket over both of us. "I'll start the car for a bit if it gets too chilly."

"Thank you." And though I thought I'd never be able to fall asleep, not in this car, not with him so close, I find that my eyelids have grown weights. It has to be a result of all the excitement, of the pleasure.

"And thank you for helping me with this, too," I murmur.

Rhys's voice is low, somewhere close to my ear. His heart beats underneath my hand. "I'm doing myself a favor too, Ivy."

The thought brings a smile to my lips, but does nothing to stop sleep from dragging me down. I don't know if he follows, but he keeps me close for the rest of the night regardless.

15

RHYS

"I thought Kenya was hot," Ivy says, wiping at the back of her neck. A few tendrils of blonde hair are stuck to the damp skin.

"Kenya's dry," I say. "Singapore is wet."

She nods absentmindedly, craning her neck to look for the approaching car. She doesn't say anything else, but at this point, I think she's figured me out. She knows I'm not someone to be spoken to around airports, not to mention on flights. But she hasn't commented on it, either.

Completely oblivious to the looks she's getting from other travelers waiting for their cars, she tugs at the buttons on her dress and huffs a sigh. "Why didn't I pack more comfortable clothes?"

"Because you didn't think this far ahead."

"Yes, that's exactly why."

"And because you sleep in silk chiffon dresses."

She levels a stare at me that is supposed to be withering, but it's anything but. It's a beautiful mixture of chagrin and embarrassment and something else, something warm. "Only sometimes," she says. "And only when I have to."

I can't help it. I step close and wrap an arm around her

waist, which I know I shouldn't in public, but fuck it. "Best night's sleep I've ever had," I tell her.

Ivy looks up at me. "You could barely fit. We had to open the door halfway through the night because it got too humid inside."

"Still the best night." I'm telling her that because I love seeing the look in her eyes, the one she's giving me now. She's remembering my fingers between her legs, and I'm remembering the way she felt. The sounds of her moaned cries against my shirt.

Yeah, I'd slept for shit, but it was still a fantastic night.

"We'll have a proper bed tonight," she whispers. Her eyes on mine are wide, golden flecks breaking up the beautiful blue. "Your legs won't hang over the edge."

"I'm a good deal taller than the national average here, so I wouldn't count on it."

"You think highly of yourself, don't you?"

"Yes, *highly* being the operative word here."

She smiles, and I wish I had a camera to capture it. I'll have to take her advice instead and take a mental picture. Her bad jokes are starting to grow on me.

This woman is starting to grow on me.

And the fact that she'd decided to trust me enough to give sex a try?

Yeah, I'm definitely taller than the average man here, not to mention anywhere, because I feel ten fucking feet tall.

I catch a group of tourists to our left eyeing us, something I've discovered is a normal side effect when you travel with someone like Ivy. She draws looks wherever we are, on planes, waiting at the gate, walking down the street, checking in at hotels.

My arm around her waist flexes a tad. It's juvenile but impossible to stop. They can look, but that's all.

We check into a hotel that is as sumptuous as it is elegant. Located in a mid-rise skyscraper, it has capitalized on the gorgeous nature that Singapore's climate supports. Trumpet trees flower in pinks outside the lobby, and an entire wall clad in tropical greens serves as the backdrop to the check-in desk.

I had to give it to him, Ben had done good. Every location was more beautiful than the last, tied in with signature logos and excellent customer service. A bellboy escorts Ivy and me to our rooms, two massive suites with a single connecting door.

"It is currently locked," the bellboy informs us with a serviceable smile. "We were not given adequate information about your status as travelers. Would you like us to unlock it so you can easier spend time together?"

It's an innocent question. Ostensibly, we could just share a glass one evening—no one would bat an eye at that.

"Yes, please," Ivy says. "That would be very convenient."

"I'll override the lock as soon as I get back downstairs," the man says. "The manual lock on either side does, of course, still work."

It doesn't take more than five minutes before the connecting door opens and Ivy peeks her head through. I'm sitting on my gigantic bed, turning my camera over in my hands, checking the gear.

"This place is fantastic," she says. "The best rooms we've had."

I lean back on the bed. "I don't know. I was kinda partial to our Jeep."

She laughs, wrapping her arms around herself. "An interconnecting door? It's like they knew we're up to mischief."

I raise an eyebrow. "And are we? Up to mischief?"

Ivy's face is one of determination as she advances on me. I hold up my hands as she climbs onto the bed with a leg on either side of me. "What's this?"

"I'm feeling mischievous."

I hold on to her hips, her body a warm weight on mine. Infinitely more interesting than my camera. "So you are," I say. She locks her hands behind my neck, like she's still unsure if she can touch me like this.

Which won't do at all for what we're planning on exploring.

"He must have seen it on us," Ivy says. "Written on our faces."

"Yours, perhaps. I'd never be so transparent."

She smiles and presses her lips to mine in a kiss that's softly determined. My fingers tighten around her hips, and beneath her, my body starts to respond.

This girl has me turned completely inside out.

"You're the one initiating kissing now?"

She grins, looking like the Cheshire cat. "I'm dedicated to my training."

"Very studious of you." I kiss her back and deepen it, meeting her tongue with my own. Just lightly, though—I always want to leave her wanting more. "I still haven't been called sensei. Not even once."

And damn me, but Ivy giggles, and it doesn't even annoy me. It sends pleasure through my chest instead, and satisfaction that I'm the one who elicited the soft sound. "Do you want to be called sensei? Is that some sort of kink?"

"Oh, we are far too early to be talking about kinks." My hands slide down and settle around her ass. As much as I don't want to be one of the assholes who objectify her, there's no denying she's fine.

Or that I'd cursed myself for being so damn stupid that the first time I touched her, the first time I kissed her body, it was in a place so dark I couldn't see an inch of her skin.

I wouldn't be so stupid again.

She cocks her head. "So, tonight?"

"We're going to plan this, now?"

"I'm a planner," she says, pushing at my chest. I let her force me down flat on the bed, but I pull her with me, until she's bracing herself with a hand on either side of my head.

"I'm not," I say. "Sometimes I make plans just so I can purposely *not* follow them."

"A rebel without a cause," she teases.

I smooth my hands up to her hips, her waist. "When there are no revolutions to fight in, you have to give yourself a few."

She rolls her eyes. "Explains your constant battle with the itinerary."

"And your constant adherence to it. But don't worry, I find you attractive even though you're so… type-A."

Her eyes widen and I'm rewarded with an indrawn breath, swiftly followed by a grin. "That's probably the first and last time I've ever been called type-A."

"Yeah, you only half fit the profile," I admit, and I should know. Lord knows I have more type-As in my family than I need.

She rolls her hips and I groan, because she's pressing down on the part of my anatomy I've tried to ignore for the past twenty-four hours. Because if I let my mind stray to the sweet softness of her around my finger, well… hardness o'clock.

"Ivy," I warn.

"You mentioned preparations."

"Yes, and I'll handle them today." In truth, we don't need much. I already have condoms and I figured I'd pick up a bottle of lube or some baby oil at a pharmacy somewhere. Not that she hadn't been gorgeously wet the other day, and damn it, now I'm hard.

Ivy feels it too, because her face becomes stunningly flushed, her eyes excited. "Ah," she says. "This, I'm very intrigued about."

"Of course you are." I grip my hands around her waist tightly. "But we're not about to explore *that* right now."

She manages to sneak a hand down and run her nails over the bulge, and sweet heaven, even through the fabric of my jeans…

I flip her over and pin her hands to the bed. "Stop that."

"Why?"

"Because we're doing this right, and that's slow and careful. I want you to have come at least twice before I'll think of being inside you, and your teasing is making it a lot harder to stick to my plan."

"You don't like sticking to plans," she whispers, her eyes on mine.

"I'm sticking to this one."

We stare at each other for a long moment, her mouth open and breath coming fast. So is mine, because despite my resolution, I'm on top of her. On a bed. And we're alone.

A faint knock breaks us out of the stand-off. I glance at my door. "It's not mine."

Ivy struggles and I let her go, watching as she flies off the bed. "It has to be the hair and makeup artist the agency hired. And I'm supposed to be showered and ready!"

I grin at her from my sprawl on the bed. "Better hurry."

"Damn it." She pauses with her hand on the interconnected door. "Stop looking so smug."

"This is just my face."

She rolls her eyes and closes the door behind her. I tuck an arm under my head and look up at the ceiling, my mind straying back to thoughts that won't make my hardness disappear anytime soon.

Yeah, I feel ten feet tall all right.

———

Ivy is nervous at my side, despite having her game face on. How do I know that? Because she's softly tapping her high-heeled shoe against the steel floor of the elevator, currently barreling us more than a hundred stories high.

"Relax," I murmur.

She glances at me. "I am relaxed."

"Mhm."

The elevator slides to a smooth stop atop Singapore's most famous building. The rooftop is one easily recognizable from movies, from pictures, and hopefully also by people interested in buying one of Rieler's travel packages.

We step out into a tastefully decorated waiting area, following the hostess. "We've set up a table for you out here…" she says, leading us to the very edge of the outdoor bar. Singapore spreads out around us, the giant, sprawling city-state on one side and the turquoise-colored sea on the other. The beautiful water is littered with container ships, ready to make port or depart.

Ivy sits down on one of the barstools, the tight dress she's wearing making it difficult for her. What's up with her agency and always putting her in the most infuriating clothes?

She pushes a perfectly blown-out lock of hair behind her ear and looks at me with eyes that are rimmed black. The makeup artist has made her look like… well, like a damn model, that's what.

The effect is almost unsettling, like she's someone else. Not the woman with rosy cheeks and sleepy eyes I'd woken up next to at dawn in a Kenyan desert.

Ivy accepts a glass of water gratefully from the waiter, but I notice how her hand curls around the edge of the table. I step closer. "Ivy, what's wrong?"

"Nothing."

"You're not a particularly good liar," I say, putting my camera down on the table. "Tell me."

She looks out at the view before quickly returning her gaze to me. "I'm not a fan of heights," she tells me. "I don't hate them. I'm just not a fan."

I nod, glancing past her to the beautiful city beyond. "But you don't have a problem with views? Through windows?"

"No, not when I'm inside. But I'm not inside, we're outside." She shakes her head. "I know it doesn't make much sense."

Well, if she's expecting me to judge her, she has another thing coming. I'm not in a position to judge anyone, certainly not with my… *aversion* to flying.

"Okay," I say, reaching out to put a hand on her bare shoulder. Her skin is warm under my hand. "That's okay. We don't have to shoot here."

The look she gives me is exasperated. "Of course we have to. It's on the list."

"Not if it's taxing for you."

"I've shot more taxing things than this," she tells me, like she's gearing herself up. "I've had a shoot that was underwater. One that had me lying on a bed of roses, and they were thorny."

"Seriously?"

"I'm a model." She shrugs. "We get all kinds of jobs."

I frown. "Okay, so we'll get this shoot done as fast as we can and then we'll be off."

She slides off the barstool. "All I have to do is focus."

"Just look at me," I tell her, taking a few steps back to get her entire form and the view. "Nothing else."

She nods and slowly, ever so slightly, her face relaxes. She slips back into the model mask I'd seen her wear before, the one where it's impossible to read her eyes.

"Good," I say. "Just look at me."

She nods imperceptibly and poses by the table, a glass of champagne in her hand. Other guests move behind me, but I ignore them, solely focused on her. And she gives me the same attention.

I don't shoot more than fifteen minutes. There might be other angles to try, but none of that matters, not when I see that her foot is constantly tapping away at the ground.

"Come on," I tell her, pulling her toward the elevators. "We're done up here."

"But... don't you need more shots?"

"Fuck the shots." I press the button for the elevator and find the small of her back. Touching her is becoming like a drug, my hands taking any excuse possible to meet her skin. She leans into me in the elevator.

"Thank you," she murmurs.

"Don't mention it." If I could figure out a way to stop flying, I'd do it too, but my wanderlust is still too powerful.

People watch us walk through the lobby in a way I've become used to by now. Ivy is dressed to the nines, the fabric of the dress she's in clings to her form, her long legs on display in a pair of high heels.

She breathes a sigh of relief when we get in the cab and she closes her eyes. "I'm sorry. That was unprofessional."

"Don't apologize." I give the cab driver the name of a dumpling restaurant, one of Singapore's best, and turn to look at her again. Her color is slowly rising.

"I should work on it."

"Not while being photographed." My traitorous hand finds another excuse, reaching for hers. Her fingers feel slender inside my hand.

Whatever spell she's cast, I'm thoroughly under it.

"Where are we going now?"

"To eat something before we go back to the hotel."

Her eyes open a tad, locking with mine. And there's no need to speak aloud for the communication that passes through us.

"Only if you want to," I murmur, my hand squeezing around hers.

She squeezes back. "I do."

I swallow at the dryness of my throat. It's been years since I've been this turned on, anticipated the first time with a woman this much. And I need to go slow—to remember the role I have to play. She wants a safe space to explore in.

Ivy gets looks when we walk into the restaurant too. She ignores them, like she so often does, but leans in to murmur something. "Do you notice how people look at you?"

I put down my menu. "Me? They're looking at you."

She smiles down at the list of dumplings. "Some are, but not all. You could be a model too. I know that's not a compliment in your book, but it's true."

I snort. "Right."

"It's true." And then she reaches up with her phone and snaps a picture of me, sitting there in my shirt and slacks, a menu in hand. She grins as she lowers it. "Two can play this game."

I shake my head at her, but the conversation pauses as the waitress arrives. She picks it right up after, though. "I thought about it," she murmurs. "When you were photographing me with Paolo."

It's petty, but my mouth sours at the mention of the Italian model. "Thought about what?"

"How the roles could have been reversed. That I could have been sitting and making pretty eyes at you instead."

All right.

I'm okay with discussing Paolo if this is what we speak of.

"I thought about it too," I admit.

"You did?"

"Oh yes."

Ivy's smile turns crooked, and then I feel a silky leg settle next to mine beneath the table. "You said something else last night… or was it the night before?"

"Time is irrelevant on this trip," I say. "I've changed the time zone on my watch more times than I can count."

"Well, you said that you'd fantasized about… well." She glances around, but the tables next to us are empty. "Taking off my underwear."

I grin. "Yeah."

"What else have you fantasized about doing?"

I shake my head. "We're not doing this."

"We're not?"

"No, for two reasons. First," I say, raising my chopsticks at her, "this is about you and not about me. Your fantasy, not mine."

Her cheeks color, but she doesn't look away from my gaze. "I want you to enjoy yourself too."

"Christ, Ivy, there's no chance I won't."

"Good." She nods. "What's the second reason?"

I lean across the table, watching her long, dark eyelashes flutter. The strength in her eyes giving way to unexpected softness. "We need to make it out of here and back to the hotel while remaining decent. And if we start talking about my fantasies…"

Her lips fall open, her eyes darting down to mine. Fuck, but she wants me to kiss her. I don't think I've ever wanted to oblige to a woman's request more than hers.

"Eat your dumplings," I say, trying to focus on my own. "We'll leave as soon as we're done."

She smiles down at her food, looking up at me every now and then as the both of us clear our plates. Something's different with her hair—they've straightened it, perhaps? It falls long and silky around her face, none of the usual playful curls.

An image comes to mind. Ivy lying on her stomach in bed, naked with a cheeky grin on her face, clad in nothing but her long hair and a smile. I'd make it black and white in the edit.

It feels like it takes forever to make it back to the hotel. Ivy's hand finds mine in the car, and she holds on tightly. It's been a long time since I've held hands with a woman like this, but with her… Fuck, but it feels right. Everything about this does.

Her foot taps against the elevator floor as we race upwards to our rooms. I nudge her with my shoulder, ignoring the other couple in the elevator. "Nervous again?"

"Never," she murmurs, but her tapping stops.

Either by unspoken agreement or simple layout, it's my hotel door we stop outside of. I hold it open for her and she steps past me on high heels and confidence. The city is a sky of lights through the floor-to-ceiling windows, and the air hums with possibility.

I close the door behind us.

16

RHYS

"You know," I tell her, heading toward the minibar, "I don't know how to compliment you."

She sits down on the edge of the giant bed. "You don't?"

"No." I open the fridge and pull out the bottle of champagne I'd called up earlier while she was getting ready.

"That seems like a curious problem to have."

I uncork it in one smooth motion. "Well, you've told me that you're tired of men fawning over you. I'm sure you're complimented every day, all the time, in ways that are... insincere. Is that true?"

Ivy accepts the glass I hand her, me standing, her sitting. She nods slowly. "I suppose that's true, yes."

"And you told me that's why you haven't felt comfortable doing this with someone."

She wets her lips. "Part of it, yes. Don't forget expectations."

"Expectations, yes." I nod. "I won't forget that. But you see, I do find you deeply attractive, and I'd enjoy letting you know just *how* much. But I'll refrain if it makes you feel... uncomfortable."

Ivy shakes her head slowly. "It won't. Not from you."

"Mhm." I take a sip to hide the smile that wants to break out. "And regarding expectations, Ivy?"

She nods. Recrosses her legs. "What about them?"

"Forget all of that with me. You tell me what you want, what you don't want. No stupid questions."

"No stupid questions," she repeats, scooting further back on the bed. She lies back on her elbows, champagne glass in one hand. "In that case, I want you to tell me just how attractive you find me."

Now I'm smiling. "Oh yeah?"

"Yeah."

I set down my glass on the bar. "I've thought a lot about the first time I saw you dance," I confess. "On the square in St. Barts."

Ivy's full lips open, my eyes tracking the movement. "You have?"

"Yes. Watching you move… well, the idea that you might be a virgin was the furthest thing from my mind." She looks away from me, her cheeks flushing. So I keep going. "Not because you were moving lewdly, but because you had complete control over your body. Knew every angle, every curve. And you looked so comfortable inside your skin that I wanted to be inside yours."

Her eyes snap back to mine, and then very deliberately, she sets down her glass of champagne on the bedside table. "You were so arrogant," she says. "From the beginning, you were so arrogant, and it annoyed me so much… but I'd never been more intrigued by someone."

"The sound of your orgasm the other night, Ivy? Best thing I've ever heard."

She swallows. Looks at me. I look at her.

Then I reach for the buttons on my shirt and start undoing them one after the other, loving the way her eyes make me feel. It's heady, this. "We have all night," I say. "Getting used to each other won't hurt."

Her eyes trail down my chest, my abs, and every hour I've

ever spent in the gym is worth it in that moment, just to have her gaze taking me in. Every drop of sweat and every early morning.

"Good idea," she breathes.

I let the shirt drop. "We touched each other the other night, but we didn't see."

"No, we didn't." She scoots to the edge of the bed and pulls me closer, tugs me down beside her. Her hands are soft and warm on my body, exploring. I reach out and wrap an arm around her waist, letting her.

She runs her nails over my chest. It's perhaps the most innocent touch, and yet it sets my blood racing.

I kiss her then, slow and soft. She's the one who deepens it and I follow along, because tonight is about her pace—I repeat that in my head, over and over, even as I feel her hike a leg up around my hip.

"This dress is pretty tight," she whispers.

"Want me to undo the zipper?"

She nods, pushing her hair out of the way. The zipper goes all the way down to her low back and the dress splits as I pull, revealing soft, tanned skin. She has two dimples on her low back, right above the edge of her panties.

My nerves feel electrified, like my body is preparing for a fight with itself. *Patience, Rhys. Not a wrong move here.*

It has been years since I'd slept with a virgin last, and even then I'd been… what, nineteen? An age ago. I'm a better man now, a better lover.

And I'll try to use all of that experience with Ivy.

She shimmies out of her dress, settling down beside me in her panties and bra. A smile tugs at her lips.

"What?" I ask, bending to run mine across her neck. Soft, fragrant skin.

"I was just thinking," she murmurs, her hand disappearing in my hair. "That the first shoot we ever did was bikini."

"Very true." I linger at her collarbone, smiling against her skin when I hear her swallow thickly. My hand traces patterns on her hip. "Were you nervous about that?"

"Of course I was. I can't think of a model, not to mention a woman, who wouldn't be."

"You fooled me." I kiss my way down to the soft, swelling curves of her breasts, hidden from me by the black lace of her bra. "You're so beautiful, Ivy," I tell her. Women are always worried about something being too big or too small, and I've never figured out why, when they're so perfect. But I know it's not to be ignored. "You take my breath away."

She bites her lip, but there's no hiding the smile on her face. "Better than a wildebeest?"

I grin back at her, the joke so unexpected and so Ivy. "Infinitely," I assure her, "but don't tell anyone."

"Ruin your reputation?"

"Exactly."

"I'll take it to my grave," she murmurs, and with her eyes locked on mine, she reaches back and undoes her bra. I slide it off her arms and peel it away from her skin, groaning at the revelation.

Her breasts look exactly like I'd imagined them in the Jeep.

Soft but firm, rosy nipples, inviting and supple. Ivy laughs breathlessly as I kiss away, my mouth racing across the expanse of skin.

"Nothing new," she murmurs.

"I couldn't *see* before," I mutter, closing my mouth around a nipple. It hardens in my mouth, and so would I, if I hadn't already been rock-hard.

Ivy's nails rake softly through my scalp. *Again*, I think. *Do that again.*

She does, and this time she mewls softly when I add my teeth to her nipple, gently worrying it back and forth. "I never knew it could feel like that," she whispers.

I switch nipples, raising an eyebrow at her. "You don't touch them while you fuck yourself?"

A breath escapes her. "Wow, Rhys…"

"What else should I call it?" I ask, grinning as I rise up on my arms. "And don't think I haven't imagined how you'd look, working with that vibrator you have."

She wraps her arms around my neck, her hair spreading out around her. "Why are we discussing my habits?"

"Because they're important." I kiss her, reveling in her sweetness. "Because they turn me the fuck on."

Ivy shivers, pulling me down flush against her, her nipples hard against my chest. "I like turning you on."

"Well, you're very good at it."

"That's what I want to explore." She spreads her legs, the movement settling me more firmly against her. Intended or not, my aching cock is now resting right between her legs, separated only by a few layers of fabric.

Ivy draws in a breath at the contact. "Yes," she says. "That's what I really, really *really* want to explore."

Well, I'm not about to argue with that.

I flip off her and start unbuckling my belt, pulling it out of the loops. She sits up beside me and her hands come to rest on my abdomen.

Her gaze flickers up to mine, and what I see in her eyes both humbles and excites me. "You can't do anything wrong here, Ives," I mumble. "Nothing that won't turn me on. And we can stop at any time."

She nods once, and then her focus is back on my pants, helping me pull them off. The bulge in my boxers is practically obscene, my whole body taut with excitement.

It goes against the grain, this. *She* was the one I'd planned on savoring for a good long while before I'd remove my own clothing. Her orgasms are what's important.

But if this makes her feel more comfortable, I'll take one for the team.

Ivy's hands settle around the waistband of my boxers. "You're going to have to show me how you like this," she tells me.

"I will. But what did I just say?"

"That I can't do anything wrong."

"That's right."

She tugs my boxers down and my cock springs free, painfully hard. A breath escapes me at the sudden freedom.

Ivy is staring at it, at me, and it twitches eagerly beneath her gaze. Her hand reaches out and I hiss at the contact. She glances up at me, a smile on her lips. "This is fantastic."

And fuck me if that isn't the weirdest and best compliment I've ever gotten. I tuck an arm behind my head and watch as she starts to slowly stroke me. Her fingers pause to dance across the sensitive head and I grind my teeth together.

This is excruciating.

It's also turning me on beyond belief.

"I never knew it would be this hard. It's not like a limb, it's... just really hard." She snorts, her hand picking up speed. "Listen to me being coherent."

It was more than I can be.

"Am I doing this right?"

I force myself to focus. She wants to learn. So I reach down and settle my hand around hers, tightening her grip. "Like this," I murmur. "And faster when you stroke."

She obliges, her hand starting to move on its own. I watch the blonde hair falling over my thigh, her hand moving, her face beautifully rapt...

Hand jobs had been consigned to the past, in my sexual life. They were usually something done quickly before a mouth was applied. At a certain point, you just graduate past them. I hadn't really missed them.

But I should have, because this is the most erotic thing I've experienced in... oh, I can't think that far back, not while my body feels like it's a running current beneath my skin.

Ivy reaches below to cup my balls, still stroking, and I bark out a breath.

"Is that okay?"

"Yes. Better than okay."

She laughs, a soft giggle that somehow goes straight to my cock, and it twitches again in her hand. Performing like some damn circus animal and loving every second of it.

I look up at the ceiling and wonder how much of this beautiful torture I have to endure. That's when she puts her mouth on me.

She kisses the head of my cock, looking up at me as she widens her lips and slips it inside. I swallow thickly. "This was not part of the plan. The plan was *you* orgasming."

She can't smile, but I can see it in her eyes nonetheless. They're glittering with determination and success. She's enjoying this—more than that, it's giving her confidence. And perhaps confidence is what she needs for this.

Her tongue swirls and I curse, looking away from her. It's the slowest, most tantalizing, most *inexperienced* blow job I've ever had, and fuck if that doesn't make it better somehow.

Ivy lets me go with a soft pop. "I've always wanted to try that," she says, breathless. "I want to get really good at it."

"Oh, you will, I'm sure of that." I reach down and run a hand through her hair. "Done exploring?"

She frowns down at my cock, her hand stroking softly. "I don't think I'll ever be *done.*"

"Well, *it* will be, unless you give it a break." That's not a lie, either. Heat had been growing in my thighs, at the base of my spine, and I need to last a hell of a lot longer tonight. This isn't about my pleasure.

Ivy gives a dramatic sigh and releases her grip. "I'll see you later," she says, and she's not talking to me.

"He's not going anywhere."

The understatement of the year.

I roll over, her legs opening instinctively for me. Nothing but the warm fabric of her panties separating us now. Taking my time, I kiss her soundly before my fingers settle around the lace edges of her underwear. I sit back on my knees, worrying the fabric in my hands.

She looks up at me, her breasts rising with every quick breath she's taking.

"I'm going to take these off," I warn her. Giving her time to protest.

She gives me a nod. *Go ahead.*

Slowly, I peel the panties off her, and this time I get to watch the whole thing. They're plain black cotton with a lace trim. Unbearably sexy.

But nothing near how sexy *she* is beneath them.

Fuck, but she's perfect in every way, and I want her so much I'm near exploding without any damn stimulation. My hands on her knees, I keep them spread for me. Admiring the view.

It isn't until she gives an embarrassed little laugh that I find my words. "You're perfect, Ivy. So fucking perfect."

"Flatterer," she murmurs.

"No. I told you once, I don't lie." My hand starts stroking up her inner thighs, the soft skin like silk under my fingers. Touching her and finding the swollen center of pleasure at the top. She shudders as I start circling right there.

"Ivy," I murmur.

"Mhm?"

"It's a fucking crime I couldn't see this in the Jeep."

Her laughter is breathless. "Didn't stop you though."

"Of course it didn't." I settle between her legs, pressing kisses to her inner thighs. Working my way up. Teasing, warming her up, not moving my lips or my tongue to the spot I know she wants me at. "I've fantasized about this too," I tell her, knowing that women can be nervous about this, not that I've ever understood why. I just don't want Ivy to be.

All I hear is a questioning *hmmm?*

I smile against her skin and settle in to work. Nudging her clit with my tongue, my fingers helping. Her heavy breathing is like music, and when she slides her hand into my hair... I devote myself to her pleasure.

Discovering which spots make her squirm, which areas

she needs harder stimulation, and where I need to go deliciously slow. I ease one finger in. She immediately squeezes around my finger, and my cock throbs in response.

"Rhys..." she breathes, but there's only pleasure in her voice, no pain.

I settle my mouth on her clit and suck gently, worrying it with my lips. Easing another finger inside of her, I curl it in tempo with my mouth.

It doesn't take long until she explodes around my finger and against my mouth, arching up on the bed like she's been pulled on a string. Looking up, she has one of her breasts clasped in her hand, her mouth half-open. It's the sexiest thing I've ever fucking seen.

And she damn near cuts off circulation to my finger with her squeezing.

I kiss her throughout her orgasm, my eyes never leaving her face. Her skin has flushed a rosy red.

She breathes heavy as she comes down off her high. "Oh my God," she says weakly. "I didn't think... I really didn't think that would happen."

I raise an eyebrow at her. "You doubted me?"

She snorts, but smiles at me. "I doubted myself."

"Foolish," I say, stroking up her inner thighs. "You can do anything, Ivy."

I run my hands up her body, down her sides, her taut stomach. There's not a part of her I don't want to have seared with my hands, like I can mark her, learn her terrain. Ivy wraps her arms around me and I hold her, feeling more desire than I ever have before. More tenderness, too. The mixture makes my head dangerously light, and it's not helped by my cock, now pushing against the softness of her stomach.

We kiss again, breaking off to breathe. "You set the pace," I murmur. "You decide."

"I want you inside me, Rhys." She glances down, a furrow in her brow. "My vibrator isn't that big, though."

"We'll go slow," I promise, wondering how the hell I'm

going to live up to that. Slow feels out of my reach, out of my vocabulary. What does the word even mean?

There's only one way to ensure this goes slow.

I grip her hips and twist us around, pulling her on top of me. Her legs settle on either side as she straddles. "You'll control the movement," I tell her. "It's better this way."

Better because I don't know if I can manage to ease in inch by inch like she needs. Reaching out to the bedside table, I grab one of the condoms.

Ivy watches me with avid interest as I undo the packet. "Another thing I want to learn," she murmurs. "I've seen instructional videos."

I snort. "Of course you have."

"I'm probably the most knowledgeable virgin ever." Her voice is breathless as she scoots down to give me access. I grip my cock in one hand and roll the condom on with the other.

It twitches in my grip, well-aware that it has a rapt audience.

"You're knowledgeable, huh?"

"Just because I haven't *had* sex doesn't mean I haven't read a ton about it." Ivy slides back up and settles on my cock, bending it so it touches my stomach.

"Reading isn't the same as doing."

"So I'm learning." She bites her lip and starts to roll her hips, sliding across my shaft. Fucking hell, but this woman is going to kill me before I've even entered her.

"That's good," I comment, which puts me in the running for the understatement of the year. I reach down and part her around me, so she's riding the full length of me. She shivers as she grinds down, using me to hit the spot she needs.

Good is definitely an understatement.

I grip her hips, and then further up, weighing her breasts in my hand. A strand of her hair brushes my hand. "Whenever you feel like it," I tell her.

She bites her lip in the way that I'm learning is unconscious, and beautiful, and makes me want to photograph her.

She lifts herself up and I grip my cock, angling it so the head pushes against her entrance. And damn it, but if this wasn't so strongly about *her,* I would have bucked my hips and pushed in on instinct alone.

Her eyes are wide and determined, her hands reaching out to rest on my chest. "Slide down," I instruct her.

She keeps her eyes on mine as she starts to sink, and she's more beautiful than I've ever seen her before. Wild and unbound, tentative and careful, focusing so strongly on what she's feeling. She's turned inwards, and yet the sensation she's searching for is one of my doing.

The head eases inside, and both of us exhale in pleasure at that. It's impossible not to. Her mouth forms a small O, a brief pinch in her eyebrows.

"Breathe and relax," I tell her. "It'll fit."

Her breath is shaky, but she keeps going. And with every inch, pleasure spreads through my body, radiating from where we join. Every part of my body is tense—focused on that spot.

"You feel fucking unreal," I tell her. "So, so good."

She laughs, but it's breathless, and it chokes off altogether when I press my thumb down on her clit.

"This helping?"

"I don't know," she whispers, "but don't stop."

Good thing I'm wearing a condom or I wouldn't last.

"I can feel you so deeply," she says, and her voice is wondrous. "I never thought about that."

I'm not really thinking at all, but I nod, my thumb still working on her clit. "Is it getting easier?"

Ivy nods, sinking down fully. I'm buried to the hilt and it's the most delicious thing I've ever experienced.

She releases a shaky breath. "Oh God."

I close my eyes at the exquisite pleasure, the tight heat of her. The pain of not moving.

"It doesn't hurt."

My eyes open, but there's only tentative pleasure on her face.

"It doesn't. I feel... stretched. But in a good way." And then she starts to move, and the sight of her coming earlier is replaced by this one as top of my list of sexiest things I've ever fucking seen. Because Ivy rolling her hips, carefully taking me in and out, hands on my chest as if I'm the only thing grounding her to earth...

With her hair a blonde halo above her, her nude, lithe body moving on top of me... Forever. I could do this forever.

And then she comes again with my thumb working her clit, and I marvel at how easy this seems to be for her compared to her earlier fears. Her breathing rises and crests, her movements growing quicker.

"Fucking hell," I mutter, not able to help myself, arching up beneath her in pleasure as her tight heat contracts around me. It's a damn near thing to hold myself back.

She collapses on top of me, her heart thundering in her chest. I wrap my arms around her waist and breathe heavily, still buried inside her and still rock hard.

"Wow," she whispers. "That wasn't... you... good."

"Beautifully phrased."

She chuckles against my chest, reaching up to kiss me. Every time she pulses, I can feel my cock twitch in response. The self-control it's taking me *not* to move feels like it's shaving years off my life.

Still worth it.

"Was I too quick?" Ivy asks. "You still haven't come."

I snort. "You say that like it's a bad thing."

She flicks her hair to the side, and it drapes over me like a silken blanket. "How do we fix that?"

"I can think of a few ways." Moving my hips chief amongst them, but I keep them still. "Ready to try a new position?"

Ivy nods and lifts herself off me. I draw in a breath at the sensation of suddenly leaving the slick, tight heat of her. The world outside is not nearly as hospitable.

She turns over on her back and I rise up on my arms above her, kissing her deeply. She wraps her arms around my back, kissing me back like she's never done anything else. Like she never wants to do anything else.

I push her legs apart with my knees, still kissing her. And then I push in slowly, watching her face the entire time. She's biting her lip, but true to her word, there isn't a hint of pain in her eyes.

My pace is faster than hers, there's no denying it, but she's more yielding now, too. So unbelievably tight and hot around my cock that it's difficult to think.

I run my hand up the soft skin of her outer thigh, pulling her leg up. Ivy gets the message and wraps them around the small of my back, and fuck yes, this is how I want her.

Fiery and soft beneath me.

My hips start moving on their own, quick thrusts that push me deeper and deeper. Ivy's eyes are on mine, her hands behind my neck.

Her mouth is a round O of pleasure and I'm not going to last for shit. This has already been the most anticipated, drawn-out sexual experience of my life. Her hand slides down to lock around my bicep as she glances down. Watching where we join.

"You like seeing it?"

She nods, tilting her hips to meet mine. I bury my head against her neck and groan, because there's no fucking way it'll ever be this good again.

Ivy holds me close. "You feel so good inside me."

Her words send my already electric body into overdrive. Pleasure starts at the base of my spine and radiates out, shooting through me, everything contracting. My hips move on their own as my orgasm barrels out of me.

I kept my face rested against her neck, breathing through the intensity of my release. Perhaps I'm crushing her. Perhaps

I should move. But I can't, not while my hips still push into her.

"Jesus Christ," I mutter.

Ivy doesn't let me go. She just holds me tight, and I wonder if I'll ever muster the strength to leave. I can't imagine ever wanting to.

"I could feel you," she says, her tone one of pleasure and wonder. "When you came, I could feel it."

I give a tired chuckle. "I'm not surprised. Fuck, I haven't come that hard in forever."

Lifting myself up on an elbow, her smile is triumphant and shy at the same time. She pushes a lock of hair off my brow. "That's a compliment I like."

"Greedy."

"Mhm, with you I am." She lifts her neck and I oblige, pressing my lips to her. The kiss is soft, but I know I need to move. Grab and discard the condom before we have a different kind of problem on our hands.

She frowns when I leave, but I return soon enough, lifting up the covers so she can slide underneath.

"So?" I ask, stretching out beside her. My entire body feels hot and tired, like I've just finished running a marathon. In some ways I think I might've. "You have to give me the debrief."

"The debrief?" The dark makeup around her eyes has smudged a bit, but it doesn't detract the least from her beauty. If anything, it makes her look wilder.

"You just had sex," I remind her. "You'll have to tell me how it was."

She laughs and reaches out to run a hand through the smattering of hair on my chest. "That's a very personal question. I'm not sure we're quite there yet."

I groan in mock disappointment. "And here I thought we were becoming friends."

"Friends? How presumptuous, Mr. Marchand."

I close my eyes. "Ugh."

"What?"

"That's what my dad is called, or my older brother."

She giggles, walking her fingers down to my abs. "Rhys."

"Much better. Now lay it on me. How was your first time? And before you respond," I say, reaching out to slide my arm under her neck, "remember that I'm a man. My ego is very fragile."

"Nothing about you is fragile, and least of all your ego," Ivy says. "And before I do, I want to know what it was like for you."

"Answering a question with a question is bad form."

She rolls her eyes. "Tell me."

"Really fucking good," I say. Ivy, naked and soft against my side. A giant hotel bed to lounge in. A foreign city right on our doorstep. "Really, *really* fucking good."

Ivy rests her head on my shoulder. "I was concerned it wouldn't be, for you. Considering I don't know what to do."

"You know what to do, all right."

She laughs, the little giggle again, and an entirely different kind of pleasure spreads through my chest. "Did I do my job well?" I ask.

"Very. You kept your word, too." She looks down at my jaw. "I came twice."

"Yes, you did." Does she hear the satisfaction in my voice? "You orgasm easily," I add. "That's a great quality."

She sighs and snuggles against me. "It feels like I've just had a workout," she says.

Seems like we'll sleep in the same bed tonight. I briefly consider if that's a good idea—and of course it's not—before dismissing it. No way am I kicking her out, not after what we've just done. Not after she's just had sex for the first time.

And, I add to myself, reaching over to turn off the lights, it's not like I mind.

17

IVY

I blink my eyes open, but there's no light. The room I'm in is bathed in a darkness so absolute it has to be artificial. Where am I?

It takes me a second to remember. Singapore. And the bed is comfortable beneath me, the comforter cozy, the man beside me warm.

Rhys is breathing deeply behind me, his arm thrown around my waist. We'd slept together yesterday.

I'd slept with someone.

It shouldn't change things, really, but it still feels like the most momentous event. I'd gone on this trip convinced that I'd never find the right opportunity, the right man, a situation where it would feel effortless to try. But I had.

The darkness is an easy cloak for my wide smile. I reach down and run careful fingers over the arm resting around me, over the dark hair on his skin. It had been so much better than I'd thought it would be, having heard time and time again how people's first times were often disappointing.

This hadn't been the least bit disappointing.

But perhaps that's understandable, considering I'm not a fumbling teenager, and Rhys probably has more experience than I feel comfortable thinking about.

I glance over at him, but I can't see a thing. He must have pulled the curtains sometime during the night.

What happens now?

The part of me who always thinks ahead, the part that's saved every penny I've ever made and follows itineraries to the letter, is staring at my sudden spontaneous side in outraged anger. *Sleep with the photographer?*

What are you thinking, Ivy?

But it's very easy to silence her, because the truth is... I would've risked a lot more to have that one night with Rhys. To experience pleasure racketing through my body, and to have his hands touch my body like he loved it. Like he couldn't wait to be inside me, like he needed me.

My smile grows wider.

And so what if I haven't looked at my physical therapy textbooks in days? There'll be time for that. Rhys goes where he wants, he does what he pleases. Perhaps I can be more like that.

I glance over at the alarm clock on the bedside table and nearly jolt up in alarm. We've slept for nearly ten hours.

Beside me, Rhys stirs and gives a low groan. The arm around my waist tightens, his leg against mine, and I smile again. Worth it.

So worth it.

He presses a kiss to my shoulder. "Morning," he mumbles.

"Good morning."

His hand smooths over my stomach, before sliding up to cup my breast. It's a casual touch, but it means the intimacy is still here. No morning awkwardness.

"Sleep well?"

"Like the dead," he says, voice hoarse. "You?"

"Same. We must have been tired."

"Clearly."

I try to turn, to see what he looks like newly awake, but I can't make out any clear shapes. "It's late," I tell him.

"The time?"

"Yeah."

"Drop the itinerary, Ives."

I push against his chest. "Not when it's our job."

He sighs and stretches to flick a switch by his bedside table. A mechanic motor kicks into gear and then the giant draperies start to slide open. We both wince at the sharp light they reveal.

"How late is late?" he asks.

"As in, I'm supposed to be in hair and makeup in twenty minutes."

"Well, that's easy." He settles back down, pulling me into his arms so I'm draped across his wide chest. "Skip it. You don't need it, anyway. I like photographing you au natural."

I run a hand under my eyes. "I never removed my makeup yesterday. You distracted me."

"Guilty." His smile is crooked.

"Do I look like a raccoon?"

"No," he says, but he has an eyebrow raised. "A panda, perhaps. They're cuddlier."

"You're very kind."

He pushes my hair back, off my face. "I do my best."

We look at each for a long moment. The deep green of his eyes is thoughtful, soft, illuminated by the morning light. I'm the one who looks away, unable to stop myself from smiling.

"What?"

"Nothing. I just... I can't believe we did that last night."

Rhys's smile is crooked. "I can."

I bury my head against his chest. "I'll probably come to terms with it soon enough too."

"Come to terms with it?" His hand settles around my bare hip, squeezing. "You wound me."

"Impossible."

"Nearly."

I look up again to see his gaze on my body, eyes focused. I force more bravado into my voice than I feel—it's vulnerable, being this intimate. "You'd want to photograph me nude, huh?"

But his voice doesn't match my teasing. "Absolutely, I do."

I rise up, a hand on his chest. "Seriously?"

"Of course." He runs a thumb over my lower lip. "I've already thought of what kind of light I'd want, knowing which poses you prefer."

There's nothing to say to that, because my mind is blank. His statement is matter-of-fact, a true appreciation. It's not lewd or leering. It's not a photographer taking advantage. It's one artist to another.

And it moves me more than I thought it would.

"So?" he asks. "No regrets about yesterday?"

"None at all." I wonder if I can ask the question on my mind. What happens now? We didn't define any parameters for this. But Rhys raises an eyebrow and barrels on—he probably has no qualms or questions. After all, when did he say his last kiss was before me? A few weeks ago?

I doubt that encounter had been limited to kissing.

"How do you feel?" he asks, glancing down. And it's silly, because he's the one who's been there, but it makes me blush.

He gives a quiet laugh. "So inconsistent, about what makes you embarrassed. It's difficult to keep track of."

"I'm sorry."

"Don't be. It's very interesting."

I roll my eyes. "So I've been upgraded from *not uninteresting* to actually being *interesting*? Thank you."

"That's a real compliment in my book," he says. "You should take it to heart."

"Oh, should I?"

He nods, flipping us over. The comforter falls off him, his hair a tumble of dark locks over his brow as he hovers above me. "You're not too sore, are you?"

"Perhaps I'm not sore at all," I counter.

Rhys shakes his head. "I don't know if I'm relieved or offended."

"Decide, and then I'll tell you the truth."

His eyes widen. "Ivy, you deceitful—"

His words are cut off by the loud sound of a phone ringing. The ringtone is mine, emanating from wherever in the oversized hotel room I'd tossed my handbag last night.

Cold suspicion grips a hold of me. "What date is it?"

"Should be the twelfth," Rhys says. "Why?"

"Damn it!" I slide out from under him, racing across the room to the bathroom. I slide into one of the giant, fluffy bathrobes. "My dad and sister are calling. They scheduled a FaceTime call for today."

"Scheduled?" Rhys calls from the bed.

"Yes, *scheduled!*" I run a brush through my hair as the signal dies. I know I'll have no more than a minute before they call again. "We knew I'd be traveling all the time, so we settled on a place and a time that would work for us both with the time difference."

Not to mention Dad is the textbook definition of punctual. Looking in the mirror, I hurry to wipe at the smudged mascara under my eyes. It's not perfect, but it'll have to do.

My phone rings again. Rhys leans against the headboard, an eyebrow raised as he watches me search for my phone.

"Interesting," he comments, as I race to the adjoining door.

"Don't speak?"

"I won't," he says, waving me away.

I hit reply and my dad's chin fills the screen. "Ivy?" he asks. "Ivy, can you hear me?"

"Dad, not so close," Penny chides him, and the phone is tugged back. There they are, my dad with his reading glasses on and gray hair, Penny sitting next to him.

She's grinning, he's frowning.

"Where is... oh! Hi sweetheart," Dad says. "Are you in a hotel robe?"

"Yes, I have to jump in the shower after this," I say. "I'm in Singapore."

"We know." Penny holds up the trip itinerary that I'd forwarded to the both of them by email. They'd printed it, and each stop I've already been to has a tidy checkmark next to it. "We've been following along!"

"How's Singapore?" Dad asks.

I launch into an explanation of the city, focusing on the buildings and new construction. It's what he's interested in, but Penny rolls her eyes halfway through. "What about the food? What about the people?" she asks.

"I've been here for less than twenty-four hours!"

"But you must have eaten?"

Laughing, I tell her all about the dumplings Rhys and I ate last night. "Oh, and have you seen the pictures I've sent you both? I've tried to take as many as I can."

"Yes, and they're *much* appreciated," Penny says. Behind her, I see the familiar outline of my living-room windows. They're in my apartment—which means Dad came into the city to visit Penny for this call, rather than vice versa.

That's impressive. If he can, he'll avoid any big city.

"I miss you," I say. "I know I've only been gone for a week and a half, but we're flying so much it feels like a month."

"You'll be home soon," Penny says.

Dad nods. "Only two more stops now. Bali, and then Sydney."

"I'll be taking a ton of pictures for you."

"How is it going with the photographer you're traveling with? Has he been behaving himself?"

I glance toward the open door between our rooms. No doubt Rhys can hear this whole interaction. "He has," I say. "Turns out, he's actually quite nice."

"What about your studies? Have you been keeping up?"

Penny elbows Dad, but he ignores it, looking straight at me. "It's been difficult to find the time," I admit, "but I don't think it'll take me more than a day or two to catch up when I get back."

It really hasn't been long at all, and I'm loving this trip, but my chest is aching with homesickness when we say goodbye, with only a few minutes to spare before the hair stylist shows up.

Rhys appears in the opening between our two rooms, dressed in nothing but a pair of slacks. His hair is a tousled mess, his abs on full display.

He leans against the doorway. "The photographer is actually quite nice?"

I groan. "You heard that?"

"I did. I'm not sure which word is more offensive. Actually, quite or *nice.*"

"You don't like being called nice?"

He shakes his head. "The weather can be nice. Having a cup of coffee can be nice. People shouldn't be described that way, least of all me."

"I'm sorry," I say, cocking my head. "Would you like to give me a list of pre-approved adjectives that may be applied to you?"

He grins, stretching out beside me on the bed neither of us had slept in. "I'll email it to you," he says. "Are you ready for Bali?"

"I'm not sure," I say, stretching out beside him. "I have no idea what to expect."

His pushes a tendril of hair behind my ear. "You'll love it," he says. "I might have asked the agency to give us an extra day there."

"You did what?"

"Good surprise?" he asks, eyebrow raised. "I figured we could both use a day's breather after all the flying and jet lag."

My smile widens. "Excellent surprise. One might even call it *nice.*"

He groans. "Not that word."

"I can't help it, I haven't been given a list of pre-approved adjectives yet!"

"You're hopeless." But as Rhys tucks an arm under his head, as we grin at each other, I'm feeling more filled with hope than ever before.

18

IVY

"You know," I tell Rhys as we trail after the Indonesian receptionist, "I keep thinking that Rieler Travels can't possibly outdo themselves. That the next place can't be any better than the one that came before it."

Rhys snorts beside me. "Are you creating marketing slogans for them now?"

"I should be. But I mean, look at this place!" The hotel looks like it's nestled into a hillside jungle, thanks to the abundance of greenery around us. The humid air is already curling my hair, but what does that matter when we're escorted past deep-blue pools?

"We've given you one of the best villas in the hotel," the hotel attendant tells us, opening the front door for us. "On your patio, you'll find a private pool overlooking parts of the forest. It has been covered in rose petals for your photoshoot."

"Thank you."

"Of course," she says, with a small bow. "Please enjoy your stay, and don't forget, don't feed the monkeys."

"Monkeys?"

She shoots me a smile before she heads back down the path we came from. Rhys and I are left alone in the bright, luxurious villa, this one with two bedrooms.

As if in a daze, I walk out onto our private patio. "Do you think someone can be too impressed? Have too many new experiences in too short of a time? Can it be fatal?"

By my side, Rhys chuckles. I hear the snapping of his camera, but I don't turn, knowing better by now. I just close my eyes and breathe in the thick air instead.

Click click click.

He wraps an arm around my waist and points at the pool. "See all those rose petals?"

"Yes." They cover the pool, placed in swirling patterns. It's an art piece.

"I'm going to send the drone up and capture a few shots of this without you, and then with you in it."

"All right, perfect."

He bends to press a kiss to my temple. As good as it feels, I push him away with a grin.

"What?"

"The hair and makeup artist will be here soon. I don't want to be seen as *that* model, you know, the one who sleeps with the photographer."

He rolls his eyes. "So I'm just the photographer again. Good to know. Once again reduced to my working status."

Laughing, I grab his hand and pull him back into the villa. "You're being ridiculous."

"That's not one of the pre-approved adjectives." He stops by my gigantic suitcase and aims a casual kick to the side. "What asinine outfits has the agency packed for you today?"

"Let's see." I sit down cross-legged on the floor and open it up, deftly finding the clothing bag titled *Bali*. I pull out a red bathing suit that's cut high on the legs and has a low scooped back.

"Well, I like that one," Rhys says.

I laugh, clutching it to my chest. "So predictable."

"Not that word again."

"I'm sorry," I say, standing. "I should get showered and

changed before the makeup artist arrives. Remember, best behavior around the others."

"I won't forget," Rhys vows. And as he starts unpacking his expensive drone equipment, his watch glittering on his wrist in the sunlight, he snorts. "Predictable."

I'm still smiling an hour later when it's finally time to slip into our private pool, amidst all the rose petals. I've never done a shoot like this, and I do my best to catalogue all of it— the euphoric feeling of being here, the beauty of our surroundings, the soft water on my skin.

These are memories I'll cherish for the rest of my life.

"Ivy," Rhys tells me, "as much as I love your smile, you're going to have to keep it under control for this shoot."

I school my features back into the carefully neutral position, the elegantly nonchalant one that I know I'm supposed to project. "Sorry. I'm just so excited to be here, you know."

"I know," he murmurs. "And it's charming."

My smile is back again. "Hey, that's one of the adjectives on *my* pre-approved list!"

He chuckles. "And I haven't even read yours."

"What does that say about us?"

"That I'm clearly more intuitive. Now stop smiling."

"Yes, sir." But it's difficult to keep it under control, and I'm glad when he calls the shoot and I can finally relax. "We have enough of the hotel?"

"Yes." Rhys rolls up the sleeves of his linen button-down. "I have a question, now."

"Oh?"

"After our little... *incident* in Kenya, do you trust me enough to get in another car with me?"

I bite my lip. "Are we driving to any deserts?"

"None."

"Then yes, I'll get in another car with you."

He puts a hand over his heart. "Thank God. My ego couldn't have handled a no."

He's rented another Jeep, this time through the hotel. It

has no windows and no roof, a monster of a four-wheel drive. "I thought," I comment, "that you once said you preferred older cars."

Rhys's smile is crooked. "There's more beauty in them," he corrects. "But I don't mind a bit of horsepower from time to time."

He takes us around the island, following the built-in GPS. It doesn't take long for me to figure out that this, too, is a place he's been before—and not just once.

Rhys Marchand is getting more and more difficult to pin down.

We shoot all over the island, both in my bathing suit and in the dress I've brought along with us. The Bali swing, the rice fields—we're everywhere, filming and shooting me seemingly having a blast.

It's not an act.

Rhys grins at me when he turns onto a dirt road. "Last stop for today," he tells me. "I have a feeling you're going to like this."

I grip the side of the car as it dips perilously into a hollow in the road. "The jungle?"

"We can go exploring tomorrow. But for today..." Rhys glances at me, "How do you feel about swimming under a waterfall?"

"Are you serious?"

"I never joke about waterfalls."

"Of course I want to!"

After a particularly muddy bend in the road, he parks the car next to a trail. "It's just past those trees," he says.

And it is, opening up like an emerald hidden amongst the greenery. A beautiful turquoise pool of water with a twenty-foot waterfall roaring into it from an outcrop of rock. A swimming hole.

And there's no one else here.

"Rhys," I whisper, because words have failed me. They could never capture this place, anyway.

His words are quiet too. "Stunning, isn't it?"

"I can't believe this place is real."

"Get into the water. You'll believe it."

"Good thing I wore my bikini under this." I tug my dress over my head and toss it back into the Jeep, stepping forward to the edge of the water. It laps against smoothly polished stones. Taking a deep breath, I know this can't be the end of my travels. This trip can't be a once-in-a-lifetime thing.

I need this again.

I'm dimly aware of Rhys shooting, but as I walk into the water, that fades away. He doesn't comment or direct, either, just takes pictures as I stand with the tepid water around my waist, the waterfall directly in front.

"As soon as you're done," I call to Rhys, "you're joining me in here."

He does, stepping into the water in nothing but his swim trunks. He looks so comfortable here, with the jungle around us and the sky reflected in the water below. Like he's made for adventure, for travel, for the unknown.

Made to bend the world to his whims.

"Are we done shooting?" I ask. "For today?"

He raises an eyebrow, knowing what I intend. "Go ahead."

I dive under the surface and swim toward him, not caring that my hair gets wet, that the carefully applied no-makeup makeup is washed away. I break the surface right in front of him and his hands find me beneath the surface.

"How did you know about this place?"

"I was here a couple of years ago with a few friends," he says. It feels like the most natural thing in the world to wrap my legs around his waist as we stand in the middle of the swimming hole, the sound of the waterfall behind us.

"You travel a lot, don't you?"

"Pretty much constantly," he says, raising an eyebrow. "Is the lifestyle growing on you?"

"It is," I say, knotting my hands behind his neck. "I don't know how I could sustain it, but it is."

He cocks his head. "What is it you're studying?"

I bend backwards in his arms so I'm floating. He keeps his arms around my waist and my legs around his.

The sky is a deep, beautiful blue above. "Physical therapy," I say. "I need something to do when I'm done modeling. I need... *meaning.*"

"Meaning?"

"Yes." I look up at him, at his thick hair, at the unusual greenness of his eyes. They're accentuated in this tropical place. "People need a purpose in life. They need to feel like their days matter. I used to, when I was dancing. As much as I find modeling fun, I don't feel like that anymore."

"But you will after you start working as a physical therapist?"

"I hope so," I say. "I worked with plenty of physical therapists after I injured my knee, when I danced. And now I work regularly with personal trainers. There's a magic, there, in the ability to hone a body... to ensure it works to the best of its ability. Easing pain and strengthening muscle." I look away from him, running my hand through the water. "Exercise has been a gift in my life. I think I'd like helping others experience it as well."

"But you're not sure."

"Is anyone ever?"

He walks us out into deeper water. "You're incredible," he tells me.

"For wanting to be a physical therapist?"

"Yes," he says, but he's smiling, and it's clear that's not all he's saying. His thumbs smooth down my hips and hook into the edge of my bikini bottoms. "Does your dad want you to get a degree?"

"Yes. He's never liked the fact that I model. Was it that obvious when I spoke to him earlier?"

"A bit," Rhys says, with that crooked smile. "I could recognize the tone."

"You've heard it yourself?"

His smile shifts into something that is more mocking than amused. "Well, I used to. But I haven't really spoken to my father in ten years."

I grip his hands on my hips. "Ten years?"

"Yes," he says. "Not one-on-one. At family dinners and events, where there's a family conversation going? Yeah. But we haven't had a conversation just the two of us in a little over a decade."

I swallow. "That must be difficult."

"You get used to it."

"What does the rest of the family say?"

His crooked smile is back. "That's the good thing about always having had a strained relationship with your father. It's accepted as par for the course."

"Wow," I murmur, stretching back into the water. Something about this place, about his tone… it's a place for secrets and for sharing, and for going carefully, lest you wreck something. "Do you miss talking to him?"

Rhys snorts. "Not particularly. We both know that if we did, it would be a shouting match of everything we've swept under the rug, so we don't."

I slide my hands over his, gripping them even as they grip me. "I'm sorry."

He blinks. "Don't be. It's not painful."

Sure it's not.

"Okay," I murmur. "But I'm sorry anyway."

Our eyes meet, me looking up at him, him looking down at me. Him standing, me floating. I think I might break if he lets me go.

"Rhys?"

"I'm here."

"Was the other night a one-time thing?"

Something flashes in his eyes. "That depends, Ives."

"On what?"

"On you. Did you just want to grab your ticket?" His fingers curl around my bikini bottoms. "Or do you want to explore more?"

I wet my lips. Pull myself up, so I'm once again wrapped around him, both arms and legs. Droplets cling to his eyelashes. "I want to explore more," I whisper.

His smile is a slash of white. "I might have died if you said you were done."

"So dramatic." I run a finger along the sharp line of his jaw and his hands tighten around my thighs.

"It's what I do best." He kisses me, in a jungle in Bali, standing in a swimming hole next to a waterfall. And I kiss him back, knowing that however this ends, I will never regret him.

19

IVY

Our villa has a connected living room, two bedrooms, two bathrooms. It's a miniature palace, one too sumptuous to really get used to. Which is good, because in less than a week I'll be back in my shoebox of a studio in Manhattan.

But until then, I'm going to make the most of the water pressure in the shower, a place so big I can actually stretch out my arms and not touch the walls. I wrap a towel around myself when I'm done, looking myself over in the mirror. Hair, clean. Skin, clean. Mind? Not so clean, not as I emerge into the connected living room in just the towel.

Rhys is sitting on the couch, his own hair wet from his shower. His camera is in his hands, and he's flipping through pictures.

He lowers it when he sees me. "This look," he says, "I like."

"You do? It's the latest trend." I turn so he can admire the fluffy towel from every angle.

"Come here." Setting the camera down, he has an arm out. I settle against his side on the couch.

"What were you looking at?"

"You, mostly."

"Really?"

He snorts. "Considering that nearly sixty percent of all my shots are of you, yes."

"Show me."

With his left hand, he grips the camera and starts flipping through images. They're of me, standing underneath the waterfall in the swimming hole.

"It looks like something out of a travel magazine."

His lips curve. "Good, since that's what it's for."

"Too bad there's an air-headed model ruining the picture."

He puts the camera down. "You're never going to let me live down that comment?"

"How could I?" I stroke my fingers over his cheek, over the faint stubble there. "Tell me what your dream photography trip would be like."

He pushes me back on the couch, bracing himself with an arm on either side of me. A wet lock of hair falls over his tan forehead and I push it back.

"Documentaries," he says.

"Documentaries?"

"Yes." His head dips lower, our breaths mingling. "I'd need a team for that, one I could finance and direct. But that's the dream project."

I slide my hands up his arms, reveling in the strength there. "You haven't shot one already?"

He shakes his head. "It takes time to build those types of connections."

My fingers wander inside the sleeves of his T-shirt, smoothing up the skin. Something about his response is so right, and yet I wonder if he's discussed that with many. If his nonchalance is a facade.

"What about your publishing company?"

"It can be expanded. Turned into a multi-media company."

"You're thinking big. I like it."

He dips his head and kisses me, the touch gentle. Like he's

gauging where I'm at. So I tell him, wrapping my arms around his neck and pulling him closer.

He moves down my neck, my chest, to the very edge of the towel. "You've gotten tan lines," he murmurs.

"Inevitable in the sun." I slide my hand into the thickness of his hair.

Tugging at the towel, he inches it downwards, tracing the line across my breast with his lips. "It's like a map," he says. "Telling me where I need to go."

"Because you couldn't find your way otherwise," I tease, and my reward is a sharp tug on the towel. It falls open to him, my breasts on full display.

Rhys grins crookedly. "You're taunting me."

"Whoops?"

Shaking his head, he kisses down my body, stopping at each nipple to lavish them with attention. His other hand slides down my ribs, to the areas that are still covered by the towel.

And there's no explaining what I do then, not in any rational way. The headiness of the moment is pounding through me, the feeling of being wanted and of finally wanting in return—of my body being an instrument of pleasure that I'm controlling.

His eyes on me are magic, and I want to preserve that gaze. So I push him back.

Rhys rises on his knees on the couch. "Ivy?"

I wrap the towel around me and hand him his camera. "Come on," I tell him, heading to our private patio. The jungle is thick around the private pool, the lounge chairs. No one can see us but wayward monkeys in the trees.

Rhys stops a few feet away from me, camera in hand, eyes on me.

I let the towel fall.

He takes a long moment to speak. "Are you sure?"

And I love that I don't have to explain this, that he gets it, that he's here with me. I've been photographed in bikinis and lingerie before—what model hasn't?—but never like this.

And this isn't for a shoot. It's not for anything else. It's for me, and him. For us.

"I'm sure."

His eyes burn, but the hands on his camera are steady as he pockets the lens. "Whatever you want."

So I pose, normally at first, like I would if I were clothed. The humidity makes my skin hot, or perhaps it's his gaze, burning even through the camera. I lean against the railing surrounding our patio. I hold a giant palm frond in front of me, and we both laugh at the silliness. "I'm Eve," I tell him.

He shakes his head at me, but he lifts up his camera, still smiling.

And when he moves closer, when he asks me to sit down, to cross one leg over the other... I do it. I rest my head in my hands and close my eyes, surrendering to the experience.

Clothed in nothing but his gaze.

It's an age later when he reaches out and grabs my hand. "Come," he murmurs, pulling me inside. Stretching out on the bed, I lie down on my stomach and look at him. Because even though I'm looking at a lens, I know it's him on the other end.

Twisting, pulling the cover half over me, I ask, "Will you be joining me on here soon?"

His finger goes still on the shutter. "I thought you'd never ask," he says, and the voice he uses isn't mocking or dry or amused. It's hoarse with emotion.

I open my arms and he rises above me, tugging off his T-shirt. "So beautiful," he whispers against my skin as he kisses his way down, as he worships me with his touch just as he'd just done with his camera. "Stunning."

And just like the first time with him, the compliments warm me. They fill me up, expanding until I think I might burst from the heat. "Come here," I tell him, pulling his face to mine. "I need you."

He reaches down to circle that aching spot right at the apex of my thighs, and it feels so unbelievably good, but it's not what I want right now.

"You," I tell him, and Rhys doesn't need to be told twice, because he curses into my neck. Pulls off his pants, the length of him free and resting against my stomach. My hands and mouth ache to explore that part of him further, to learn just how best to please him, but they'll have to wait.

I need another ache stilled first.

Rhys puts on the condom with practiced moves, and then he nudges my legs wide, eyes on mine. His thumb circles as he pushes inside of me slowly, inch by torturous inch.

His darkened eyes meet mine, and I nod, even though he hasn't spoken. My body is lightly sore from the other night, but it's not painful. It's a dull ache, evidence of him. Of what we'd done.

Rhys pushes himself in to the hilt. Eyes rake down my face, my chest, my hips, to the place where we're joined. I watch, too. Transfixed.

Amazed at how easy this is with him, compared to how difficult I'd always imagined it would be. Once the fears melt away, the exploration itself is nothing but an adventure.

The heat inside of me grows with every second he stays still. Stretching me, and I take a deep breath, relaxing into the sensation.

"Rhys," I beg, raising my hips.

He reaches down to grip my thighs, pulling my legs up to rest on either side of his chest. And then he starts to move.

My hands fist in the comforter beneath me. "Oh God," I murmur, over and over again, because it's so deep this way, like he's moving somewhere in my center.

Rhys rolls his hips, over and over again, turning his head to press a kiss to my ankle. "You feel so good," he tells me. "Fucking unbelievable how good you feel."

There's no real response to that, or if there is, it's beyond me. My entire body is focused on where we join, and on the sheer intensity of it. I never knew it would be this intense—to have someone inside you.

But of course I should have, because how couldn't it be?

I reach up to grip the headboard when he speeds up. Faster and deeper he goes, like this is a race we're running, and maybe it is because my own pleasure grows in turn.

"Touch yourself," he tells me, hands gripped around my thighs. My legs are still braced against his body.

A fleeting moment of embarrassment, but it doesn't linger. I circle the throbbing spot between my legs, right above where he's working, and the pleasure grows.

"Yes," Rhys growls, "just like that, Ivy. Just like that." He shifts forward, bending me double, bracing his hands on either side of me.

The depths he's reaching make me gasp.

"Too much?"

"No, no, no." I shake my head too, for added emphasis. "Good."

A smile ghosts across his lips. "Good," he echoes, and then he surrenders to the job and I surrender to him. The height of my pleasure is a mountain easily climbed with him so deep inside, and I break and shatter, moaning. Surrender any semblance of control.

"Fucking hell, Ivy," Rhys growls, and then he comes too, and I watch his face as his eyes shut, as he groans, as the thrusting becomes erratic.

It's the most erotic thing I've ever seen.

I reach up to pull him down, to have him stay with me after, but Rhys rolls off right away. "Condom," he tells me by way of explanation, throwing it out. But then he returns, stretching out nude on the bed next to me.

We're both breathing hard.

"That was faster than I'd intended," he says.

"Was it?"

He runs a hand over his face. "There are still a ton of

things you haven't explored. Things I was looking forward to showing you. Turns out I couldn't wait."

"Neither could I," I say. "And we still have time to explore, don't we?"

He glances over at me, an eyebrow raised. "You might regret saying that."

"Will I?"

"Yes. Because there's no role I enjoy more than that of tutor."

I roll over on my stomach and slide my arms beneath a fluffy pillow. "It lets you be suitably pretentious and snide."

"Finally someone who understands me."

I laugh, reaching over to trace the length of his arm with my finger. "Is this something you do often?"

"Define 'this,'" Rhys asks, reaching up to tuck an arm behind his head. In profile, with his straight nose, full lips, strong chin... *he should be the model.*

"Tutoring impressionable young virgins."

He barks a laugh, and I join. My finger doesn't stop tracing the length of his bicep. He has a few freckles here, from sun and saltwater.

"No. It's been a long time since I've slept with a virgin."

"Two days ago," I correct.

He raises an eyebrow at me. "Smart-ass."

"I've learned from you." I turn my finger up, trace the other direction. Across the width of his shoulder. "But what about sex in general?"

He closes his eyes, a smile playing on his lips. "Men are usually the ones to ask about that."

"They are?"

"Demanding lists of former sexual partners, plotting a strategy to best every single one of them in performance."

"Would you have done that to me? If I had a list?"

He snorts. "I don't know. As it is, I'm just glad you didn't have one."

Questions swirl around in my head, questions that don't

have an answer. Things had changed these last few days, but had they changed more than the two of us becoming friends who've slept together?

Do I want them to?

"I'm allowed to ask any sex-related questions I want."

"Did I ever agree to that? I can't remember."

"Oh, you did."

Rhys turns his head to mine. "What was the question exactly? Do I have sex often?"

"Yes. I can specify, if I must." I duck my head down, looking at him. "When was the last time you had sex before me?"

"Two weeks ago, I think? Well, three and a half now, I guess."

"The person you kissed?"

"The very one."

The response isn't the one I wanted, and perhaps he notices that, because Rhys's smile is crooked. He runs a hand down my bare back and my eyes flutter in pleasure at the simple touch. "Not a relationship, just a casual friend."

"You have a lot of casual friends?"

"I only have casual friends," he says, smoothing up my spine.

"How come?" I ask. "You know why I haven't had serious relationships, but what's your excuse?"

"Lack of interest in one," Rhys says, his hand continuing its movement over my back. His fingers are lightly callused, reminding me in yet another way how different he is than the man I'd thought he was.

"I can't believe that."

He raises an eyebrow. "You can't?"

"No. I think everyone wants deeper human connection. It's a need, like thirst or hunger."

He reaches over to rest his forehead against mine, and my eyes flutter closed. "You," he says, "are starting to overthink this."

I release a breath. "Is it that obvious?"

"A little, which is fine. Only natural." His hand settles around my hip. "I did let you ask any questions you want, and these are no different."

"I guess I'm just curious about what happens when we get back to New York."

"If we'll keep exploring, you mean?"

"I suppose, yes. Or if we'll even continue being friends." A thought strikes me. "Because we truly are friends now, aren't we?"

Rhys's lips curve into a smile. "We're friends. And to answer your question, I don't know, Ives. Let's live in the moment and see where the days take us."

Live in the moment. The one thing an inveterate planner is not good at. But I relax into his touch and close my eyes, determined to try. After all, we have a lot of exploring left to do, and I don't want to waste a minute of it.

20

IVY

Rhys has his eyes closed in the first-class seat next to mine, but he's breathing through clenched teeth. I'd noticed his dislike of flying on our first flight, and the subsequent bad mood, but I couldn't think of a way to help him then. I still can't, but we're not strangers anymore.

So I put a tentative hand over his on the armrest between us. "Is there anything I can do?"

He looks over at me, eyes blank and expression harsh. But then something like embarrassment flickers over his expression and his clenched jaw softens. "No," he says.

"I wish there was." I keep my hand on his, my thumb moving in small circles. "My sister doesn't like flying either."

"Hmm." His hand is still clenched beneath mine, but he's looking at me.

"She's two years younger than me."

"Mine is four."

"Your sister is four years younger?"

"Just about." Beneath my hand, his relaxes on the death grip. "Tell me about yours."

"Her name is Penny," I murmur. "She's completely fearless, not at all like me. She'll rush into any situation, convinced she'll be able to manage. She most often does, too, but I can't tell if it's a consequence of her attitude or skill."

Rhys snorts softly. "Sounds like my sister too."

"Really?" I settle back into my seat and run careful fingers up his arm, back down to his hand again. "We're really close. Always have been, but I think our mother leaving helped with that. With us turning to one another, I mean."

He nods, eyes on mine. "Mhm."

I turn in my chair, tucking my legs up beneath me, and thread our fingers together. "What do your siblings think of your father?" I ask. "Considering you don't speak to him, they must have thoughts on him too."

Rhys gives a single shake of his head. "We're not making this flight any worse than it already is by adding a discussion of my dad on top of it."

"You're right. My bad." My thumb rubs a circle on the back of his large hand. "But should I keep distracting you?"

"Yes."

I nod, thinking, and let my gaze travel down his form. His legs are stretched out fully in front of him. "You're very tall," I comment. "How do you manage when flying coach?"

The familiar smirk ghosts across his face. "I don't."

I snort. "Right. I forgot you were richer than the federal government."

"Oh, we're not *that* rich." He waves a dismissive hand before returning it to the armrest. "People always like to inflate fortunes."

"After a certain amount of money, rich just becomes rich to the rest of us," I tease. "The nuances are only important for the wealthy themselves."

"That's most definitely true." Rhys tugs at the top button of his shirt, but doesn't move his hand locked in mine.

"Thank you for the extra day you got us in Bali."

His gaze lands on mine. "I was perhaps a tad selfish in requesting it."

"I enjoyed it. I enjoyed the jungle…" I bend to press a kiss to his hand. "I enjoyed the beach..." I press a kiss to his cheek. "And I enjoyed your lessons."

He turns his head for my third. It's a slow, soft kiss, one that makes my insides melt. "This," he murmurs, "is an *excellent* way to distract me."

I grin. "I figured it might be."

His hand clenches around mine. "Tell me what other lessons you want us to explore in Sydney."

And so, thirty-five thousand feet in the air and above the roar of the engines, I murmur my fantasy of the two of us and a large shower into his ear, until Rhys curses against my lips and requests a distraction from the distraction.

"I can't believe we're in Australia and we only have two and a half days here. It feels criminal."

"You'll be back one day." Rhys keeps a hand on my back as we walk down the hotel corridor.

"You think?"

"Absolutely. Come on," he says, leaning down to brush his lips against my ear, "can you honestly tell me you're ready to return to New York and settle down for good? To never travel again?"

A shiver runs down my spine that has little to do with his words and lots to do with his warm breath on my earlobe. "No," I whisper. "I'm not."

He presses the button to the elevator. After a full day of traveling, the two of us are ready to explore Sydney by evening and find a place to eat. The Rieler hotels might have terrific dining, but we've both agreed we're done with that. The streets of the city beckon instead.

"I've been thinking about our discussion on social media," I tell him, leaning into his side in the elevator.

"You have?"

"Yes. And I'm going to start being more real. More

behind-the-scenes, talking about things that matter to me. Post less pictures of me that are staged or posed."

Rhys's hand curves around my hip. "And your agency?"

Looking him straight in the eye, I smile. "Fuck my agency."

He grins wide at that. "Ivy, have I been a bad influence?"

"Perhaps, but I'm starting to like it."

He tips my head back and presses a kiss to my lips. I'm dimly aware of the elevator doors sliding open, but they're secondary to the feel of his mouth on mine.

"Good thinking," he says finally, pulling me with him out of the elevator. But there's someone standing there waiting for us, someone in a suit.

Ben Rieler, to be exact.

And he's grinning.

"Hello you two," he says. "Care for dinner, or am I interrupting your plans?"

I step out of Rhys's arms. He just inclines his head. "Ben."

"I came to join the two of you for the final leg of your trip." His eyes sparkle as he looks between the two of us. "I'm glad to see you're getting along."

I feel nauseous.

This man is the one hiring my agency, and by extension me. And he just saw me getting chummy with the photographer. It's nothing new, nothing that doesn't happen over and over and over again in the modeling world, but it has never been *me*. I have never been cast in this role before.

I've been so careful to *never* be this kind of model.

Ben pulls Rhys in for a half-hug. It's a familiar motion, the one men do when they know one another well.

"You flew out to Sydney just for us?" Rhys asks. There's tension in his voice. He can't be happy that our employer saw us, either.

Ben snorts. "No, I have more faith in you than that. We're expanding out of Sydney, so I came here for meetings and to view the properties up in Queensland. Figured I'd catch up with my favorite photographer-model duo while I'm here." He smiles at me. "How have you been, Ivy?"

I knot my hands together. "Great. Your hotels and staff have been wonderful."

It's flattery. It's the truth. And I'm just glad I've managed to speak around the lump of horror in my stomach that he saw us, Rhys and me.

"Good," Ben says, "because I gave the entire company strict instructions to provide you the best experience possible."

"Well, you succeeded." Rhys's tone of voice is impossible to decipher.

We walk to a nearby restaurant, apparently one of Sydney's best, if Ben's to be believed. My running shoes still have the red clay of Kenya stuck to the sides, and the jeans I'm wearing aren't fit for linen-clothed tables. The plan to walk down to the Opera House has been abandoned entirely.

Rhys might be comfortable around Ben, but I'm not.

I smile at the waiter who pulls back my chair. The men follow suit, and it's not long until Ben has ordered us a bottle of Australian white wine.

"They have some good ones down here," he tells us, and Rhys gives a small hum.

"Yes, well, I know *you* don't agree," Ben says. "Sometimes you really do have the French mindset."

"Something was bound to rub off," Rhys comments, looking through his menu.

I look at mine unseeing, my fingers toying with the edge of the paper. My eyes fixate on the prices. It's more than the per diem Rieler allowed for the trip, but it's a small worry in what feels like an ocean of mistakes.

We order. Ben leans back in his chair, draping his arm over the one next to him, and looks at me with a smile. "Ivy, how have you enjoyed traveling with Rhys here? Has he been behaving himself?"

Rhys shakes his head, muttering something that sounds like, "Christ, Ben."

"It's been good," I say, the most noncommittal answer I can think of. "He's really knowledgeable about the places we've visited, which I think has led to some great shots. In Bali, for example, he knew the location of a waterfall without any other tourists."

Ben looks over at Rhys. "All your traveling has come in handy."

"So has my shooting. We've gotten some excellent footage."

"I'm looking forward to seeing it."

I take a sip of my wine. "You two know each other well?"

Rhys opens his mouth to speak, but Ben is the one who responds. "Oh, we do. We went to college together."

"You did?" I glance over at Rhys. "Where?"

"Yale," Ben replies, thanking the waiter when our food is delivered. "Although we only got the first two years together."

Rhys's hand is knuckled around his fork. "Circumstances changed."

"They did, yes. But to answer your question, Ivy, we stayed in touch." He raises an eyebrow to Rhys. "And he critiqued my travel ads and promotional material *one* time too many, saying that they were soulless… so I hired him."

"That does sound like him," I say. Ben laughs and Rhys shoots me a look, one that's equal parts amused and annoyed. But not at me, I think.

No, neither of us had planned on having dinner with someone else tonight.

Rhys's phone rings, and he scoots back to turn it off. But then he sees the name on the screen—I catch a glimpse, too. *Lily.* "I should take this," he says, looking at me and Ben. "I'll be right back."

"Don't worry about it," Ben says, waving a hand good-naturedly.

He nods to my plate of lamb when we're alone. "Enjoying the food?"

"It's delicious. A good choice of restaurant."

He nods, reaching for his wine. "I'm glad we got this chance to have dinner together. Your face might be the one I'll see for years, you know, whenever we put together new brochures or video ads. I'm happy to know a bit more about the person behind the image."

"And after having seen your hotels, I'm happy to be part of it," I say. "You have some terrific staff. They've really made this whole trip a joy."

"You're good," Ben says, nodding at me. "Very good."

"Sorry?"

"That would make an excellent testimonial."

I laugh politely. "Well, it's the truth."

"Even so, I'm happy to hear it. Truthfully, I'm impressed by what the two of you are doing. Traveling this much in such a short period of time is taxing." He raises his fork, chewing. "Trust me, I know. I do it often."

"You're not wrong," I admit. "But it's been an adventure."

"You're not a complainer," he notes, leaning back in his chair. "I admire that. And, judging by what I saw earlier, it seems like the two of you get along famously now."

My cheeks scald, but I don't turn away from his gaze. "We've gotten to know one another, yes."

"Oh, don't be embarrassed about that. He's charming," Ben says, slicing through his lamb. "It happens."

"Right, yes. I'm sure it does."

"He never could resist a model, either." Ben chuckles.

I reach for my glass of wine, at a loss for what to say. My fingers are tense on the stem. Time has flowed irregularly on this trip. With only one another for company in the face of so much travel, it feels like I've known Rhys for months. But that familiarity is false. It's only been two weeks, and with Ben here, that knowledge sharpens into a blade.

The owner and CEO of Rieler Travels doesn't look at me to

see how his words landed. I wonder if he, too, can't resist a model. Like we're a species and not a profession.

"I'm sorry about that." Rhys's voice is deep, a hand on the back of my chair as he sits down.

"Not to worry," Ben says. "Gave me the perfect opportunity to get to know Ivy a bit better."

He raises his glass and I raise mine. Rhys joins, but sends me a questioning look. He doesn't seem fooled by my returning smile.

The sun has long since set when Rhys and I walk back to the Rieler hotel in Sydney in silence. With half the interiors still under construction, we're two of the first guests to stay there.

"I didn't know you two knew each other like that," I say. It comes out like an accusation, my arms wrapping around my torso.

Rhys's hand lands on my lower back, his other unlocking the door to his hotel suite. The mirror image to my own, it looks just like all the other Rieler suites we've stayed in these weeks. Same color scheme. Same furniture.

"We're friendly," he acknowledges, leaning against the wall. "Ivy, he's not going to make a big deal about seeing us kiss. I promise you that."

My shoes dig into the plush carpet as I pace. "You can't promise that. No one can. Rhys, this is what gives models in my business a reputation. Sleeping with photographers."

His jaw tenses. "I'm aware. Trust me, I am. If I'd had a clue he would be here..."

"It's just so *embarrassing.*" I sink down onto the edge of his giant hotel bed, kicking off my sneakers. "He's the head of a company that's hired me. He hired my agency."

Rhys tugs off his jacket. Runs a hand through his hair, and sits down next to me, close enough that our bodies are touching shoulder to shoulder and thigh to thigh.

"Ben's knowledge doesn't change anything," he says.

I reach for his hand. He lets me take it, holding it in both of mine on my lap. "I'm not the first model you've slept with, right?"

His hand closes around my fingers. "Where did that come from?"

"Ben mentioned something to that effect."

Rhys groans. "He has never known how to be tactful."

A sinking feeling in my stomach. It's true, then. It shouldn't matter. We're not anything, not really. And yet it feels like it does.

"Ivy," Rhys says, turning to face me. His free hand curves around my cheek. "You know I wasn't a virgin before I met you."

My cheeks flush again, this time in mortification. "I know that. I never expected you to be. But considering you made your low opinions of models so clear…"

He's shaking his head before I finish my sentence, a furrow between his dark brows. "I have dated women who worked in modeling, yes. And I'll readily admit that what I've seen of the industry, or the concerns of those women, didn't… well. I didn't have a high opinion about all of it before I met you."

"So you slept with models, but you didn't respect them?"

"Christ, Ivy." He pulls his hand back from mine and rises, walking in front of me where I sit on the bed. Tension radiates from his form. "Yes, I've had a fair share of casual sex. Most sex I've ever had, truthfully, has been casual. But I've never deceived anyone. It's never been anything but honest. The models you're referring to? They gained things from me, too."

I track his familiar features. The thick, dark fall of his hair. The tanned skin and broad shoulders. Hands that have long fingers and broad backs, made to pitch tents and take photographs and drink wine.

"I understand," I murmur. "I do, Rhys."

He pauses in front of me, dark green eyes swimming. "My past has no bearing on what happened between us."

"I know," I say, reaching for him. He steps closer almost

reluctantly, not relenting until I tug him down beside me on the bed. We stretch out next to one another like we've done so often in the past week.

"I'd rather you ask me," he says. "Whatever you're thinking. Even if it's ludicrous. *Especially* if it's ludicrous."

"Brutal honesty," I murmur.

He nods, lifting himself up on one arm. Watching me with those inscrutable eyes, the ones that had intrigued me in the beginning. Infuriated me in their unreadability.

They're my favorite feature now.

"Your sister called during dinner?"

"Yes," he says. "She's being a nag."

It's so unexpected in the context of our conversation that I chuckle. His lips curve into a fond smile. "What is she nagging you about?"

"My father's birthday is the day after we return to New York. It'll be a grand affair," he says, using the words mockingly.

"You're not planning on going," I guess.

"No."

I reach out and run my fingers through his hair. The fear of these casual touches had disappeared days ago, shifted into comfortable intimacy. "You went to Yale."

"I did," he confirms. "For two years."

We look at each other, the tension from Ben's sudden arrival leaking out of me. Rhys is right, in the end. Him knowing changes nothing between the two of us.

He crosses the distance between us and kisses me, the touch of his lips setting off an ache in my chest. My arms twine around him in response.

"We still have two days, right?"

He nods, his hand slipping under my shirt to find the curve of my waist.

I grip him tighter. "We're going to use them well, then."

"Ivy," he murmurs against my neck, his lips sending shivers across my skin. I stretch my neck to give him full access to the sensitive skin. But he pauses, rising on an arm as if a thought has just struck him. "I respect you," he tells me. "And I don't think any less of you for working as a model."

I pull him back down to my lips, his words setting off the same ache in my chest again. The one that warns me I've already fallen too deep.

21
—
IVY

We land in New York after more hours of flying than I like to count, the both of us quiet and tired. It's mid-afternoon here, but it's the Wild West inside of me time-wise. I'll need a week or two to fully recover from the jet lag.

"Welcome home," the passport controller tells me. It's a professional tone, but the words are beautiful. I can't wait to collapse into my own bed.

Rhys rolls my giant suitcase as well as his own. The agency hadn't arranged transport back home for us from the airport, but I've decided to splurge on a cab.

"Solid ground," he mutters.

"Feels good, huh?"

"I'm never flying again."

"Yes, you are," I tell him. "But not anytime soon."

"Did you know I sail?"

I shake my head. "No."

"Well, that's how I'll travel from here on."

We turn the corner and emerge into the arrivals hall, walking past lines of people waiting for their loved ones. Seeing it makes me smile.

But Rhys stops in his tracks. "Fucking hell."

"What's wrong?" I follow his gaze to a man. A man who's

staring at Rhys, and who Rhys is staring right back at. "Oh. A friend of yours?"

His voice is short. "My brother."

The man approaches us. Nearly as tall as Rhys, with the same hair, similar features, the two of them almost the same age. Their expressions are perfect replicas of one another. They look like mirror opposites, carved from the same stone but by different sculptors.

"You sent Lily your itinerary," his brother says by way of greeting. "I'm heading up to Paradise and you're joining me."

Rhys's eyebrow is lifted, but it's not mischievous. "Am I?"

"Yes."

The temperature between them is glacial. It's the kind of conversation I shouldn't be here for, shouldn't be overhearing.

But then his brother blows out a tired breath. "Your sister has missed you. Mom's missed you. Just stay for the night, man. The cottage is yours."

I can tell Rhys is gearing up to refuse. It's in his tense form beside me. I grip his arm and look at his brother. "Will you give us a moment?"

He turns to me for the first time, as if only now realizing I'm there. "Yes, of course. I'm parked right outside."

And then he disappears through the sliding doors, shoulders back and bearing straight.

Looking so much like Rhys.

Was that Henry? The older brother who's designing the New York Opera House?

I turn to Rhys. He's running a hand through his hair, looking at me. Waiting for me to speak.

So I nudge his shoulder with mine, forcing my voice to be light. "Feel like going on another adventure? I'm up for it, if you are."

His eyes widen. "You'd come with me? To Paradise Shores?"

"Why not? I've already played buffer once for your family. I can do it again."

"You were excellent at it last time."

"All I had to do then was flutter my eyelashes. This crowd might be tougher, but as long as there are no Jeeps and deserts, I'm in."

"None." Rhys looks at me for a long time, eyes dark. But then his lips curve into a crooked smile. "I'll take you sailing while we're there."

"I'd love that."

"And it won't be for more than a night or two."

"Sounds great. I'm not working this weekend, anyway."

Rhys grabs one of my suitcases along with his. "Paradise Shores is north of New York. A two-hour drive."

"We'll go with your brother, then?"

He nods again, and we head toward the sliding doors. "We'll go," he says.

And just like that, I'm whisked away into a large car, seated in the backseat while Henry and Rhys Marchand converse quietly in the front. Like slipping onto a different path, accepting an offer, and life shifts. The weekend unfurls in front of me with the promise of new experiences, instead of the one filled with laundry and studying I'd been expecting.

Excitement drums through my veins like a second heartbeat, and I wonder if that's what life is always like around Rhys, if he regularly bends the rules of normalcy.

And I wonder how far I'm willing to bend with him.

———

"We're staying *here*?"

Rhys pushes the door closed behind him and rolls my giant suitcase against the wall. The living room is tastefully decorated, the windows opening up to a view of the ocean.

"Yeah," he says. "The cottage is for guests."

"You guys call this a *cottage*?"

He grins. "You're welcome to re-name it. Now, come on."

"Where are we going?" But his hand is already on mine, and he's pulling me toward one of the bedrooms. A giant master bed opens up before us. "Rhys…"

But he heads to the bathroom instead, nodding to the giant walk-in shower. "We've been traveling," he says. "I need a shower. Care to join?"

I put my hand on the giant bed, pressing down into the soft mattress. It's impossible to tear my eyes away from the cloudy pillows, the down in the comforter. With every passing second, my eyelids grow heavier. "This looks like heaven," I tell him.

There's a smile in Rhys's voice. "It's late enough," he says. "Sleep off the jet lag. We have the whole day tomorrow."

It's a difficult choice, watching the tall frame of him silhouetted against the bathroom. But tiredness is fighting with me every step of the way, and the few hours of sleep I'd managed to snag on the plane were not enough. "Over twenty hours," I tell him. "We've been traveling for twenty hours."

He rests a hand on the doorframe. "Sleep, Ivy."

"When's your dad's party?" But I'm already sitting down on the bed, pulling off my socks.

"Tomorrow evening."

"Mhm." I lie back, fully intending to take off my yoga pants, but first I have to test this bed out, like Goldilocks and her bears. Is this one just right?

It's more than just right, and I close my eyes, just to get the full effect.

The next thing I notice is a room in darkness and someone large shifting in bed next to me.

"Rhys?"

"I'm here," his deep voice comes out of the darkness, from my left side. I relax against the sheets.

"We're sharing a bed," I mumble.

There's a pause in the darkness, a questioning silence. "There's a guest bedroom. Do you want me to go?"

My yawn makes my reply near unintelligible, so I have to repeat myself, struggling to pull off my sweater at the same time. "No."

"Good."

I finally get my sweater off and climb back under the sheets in nothing but yoga pants and a camisole.

"I'm going to marry this bed," I murmur.

"Not if I propose to it first."

"Dibs," I mumble, reaching out to find warm skin, shifting beneath my fingers as he moves closer.

His voice is the last thing I hear. "Thank you for coming with me."

I don't reply, drawn down through the layers of sleep to where unconsciousness beckons.

22

RHYS

The ocean is a calm presence outside the cottage's windows, and the sky a tentative blue above it. For every photograph I edit, I have to look up to the vast expanse of blue beyond, as if to make sure I'm not dreaming.

I'm really in Paradise Shores, and Ivy is here.

Such a thing had felt unimaginable, just a week ago, but here we are. Her and me in my sister's old house, with her living right next door. No doubt Henry told her last night that I'd brought someone. No doubt she'll be here as soon as she can, knocking on the door with curiosity burning like candlelight in her gaze.

I step away from my laptop, the motor in the external hard drive humming, to peer into the still-dark bedroom. Ivy isn't sprawled where I'd left her, and I hear the shower running.

I pour her a cup of coffee and return to my laptop, to the image I'm editing. She's standing on the beach in St. Barts, her face upturned to the rays of sunshine and her feet buried in the turquoise water.

The surroundings are gorgeous, and I reluctantly up the saturation, the glossiness, until it looks like a travel photograph. I'll have to meet Ben halfway here if I'm to have a shot at winning this bet.

Ivy emerges into the living room in a fluffy robe, hair wet down her back. "I can't remember the last time I slept this long."

"Jet-lag knockout."

"Completely."

I pull her onto my lap and she settles there gracefully, leaning back against my chest. "Are you editing?"

"Yes." I flick through some of the photos, all from St. Barts, and nearly all of her. Walking past beautifully colored houses, dancing on a square. They showcase the best the place has to offer, all with her as the protagonist.

"Wow," she breathes. "I didn't know you got me dancing."

"Of course I did."

"Is this what you'll submit to Mr. Rieler?"

"Most likely, yes. It'll take a while to sort through and edit, though." I shake my head, muttering, "Mr. Rieler."

"I can't call him Ben just because he's *your* friend," Ivy says, nudging me. I tighten my arm and she leans her head back against my shoulder. I press my lips to her neck.

"What happens today?" she asks.

"We have the whole day." Her robe has fallen open to reveal the length of a tan thigh, and I settle my hand there, smoothing over the skin. "It's very early still, you know. The town isn't awake yet. We're the ones who are on a different schedule."

"Right," she murmurs.

"Let me take you sailing this morning." The ocean always drew me when I was here, a siren's call. Not to mention my sister couldn't question the two of us if we were at sea.

"And you're sure you know what you're doing?"

I snort. "Yes. This won't be like the Jeep-in-the-sand incident."

She slides off my lap and turns with a wide smile. "I've never been sailing before."

And just like that, she sweeps my legs out from beneath me, like she has so many times during this trip. Her honesty and enthusiasm is so genuine it disarms me.

"You'll love it," I tell her, smiling back.

Paradise Shores is quiet and empty as we head down Ocean Drive, parking by the marina. This place that is as familiar to me as the lines in my palms, a place I've both run to and run from.

The *Frida* is lying calm and steady in the water, and seeing her proud mast is the truest homecoming of all.

Ivy has never sailed before, but she follows orders like she was made for it, her hands tidy as she ties the most basic of knots. We cruise out of the marina on engine power, the docks and shore devoid of people. There's one good thing about jet lag, at least. It reminds you that life can start early in the morning, if you only have the discipline to let it.

"You're good at this!" I call to her, sitting in the bow. "Sure you haven't sailed before?"

"No!" she calls back, grinning widely at me. "But I'm used to following orders from my dad, when we went camping. This isn't that different."

I shake my head at her, keeping our course steady. "Comparing a boat to a tent! You should walk the plank for that."

"Do you have one?" Tendrils of blonde hair have escaped her braid and curl around her face in the wind.

"It's somewhere around here," I say. "Don't go anywhere while I get it rigged up."

The sound of her laughter on the wind mingles with the birds above and the waves below, and I close my eyes, drawing in the scent of it all. Of salt and sea and life.

We anchor off an abandoned bay and Ivy pulls out the sandwiches we'd bought at the gas station. The early morning sunlight is bright but not strong, letting me lie back on the deck and close my eyes without shades.

"You've had adventure on your doorstep your entire life," she tells me, a smile in her voice. "No wonder you seek it in adulthood too."

I put an arm beneath my head. "Never thought of it like that before."

"Hey, that's why you dove in after us? Jordan and me, in the Hamptons, I mean. You grew up on the water."

"I dove in after you because you needed help."

"Well, that too."

We eat in comfortable silence for a while, the sea rocking the boat gently. It's a motion I've missed.

"What are you going to introduce me as to your family?"

I laugh. "That's what you're thinking of right now?"

"Well, it's important." A pause as she takes another bite. "Just so I know how to better play my role as a buffer."

"What do you want to be introduced as?" I ask, smiling up at the sky. Waiting for her answer, for whatever she says to shock me.

She's so good at that.

"Whatever will make my role as buffer most efficient."

I chuckle. "So committed to your job."

"That's me," she says. "*I* take things seriously."

"As opposed to me?"

"I'm itinerary-girl," she says, a shrug in her voice. "You're... chaos-boy."

"Those are terrible superhero names," I protest. "I refuse to let either of those two stick. Sexville I accept, but not these two."

Ivy's voice is teasing. "You haven't answered my question, though."

"My friend," I suggest. "My colleague. Aren't both of those correct?"

"They are, I suppose."

"But I think I'll go with date."

There's a smile in her voice. "I like that one the best."

I glance over to watch her reach her arms to the sky, stretching. She's graceful even seated, as if the curves of her body always carry the memory of dance.

"I'm going to photograph you dancing one day," I tell her. "In a studio, just the two of us."

Her eyes lock on mine, surprise and warm joy filling them. "I'd like that," she says.

"Good, because you're not getting rid of me yet."

"Not trying to."

Something warms in my chest, and it's not just the sunlight or the waves beneath us, even though it's a rocking I've missed. Give me a good boat rather than an airplane any day of the week. If I have to die, let it be by ocean rather than sky.

"Will I ever find out what's between your rift with your dad?"

I close my eyes. "Get me drunk enough tonight and you might."

She groans. "Rhys."

"I can't be serious for more than a second," I say. "Not my fault. It's probably programmed into my genes."

"Why is the boat called the *Frida*?"

"You're full of questions today." I open my eyes to see her sitting by the edge of the railing, folding herself down so her legs can rest over the edge.

She grins at me. "I've always been full of questions," she tells me. "I'm just not afraid of asking them anymore."

I raise an eyebrow. "While you're on a boat alone with me? Unwise."

"I've never claimed to be wise in relation to you."

"I don't know why the boat is named *Frida*. My father named her decades ago, and none of us have ever figured out why."

"Your grandma?"

"Her name isn't Frida."

Ivy looks back out at the sea, her legs dangling over the edge of the sailboat, her hair loose. It falls in golden waves down her back, tousled in the wind.

My hand aches with the absence of a camera. Capturing her here, on the ocean, on this boat, feels like a necessity. I need it like I need air.

But there's no camera, so I'll just have to bring her out here again.

"Ivy," I say, lifting the hem of my shirt.

"Yes?"

"Feel like swimming?"

She turns to look at me, eyes widening as she sees my hands resting on the zipper of my pants. "Sure."

"Let's skip the swimsuits."

Her eyebrows rise. "You can't be serious."

"Why wouldn't I be?" I spread my arms out. "It's a beautiful summer day. There is no one here."

She bites her lip, but doesn't look away from me as I kick off my shoes. The decision is being made, I can see it in the lightness of her eyes, the way she surrenders to adventure.

Ivy reaches for her own shirt. "I can't tell if you're a bad influence," she says, "or if you're the best influence."

"The best," I say, watching as she undoes the clasp of her bra. She's magnificent, and my body responds on instinct.

She notices when I kick off my boxers. Her cheeks are the flush of a pale rose, her smile that of the dawn. "I thought you said we were *just* skinny-dipping."

I nod to her body, glorious in the sunlight. The sea suits her. "Can't help it," I say. "But don't worry, the water will get rid of it."

She looks over at the edge of the boat, her thumbs hooked into the edge of her panties. "Is it cold?"

I raise an eyebrow. "Changing your mind?"

She meets my gaze squarely as she pulls off the last stitch of fabric, as she backs toward the edge. One last triumphant glance and then she dives clean off the boat, a nude streak against the deep blue of the ocean.

And as I dive off the boat after her, her words come back to me—that I'd always had adventure on my doorstep. Maybe, with her, it can always be one in the future.

After our swim, we lie on the deck of the *Frida* under the warm summer sun. There's no need to talk, but words rise to the surface regardless.

"I haven't had a plan in a very long time," I murmur, smoothing my hand over her back. "For a long time it was just to do whatever my family *didn't* want me to do."

"That sounds like a general direction at least," she says, her hand smoothing over my chest. Her voice is drowsy. "You know, a pre-planned rebellion feels like an oxymoron."

I snort. "You're too smart for your own good."

"You love it when you're challenged."

"Of course I don't. Can't you be a bit more obsequious?"

"*Obsequious?*"

"Just because I dropped out of college doesn't mean I'm not well-read." I press a kiss to her forehead. "That's a very elitist sentiment of you."

"I've never said anything of the sort."

"It was in your tone," I tease.

Ivy glares at me, but there's laughter hiding in those eyes. I stroke down her back, wanting us to stay like this forever. On an adventure with no beginning and no end, with her the biggest mystery of all.

"I think I would have hated you in school," she says.

It's so unexpected that I burst out laughing, until I have to sit up, until I can barely look at her or risk breaking out into guffaws again. "Ives, that might be the truest thing you've ever said."

She has the widest smile on her face. "Imagine how much we would have argued."

Still chuckling, I tuck her against my side again, right where my body is getting used to her living. "I'd have teased you for all your planning. You would have hated me for my lack of it."

She curls up against me. "Good thing we met as adults, then."

"A very good thing indeed," I say, gripping her close.

23
IVY

Rhys's hand rests on my low back like a talisman. "Don't be nervous," he murmurs in my ear.

"I'm not." I shoot him my winning smile, practiced from years of modeling. It's not enough to convince him, judging by the raised eyebrow. "At least I'm allowed to talk at this party."

He gives a crooked smile, but the tension around his eyes doesn't fade. "A big improvement from the last party we attended together."

"Do you think we'll end up in a pool at this one too?"

"It would be a shame to," he says, his hand curving around my hip. "You look stunning."

So does he, tall and poured into a tailored gray suit, no tie, the expensive watch glittering at his wrist. He's a different man from the one I've travelled with, the teasing glint in his eyes elevated.

"Good thing my agency packed all those unpractical clothes, you mean."

"I'll admit that they do *look* beautiful."

"And as for unpractical…" I smooth a hand over the red silk of my dress, the same I'd worn walking through St. Barts.

It's a risk, wearing it tonight, when it has to be returned. "Well, I don't expect having to run from any lions tonight."

"I wouldn't count on that," Rhys mutters.

We pause in front of a large three-story house, white with shutters and a wrap-around porch. It's perched right by the sea, close enough that I can just make out a private shoreline.

The sound of a live band reaches us, soft notes and guitar strings. Laughter rises up from the lawn.

"This is where you grew up?"

Rhys nods. "I'm surprised he agreed to host the party here."

"You are?"

"Yes. He'll pretend to be reluctant about all the attention he's getting, but he's going to be counting all the congratulatory cards he's received tonight."

I grip his hand and pull us toward the music that beckons. To think he grew up here, by the ocean and the old wealth of this town... "But your siblings will be here?"

"They will. Not to mention there'll be tons of good food and an open bar."

"There will?"

"My mother only uses the best caterer."

He weaves us around a throng of people without bothering to say hello, ignoring the curious looks they cast him. I give them all a polite, sheepish smile. Inside, my heart is pounding. Of all the adventures Rhys and I have gone on the past two weeks, this might be the scariest.

A beautiful woman with auburn hair spots us, a smile breaking like the dawn across her freckled face. She heads our way, a faint limp to her walk. Rhys's own steps quicken.

"You ghost!" she scolds him. "I hear you arrive at the cottage, but you don't say hi. I come over in the morning, and you're already out!"

Rhys's grin is unapologetic. "Whoops."

"Was it punishment?" she asks. "Because I sent Henry your itinerary?"

"I hadn't thought of that, but if you want to see it that way, by all means."

She rolls her eyes before turning to me. "And I heard you brought a friend. Hi!"

"Hi." I shake her extended hand. "I'm Ivy."

Her smile grows wider. "And I'm Lily. We're both named after plants."

"Although only one of you is poisonous," Rhys points out.

His sister shoots him a look. "Well, that's not kind of you."

"Don't worry," I say, liking her already. "I'm used to it by now."

At my side, Rhys snorts. "She's exaggerating."

"Only a little."

Lily glances from me to her brother and back again. "So the two of you have been on a trip around the world, from what I've heard. I want to hear all about it. Rhys hasn't sent me a *single* picture."

"And he's taken a thousand," I tell her.

"Hey," Rhys tells me. "Whose side are you on here?"

I laugh, and so does his sister, shooting another speculative look at him. Our little group is interrupted by the brother who'd driven us here.

"Save me," Henry says, wearing a suit and a pained expression.

"Investors?" Rhys asks.

His brother grimaces, the expression minute. "Legions of them. Is this a birthday party or a conference?"

"Both," Lily says. "Always both."

"We should form a sub-party," Rhys says. "Like the old days."

Henry groans at the same time as Lily gives an excited whoop. I glance between them. "A sub-party?"

"It's when you steal a few bottles from the open bar and find an abandoned room," Rhys says. "Very useful in a pinch."

"And very adolescent," Henry says. "Ivy, it's nice to see you again. Did you enjoy sailing?"

"Smooth," Rhys says. "Not obvious you changed the subject at all."

His brother gives him a level look. "Thank you."

I bite my lip to keep from chuckling. "I did, yes. This town is beautiful. And I want to thank you for letting me stay in your cottage, Lily, and the hospitality. I know I'm an unexpected plus one."

Rhys shakes his head, reaching for a glass from one of the circulating trays. "I invited you," he says.

"Yes, well this is still a family event."

Both of Rhys's siblings look at me like I've misunderstood something, Henry with a raised eyebrow just like his younger brother, and Lily with a wide smile.

"Oh," she tells me, "this isn't just a family event. We don't have *this* much family."

"Not on this side of the sea, at least," Rhys mutters.

"This is a conference masquerading as a cocktail party." She raises her champagne glass. "Welcome to Paradise, Ivy. We're happy to have you here."

I let my glass clink against hers. "I'm happy to be here."

"Where's Hayden?" Rhys asks. "Not to mention Faye?"

"She's charming the old man," Henry says, nodding his head at the throng of people on the other side of the lawn.

Rhys smirks. "How does it feel to be replaced as the favorite by your own fiancée?"

Henry rolls his eyes, the gesture familiar. The two of them carry themselves in the same way, with their brightly shining sister in between them. "It feels great," he says. "My shoulders were sore from the burden."

Rhys snorts. "Not untrue."

"Hayden's with Parker, around somewhere. That's my husband," she tells me, threading her arm under mine. "Parker's our third brother. I'm sure it's all very confusing, and you don't have to commit it to memory in one night."

"You should," Rhys tells me. "I might give you a Marchand pop quiz later."

"Marchand Jeopardy, perhaps," Henry suggests. "More dignified."

"If it's dignified we're after, we should break out the Marchand Pursuit."

Lily blows out a breath. "You're both incredibly witty, but you can dazzle us with it later. Rhys needs to pay his respects."

He takes a deep sip of his drink. "I hate genuflecting," he mutters. But the smile he gives me is true. "Ready to meet the lions?"

"Never been readier." The butterflies are back again, spreading their colorful wings in my stomach.

"Let's go," he says, still looking at me. "Henry, my man, start working on that sub-party."

"You know I won't."

"Lazy," Rhys throws over his shoulder, his hand finding my lower back again. "I expect more from you!"

There's laughter behind us, but we're already gone, weaving through throngs of people on the lawn. The sound of music intensifies as we pass by the small band, a group of musicians playing old-school classics.

"Crab cake?" a waiter asks me. I shake my head and smile, already pulled in the opposite direction by the force of Rhys's momentum.

I put my hand around his forearm. "How do you talk to him?" I ask. "If you don't, you know, *talk* to him?"

"Watch me work," he murmurs back, stopping in front of a woman with neat, coiffed hair. She turns from the women she'd been speaking to, and a smile erupts across her face. "Rhys, darling."

He bends to kiss her on the cheek. "Good to see you, *Maman.*"

"I'm so happy you came." The sincerity in her voice is obvious, her hand curling around Rhys's arm. "*Henri* told me you.... oh, hello."

"Hi," I say. "It's a pleasure to meet you."

Rhys's hand returns to my low back. "This is Ivy. We worked together on a campaign recently."

My smile widens. The word *recently* feels like a bit of an understatement.

"I'm Eloise, Rhys's mother. You're very welcome here," she says, but the look she tosses Rhys is heavy, with something like motherly chastisement in it. "Your dad is with Faye. They went to fetch a bottle of whiskey in the cellar."

"He's opening one of the vintage bottles?"

"It's his birthday," she says. "If not now, when?"

Rhys takes another sip of his drink. "What a shame," he says. "Tell him I said happy birthday."

His mother sighs. "He'd really appreciate it if you said it in person."

"Sure he would."

"He's not infallible."

"Oh, I know that."

His mother shakes her head, manicured nails closing around a champagne flute. "I've given up mediating," she says. "Have you said hello to your sister?"

"Of course I have."

Her gaze returns to me. "Enjoy yourself, Ivy. I'd particularly recommend trying the oysters on ice, over by the bar."

"Thank you, I will."

Her free hand lands on Rhys's arm, giving her tall son a pat. "Glad you came, son."

Rhys takes a sip of his drink and watches as she drifts toward another group of people. They welcome her into their circle with wide smiles.

"Just what you'd expect," Rhys comments.

"Did she not approve of me being here?"

He raises an eyebrow. "She knows what I'm doing."

"That I'm a buffer?"

"Yes."

"Hmm," I say. "Do you bring dates to these parties often?"

There's not a trace of his usual arrogance or smirk. "No. It's happened once or twice, that's true. More often than not I'm not here, not when it's something for my dad or his company. Haven't been for years."

I swallow. "Oh."

"But," he murmurs, bending to press his lips to my cheek, "I'm finding it's very nice to have you by my side here."

I shiver at the light touch of his lips, my gaze returning to his. And I can't imagine ever looking away, the fierce aching in my chest returning. My lips curve into a smile. "I'm glad to be here," I tell him. "And if—"

"Rhys!" a man calls. "Give us a hand!"

I turn to see two men walking from a nearby beach cottage, carrying a crate between them.

"My brothers," Rhys murmurs. "I'll be right back."

He jogs toward them with ease and helps carry the heavy thing. Reinforcement. They carry it to the back of the lawn, disappearing behind guests. Setting up a lawn game.

I take a sip of my champagne and turn my face up to the evening sunlight. The smell of salt and sea hangs heavy in the air. We'd lived miles and miles from the ocean growing up, and the closest place to swim had been a muddy lake. What would it have been like to grow up here?

I blink my eyes open to voices near me, as a man and a woman walk down the back porch steps. She's dark-haired and stunning, the silk of her dress flowing gracefully around a rounded stomach. The gray-haired man by her side is carrying a whiskey bottle. "A shame you can't drink it," he tells her.

"Just you wait until I can," she responds. "I know where the cellar is now."

"Am I going to have to put a lock on it?"

"Oh, I'd get a fingerprint scanner if I were you." She smiles, putting a hand on his arm. "I'll tell one of the waiters to bring out the whiskey glasses."

He makes a noncommittal sound in response as she heads off, inspecting the bottle in his hands. There's no doubt in my mind who he is. The resemblance, despite the difference in age, is too great.

Michael Marchand looks over, noting my gaze. He lifts an eyebrow in an achingly familiar way, this man who commands a real estate empire. "Yes? Can I help you?"

It's the same thing Rhys had once asked me, at that fateful party in the Hamptons.

"I'm sorry, sir, I don't believe we've been introduced."

"No, we haven't. I would have remembered."

"Ivy Hart," I say, extending my hand. He shakes it with the firmness of a man used to the grip. "I'm here with Rhys."

An amused glint in his deep green eyes. "Ah. Of course. I'm Michael, his father."

"I suspected as much. The family resemblance is obvious."

His mouth quirks. "Right."

"We recently worked on a campaign together, actually. Got back just yesterday." No idea if that's the right thing to say or not. I'm acutely aware of the fact that he hasn't had a direct conversation with his son in a decade, but here I am, my words spilling forth.

"A campaign," he repeats. "Yes, well, I'd rather he focused on growing that publishing company of his. Nothing personal against you, of course."

My throat goes dry. "Yes. Well, his photography is impressive."

"Hmph." Michael looks past me to the guests beyond, but his silence is heavy with expectation. He wants more.

So I give it to him. "We've just completed a campaign shot in eight different countries, and he captured each of the locations perfectly. Understanding the camera equipment, the light, the locations... it's an art and a science, and he's talented at it."

Michael gives a curt nod. "And I suppose you were the star?"

"I was just there to make the scenery relatable," I say. "The locations were the true stars."

"And he flew to all of these places?"

I wet my lips, nerves dancing down my spine. "Yes, he did."

Another noncommittal sound, another glance over my shoulder. But I have him. So I take a step closer and wonder if I'm wildly overstepping the mark, or if I'm doing my job as a buffer, whatever that truly means. I'm not sure Rhys knows either.

"He's brilliant. He took me sailing this morning, actually, for the first time."

"And he docked all right?"

"He did, yes."

Rhys's father rolls his shoulders back, giving me a nod. The tense press of his lips has softened somewhat. "Good of you to come with him," he tells me.

I don't think he's referring to sailing.

"It's a wonderful party," I say. "Happy birthday."

"Thank you." He steps past me, shaking his head. "Although after forty, one should really stop counting. Enjoy yourself."

I release a shaky breath after he's gone. Rhys finds me not long after, raising an eyebrow at me, so like his father. But the concern in his voice is all his.

"Is everything all right?"

"Yes, yes. Absolutely."

He puts a hand on my low back and kisses my forehead. "Come," he tells me. "The oysters really are amazing."

It's late when we finally make it to his sister's house, located right next door to the cottage we're staying in, to play cards with his siblings.

They're all there, the ones I know and the ones I don't. Rhys's youngest brother Parker endures a few good-natured jabs about having bought the town's yacht club. Internally, I marvel at that, how casually it's mentioned. Like an ice tray of oysters in the middle of the summer heat, their wealth is obvious and understated.

"You're supposed to get *out of* the town you grew up in," Rhys tells him. "Not find more reasons to stay."

Parker grumbles good-naturedly at that, but Henry's the one who raises his glass to salute his youngest brother. "Don't listen to Rhys," he says. "If you never try at anything, you can never fail, but that's not a way to live."

Rhys gives a hoarse laugh at the jab, but I don't join in, gazing between the brothers instead.

Lily and Faye return from upstairs, where they've checked on Lily's son. Jamie, he's called, though I've yet to meet him. He'd been asleep when we'd returned to the house.

"All good," she tells her husband and perches on the armrest of his chair. "Now, if you're all ready, I'm planning to crush you in cards."

Her brothers groan at that, but Faye and Hayden laugh. "It is her turn," her husband adds.

"And I'm in a crushing mood," Lily declares.

She wins two of the four rounds, in the end, so she is declared the winner. Rhys wins the other and Faye the final, raising her non-alcoholic mojito high.

They wave us goodbye and toss *see you laters* over their shoulders when Rhys and I leave, the night sky dark above us. They'd given me more than a few curious glances, but no one had asked about our relationship outright. I wonder if they'd not dared to, or if he'd instructed them not to.

My eyelids feel heavy with sleep and my bones loose with the drink, but I'm not ready to go to sleep yet. No, not when the waves crashing against the beach beckon.

Rhys laughs when I tell him. "You've had too much champagne."

"And you've had too much whiskey. See? We can all make pointless accusations." I pull him across the street and onto the beach, pulling off my shoes and sinking my feet into the cool sand. The waves lap against the shore like a lover's touch, the summer air warm against my skin.

This town is aptly named.

Yet another place I've now seen, even if it isn't as far away as Kenya or Australia. But watching the full moon above us and listening to the ocean close by, I'm not sure it's any less impressive because it's close to home.

I sink down into the sand cross-legged. "Come on," I tell him. "Sit with me."

He sinks down without protest, long legs stretched out in front of him and his feet in a pair of worn boat shoes. "Not a desert in Kenya," he comments.

"Close enough," I say and let a handful of sand trickle down my fingers. "Your entire family is great. I get how you can be adventurous and travel, when you have this to come back to."

"I've recently come to that realization as well." He lies back on the sand, looking up at the sky. "The stars are out. Remember the ones we saw in Kenya?"

"Yes." I settle down beside him. "All the constellations I'd never seen before."

He hums. "I've always loved watching the stars."

"I don't think I've ever really done it enough." The sand is soft beneath me and I bury my feet in it, rearranging my head to fit better. I'll have to wash my hair later, but not for all in the world would I let it stop me.

"You've surprised me, you know."

"I have?"

Rhys's voice deepens. "Yes. Coming here with me. Spending time with my family. And through it all, you haven't complained once."

"Of course I haven't. What kind of friend would I be if I did?"

There's a smile in his voice. "You'd be a normal person, Ivy, in the normal world. Very few are willing to give something up for others."

I frown up at the night sky. "That's not the kind of normal world I want to be a part of."

"So I've learnt." He reaches up and in a move that's so him it makes my heart ache, he tucks an arm underneath his head. "Thank you for talking me into coming this weekend."

I swallow. "I spoke to your father tonight."

"Did you?" He doesn't sound surprised.

"Yes. When you were off with your brothers."

"And what was your impression?"

"He seemed to enjoy hearing news about you," I tell him. "Everything I said, about our trip, your photography, even sailing, he wanted to hear."

There's skepticism in his silence, so I ask him. The drinks have loosened all kinds of inhibitions. "What is it between you?"

Rhys is quiet for a long while, stretched out beside me to watch the stars. But then he speaks. "I learned early on that most people are only looking out for themselves, and my father was always the prime example. He cared for status and prestige when it benefitted him, seeing money as a token of worth and his children as prize ponies. Our accomplishments mattered a great deal to him, as did how they reflected on him."

I'm afraid to turn my head to look at him, lest these words stop. So I give a nod. "I see."

"As soon as I got that, I also realized that the opposite was true. He took every misstep, every rumor, every failed test as an insult. He believed it made him look worse," Rhys says, shaking his head. "I abused that knowledge for years. I'd receive an F on a paper and feel nothing but vindictive delight. Teachers would ask a question I'd know the answer to and I'd give them the wrong one, just because. The more outrageous the better."

"To shock them?"

"I suppose, yes. Every expectation, I've hated. Tried to subvert." Rhys is quiet for a beat. "Until college."

"Yale?"

"Yes. You didn't see it, but there are four diplomas hanging in their house. One for each of my siblings from Yale. And above it, my dad's diploma."

"But none for you?"

"No," he says.

The silence stretches again, but it's not heavy. I rest my hands on my stomach and close my eyes. "Seems like it would be the place for you. I can see you in sweater vests, sitting on a windowsill reading Faulkner amongst ivy-covered brick."

The joke releases tension, and he chuckles beside me. "I would never wear a sweater vest."

"A checkered blazer?"

"Perhaps." He sighs, soft as the waves that assail the shore. "During my second year, my little sister was in a car accident."

"Lily?"

"Yes. That's why she has that faint limp, now. She was in the hospital for… well." Rhys clears his throat. "It changed things for all of us, in different ways. Her husband was the one who drove the car."

"Oh, God."

"He left and broke my sister's heart. I hated him for years, for that, even though I know my parents had pushed him toward the decision. My father, more specifically."

I wet my lips. "Oh."

"She lay in bed for months healing, in pain in more ways than one over Hayden's sudden disappearance. And all my father said was how happy he was that the boy was out of our lives and that she'd be returning to Yale.

"It all collapsed for me then. Why should I play to his rules, his vanity? When it drove my siblings to tears, to frustration, to pain? If I could, I'd be the complete opposite. Stop doing it in half-measures and commit. So I dropped out." He gives a self-deprecating laugh. "I committed myself thoroughly to debauchery for a while, Ivy. Traveling as far away from Paradise Shores and my brothers' ambition as I could. Far from the reach of my father. Went months without touching my trust fund, seeing how long I could do without his money."

I switch onto my side, propping up my head. "How long could you last?"

He runs a hand over his face. "I didn't make it to my sister's college graduation," he says, voice half-muffled. "Stuck on a godforsaken island in the Pacific, with an old camera in hand and my resolution not to touch my inheritance in the other."

The shame of that decision is clear in his voice. Pride had won that day, but it had cost him, too.

"Why photography?"

He looks over at me, hands dropping to his chest. "It's one of the few arenas where money doesn't matter. I'm either good enough or I'm not. And if I want to shoot the things I want to, if I want to create photography books and tell stories, I have to have credentials. Money or status can't buy those."

"And your father dislikes it?" I hedge.

Rhys snorts. "He sure does."

I wet my lips and wonder if I'm making a terrible mistake in speaking the next words. But something about Rhys makes me think that's a difficult thing to do. "You once said you prefer brutal honesty."

"I did," he says, an eyebrow raised. "Tell me whatever you're thinking, Ivy."

"Well, only that defining your life by what will make *someone else* unhappy strikes me as a terrible way of making *yourself* happy."

Rhys shakes his head, but it doesn't seem to be at me. He looks back up at the sky, so I turn my head and do the same thing, the stars expanding above us. I wonder if this is the most honest conversation I've ever had.

"I'm sorry, Ivy. That I ever called you air-headed and vain."

I smile. "Yes, well, I've forgiven you for that."

"Yes. You're wiser than me in that way, too. I've seen how willing you are to change directions in life. To go after your dreams, or to re-evaluate them. How your father's dislike of modeling didn't seem to derail you."

"At the end of the day, it's my life," I murmur. "My dad doesn't always understand, but his opinions just mean he cares. They don't drive us apart."

"An absolute revelation to me," Rhys says, but there's a note of teasing in his voice. "The idea that one could have an uncomplicated relationship with your parents."

I chuckle. "Revolutionary."

"You helped me in other ways too."

"Oh?"

His voice deepens, and something about it sends shivers over my skin. "You were so open with me. Hid nothing at all, not even the one thing you claimed you were most insecure about."

"Hmm. Well, I never intended on sharing that."

"And yet you did," Rhys murmurs. "I'm happy you did, by the way. The effects were very pleasurable."

My heart is dancing in my chest, words unspoken twirling on the tip of my tongue. I open my mouth to let them out when Rhys gets there first.

"I'm glad I met you," he says.

"I'm glad I met you too," I murmur.

He reaches out, tucking me against his side on the damp sand. I should care about the dampness on my borrowed dress, or the sand getting in my hair, about the late hour. But those things all seem trivial compared to the importance of living.

"You already have your ticket," he says, his hand smoothing over my arm and raising goose bumps in its wake.

"My expression has really stuck, huh?"

"Unfortunately."

"Are you asking me if I still want to explore?"

"I'd never say anything so crude." He turns over and rises above me, blotting out the stars above. "Remember when you blushed, ordering that drink in Australia?"

I shake my head. "Rhys..."

"What was it called?"

"Sex on the Beach," I admit, my leg hitching up to his hip. "But that would be crazy."

"Would it? It's dark out here, and there's absolutely no one around." He bends so his mouth fits over mine, kissing away fears, objections, thoughts, until my senses are ribbons in the wind. "I want to be a part of your every first."

"You already are," I murmur, my hands sliding up to his shoulders.

His mouth trails my neck, slipping down my body. I glance around us, but the narrow stretch of beach is deserted, the boardwalk empty, and the night covers all in a blanket of darkness. I barely make out his shape under the full moon.

So I guide his hand to my thigh and up the hem of my dress, because there are times in life when all you can do is focus on living.

24

IVY

I wake up to an ocean of pillows, comforters and soft mattress. It's warm and cozy and leaving is out of the question. So I quest across the sea for Rhys, but he's not in bed, his side cold and empty.

Yawning, I sit up. Judging by the light streaming in through the windows, I've slept a lot longer today than yesterday, slowly adjusting back to Eastern Standard Time.

Pulling a bathrobe around me, I head to the kitchen. A faint headache is hovering around the crown of my head and I drain an entire glass of cold water. But it had been worth it, for last night, for getting to know his siblings.

I smile at the memories of what had happened after. The whisper of his voice in my ear on the beach. *I'm glad I met you,* before we'd made love under the stars. Because that's what it had felt like, just the two of us and the waves and the slow, building certainty that I'm falling in love with him.

I trace my lips with my finger, wondering at the heat that arises between us with so little effort. The desire is obvious, evident, despite it being absent with so many men before him. Effortless, even, built on foundations that seem rock-solid. Trust and friendship and shared adventure.

My gaze snags on a piece of paper on the dining room table, right next to his closed laptop.

Ivy,
I'm out for a run, will grab us some breakfast on the way back.
While you wait… open my laptop and look at the first picture.

I do as he's instructed. His laptop comes to life, opening a picture that makes my heart stop.

It's me, and yet it's not.

I'm sitting on the patio to our villa in Bali. The jungle opens up behind me, a sprawling expanse of green. I'm nude, one leg crossed over the other, half-reclining back on my arms. My eyes are closed and I'm looking up at the sky, a smile on my lips. The rose petals drifting in the pool beside me add to the magic, the illusion that I'm surrounded entirely by nature. Of it, and from it.

It might be the best picture ever taken of me.

It barely looks like me, this ethereal, otherworldly creature of nature.

I'd thought I'd be mortified seeing these pictures, but looking at it now, it's art. Without Rhys I would never have dared be a part of its creation.

A notification pings on his laptop, the text coming up on the top right corner. My eyes skim over it on instinct.

Ben Rieler: Just looked at the preliminary photos. I don't want to lose the bet, but they look great.

The bet? A second text follows right after the first, this one, too, appearing in the notification bar.

Ben Rieler: Still waiting on my thanks for finding the model from the Hamptons party for you, by the way. You didn't seem too upset about it in Sydney, but then, you always did love blondes.

The world tips slightly, falls off-keel, the words slicing through me like a sharp knife through butter. The first question spawns a thousand others, my mind fracturing like a kaleidoscope. I sit frozen in front of the computer as the notifications slide off screen and leave me alone with the portrait of me, naked and happy in Bali.

The model from the Hamptons party.

Had Rhys been the one to ask for me?

I dismiss the idea as soon as I think it. His shock at seeing me in the office room in Rieler Travels had been too real to be anything but. Which means…

The Hamptons party.

I hadn't been paying attention to the other men, the ones sitting around Rhys, caught in his spell… but Ben must have been one of them. Hadn't they discussed something about Sydney? He chose me. He chose me from my agency, not because of my skill, or my portfolio, or because I was the right fit for Rieler. He chose me as some elaborate prank played on his old friend, then, because of our argument and our tumble in the pool. An amusement of rich men, this sport.

I put my finger to the keyboard and start flicking through the images, away from the beautiful one he'd wanted me to see. And it's all images of me, all naked, all edited with the lighting. My own face taunts me in all my happy, relaxed ignorance.

Each image makes my cheeks flush darker, the shame deepening. Ben had chosen me as a prank, and Rhys had known, and hadn't told me. *You love blondes.*

Until I come across an image that isn't me at all. It's another woman, posing suggestively on a bed, sheets wrapped around herself. She's looking at the camera like it's all she's ever wanted.

Like she's seeing the man behind the lens.

Exactly like I'd done.

The sick feeling rising up doesn't stop me from scrolling quicker and quicker through images of a few other models.

Other places. No clothing. Nothing is lurid, I'll admit, and perhaps I could appreciate the beauty of these nude portraits if I wasn't being choked by my own furious humiliation.

I've never felt cheaper than I do right then.

He never could resist a model.

I highlight all of the pictures of me sans clothing, every stupid one, and hit the delete button on his computer. Then I empty the trash for good measure. All my old fears combine with this new evidence, the images of other models swimming in front of me. His honest response to the last time he'd slept with someone. The way he'd described his casual entanglements.

It's like a house of cards toppling, the image I'd built in my mind of who I could be around him, the carefree, effortless woman who took what she wanted. Who slept with a man without expecting to catch feelings. Who just wanted to explore.

Because I'm *still* the girl who would have hated Rhys in school. Who plans and plots and writes to-do-lists. Who wants a man who loves her, who wants a relationship, who wants to be *more* than just a sexual partner.

And the worst part of it all is that he's never promised me anything, never been anything but honest about the whole thing, and I still feel like he's lied.

Like he's made me feel more special than I am.

But I'm the one who's inferred that—it's myself I've been lying to.

I'm still sitting by the table with a pounding heart and a constricted throat when Rhys comes home. He's carrying a paper bag and coffee, dressed in shorts and a T-shirt. A damp curl of his dark hair hangs over his forehead.

He stills when he sees me. "Ivy?"

"Ben was at the Hamptons party, where you and I... where we met. Was that why he chose me for Rieler's travel campaign?"

Rhys sets down the food on the coffee table with an exaggerated stillness that sets off hairline fractures along my heart. "He did, yes."

"I didn't recognize him in the meeting. I didn't... I thought..." I push away from the table and tie the bathrobe tighter around my waist. "So what was I, to the two of you? A joke? A prank? Something to prove a point to the other?"

His eyes look miserable. That, if anything, makes my chest ache. "It started out that way, Ivy, at least from his part. I'm sorry you were dragged into it."

"How could you not tell me about it?" I step back in response to his step forward, his throat bobbing as he swallows. "In his text, he mentions a bet. What bet?"

He runs a hand through his hair.

"Tell me, Rhys."

"I complained about his traveling campaigns one time too many. The cheesiness of it. How staged they were. He made me a bet, then. To see if I could shoot a campaign that was better than one he paid a professional marketing firm to do. He'll compare the two of them when they're finished and choose one."

I laugh. It sounds shrill. "Right. So this entire trip has been some weird, masculine contest? Who has the money to do something like that?"

"It started out that way. It started out silly, and wasteful, a bet between us to see whose word was true. You were never meant to be caught in the middle of it."

"But I was," I reply. "Which means you knew, the whole time, why we were traveling without a single designated stylist or assistant?"

"Yes." His admission is simple, plain. It's there in his face, too, completely devoid of a smirk or his raised eyebrow.

"How could you not tell me, Rhys? *How?*"

"There's no excuse for it," he replies, voice hoarse. "I know there isn't."

"So much for brutal honesty."

"I can't be brutal with you, Ivy. It's the one thing I can't be."

"But you can lie to me." I gesture to his laptop, now closed again on the dining-room table. Tears of anger threaten to overflow. "I saw a ton of other pictures there, by the way. And as Ben so charmingly put it, you can't resist a model and you love blondes. What was I? A prize? A trophy? A way to settle the bet more effectively?"

"It was none of those things, Ivy. What happened between us had *nothing* to do with him, or with the campaign, or with any other women."

I wrap my arms around my chest. "Are you sure? Because if that was the truth, you would have told me about it."

There are a lot of feelings in this world that are unpleasant, but I'm not sure there's one worse than the feeling of foolishness. Of knowing you had suspicions and those suspicions were correct, that you let your heart do the thinking and not your mind. I turn away from his dark gaze, unable to hold it. The agency hadn't believed in me. They hadn't chosen me for my work.

I'd been chosen because I'd accidentally argued with a rich guest at a Hamptons party. *I'm immune to beautiful women*, he'd said then. Judging by the pictures on his computer, it seemed rather to be the opposite way around.

"Ivy, everything I've told you has been the truth. What happened between us, what I want in the future… I haven't lied."

I shake my head, unable to see through the sudden film of tears. "No. I can't hear it."

"The last person I wanted to hurt was you. The last person. Do you hear me?"

"Your actions say something completely different. God, I'm such an idiot. Just another beautiful woman for you, right? Another casual entanglement, something to amuse yourself with. And I never asked for more." My chest feels like it's breaking. "I can't talk to you right now."

"Ivy, please, let me—"

I retreat again. "Please, Rhys. Give me some space."

He stops by the door to the cottage, looking like he has more to say and no idea how to say it. The weight of his gaze feels heavy, but I don't look away, not even through my haze of tears. "I'll be back in an hour," he says quietly. "Please, Ivy. Let me try to explain then."

I don't nod. After another beat of silence, he disappears out the door, closing it behind him.

I let myself fall apart then, as I rush through the house, tears gathering in my eyes and rolling silently down my cheeks. There's only one thought in my head, and that is escape. My hands don't tremble as I pack the few things I'd removed from my two giant suitcases. The agency's red silk dress looks ruined. I'll have to take it to the dry cleaner's in New York before I can return it.

It's depressing that *that's* the thought that breaks me, but it does, as I sink to the floor of the bedroom. I won't be able to look at that dress without thinking about him and me on the beach.

And that's not a thought I can afford to revisit right now.

It takes me a few minutes, but I manage to control myself, storing the hurt at his lies of omission somewhere deep inside. I've worked under stressful conditions; this shouldn't be much different. I carry one of the suitcases to the curb, returning for the second. Does Paradise Shores have a taxi service? As long as I can get to a train station, I'll be able to figure my way back to New York. I've never longed more for my tiny Manhattan apartment than I do right now, not even with the ocean a stone's throw away and the bright summer sunshine.

"Ivy?"

My heart leaps out of my chest before I realize it's not him. "Hi, Lily."

She smiles at me from her lawn, holding the hands of a

tiny toddler. He's standing, albeit with a considerable dose of help from his mother.

"No sleeping in when you have a one-year-old," she says, smiling down at Jamie's thick brown hair, the same as his father. "Are you heading somewhere?"

Perhaps it's in the silence of my response. Perhaps it's the look on my face. But she scoops Jamie up onto her hip and steps out on the curb. "Ivy, is everything all right?"

"I need to get back to New York."

"Okay," she says. "Do you have a train ticket booked?"

"No, not yet."

"Okay," she echoes. "I'm sure Rhys can drive you to—"

I shake my head. "I need to leave now."

"Right. Well," she says, bouncing little Jamie on her hip, "how about I drive you to Bridgeport? We can grab a drive-through coffee on the way, and—no, no playing with Mommy's hair—then you can board one of the Amtrak trains back to Grand Central."

My throat feels thick with sudden emotion. "I can't ask you to do that."

"You're not asking, I'm offering," she says. "Let me just drop off this rascal with his father, and I'll be right back."

"Okay. Thank you."

Five minutes later I'm in the passenger seat of Lily's car, leaving the glittering ocean behind me in the rearview mirror. She turns on the radio, keeping the music down, her fingers drumming on the steering wheel.

"Sorry for this, truly," I say again.

"Oh, don't apologize. It's not a problem at all. And even if it was a problem, I'd still do it."

I swallow before speaking his name, but it still grates on my tongue. "You and Rhys... you're close?"

"I'd say so, yes," she says, face softening. "We're both the rebels of the family, in a way. I run an art gallery, he has a publishing company. It's not construction or real estate and it's not going to land us in *Forbes*."

"And those two things are important to your father," I murmur.

"They were," she says. "They've become less so now, but they still hover above our heads, in a way. How about you? Did you always want to be a model?"

"No. I wanted to dance when I was younger, but I injured my knee, and had to stop. I worked with a lot of physical therapists afterwards. I'm studying to be one, now, part-time. Modeling is how I pay for college."

Lily nods. "What kind of injury?"

"Tore a ligament in my knee, and the recovery was pretty rough. It can handle a lot now, but it can't handle hours of dancing every single day."

"A shame," she says softly. "Did Rhys tell you about my injury?"

"A little, yes."

"Well, one of my legs is pretty bad too. Not terrible, but dancing is pretty much ruled out for me as well." She shoots me a grin. "It probably was before the accident too, to be honest."

I smile back, even if my heart feels like it's shattering. They're all being so nice to me, and here I am, running away.

"So," she says. "If you want to tell me what my brother has done to piss you off, I'll listen. Lord knows he's pissed me off too many times to count."

I look down at my hands. "This might be a bit different."

She snorts, sounding so like Rhys. "Probably. But I'm a good listener, and I don't gossip."

I stare out at the passing landscape and think of what to say. What will be true, without going into all the gory details. My throat still feels tight with tears. "Well… I think we're on different pages, in regards to us. How serious we were, or where we're heading."

Lily is quiet for a long moment, and when I look back at her, a frown is tugging at her lips. "Was that too much info?"

"No," she says. "It's just, I've never known Rhys to be anything but honest. I don't like thinking he's misled you."

"He's your brother," I say quietly. "I don't want to come in between that, somehow."

She shakes her head with a kind smile. "Don't worry, you won't. And I completely understand if you don't want to say more. I'll still give him an earful later."

I chuckle at that, despite myself.

"He's often difficult," she says. "He goes his own way. He makes his own path. He claims to love debate, and truth, but that doesn't mean he's always good at putting himself in other people's shoes. But if there's one thing he is, it's loyal, right down to the bone." She's quiet for a long moment, even as we pull up to the Bridgeport train station, turning the car off in the parking lot.

But then she turns to me. "I've just met you, Ivy, but on account of us both being named for plants…," a smile curves her lips, "let me tell you that I've never seen my brother laughing with a woman the way he did with you last night. And I don't think he would have come to our father's party if he didn't have you there by his side."

My mouth feels dry, my heart heavy. "Oh."

"Yesterday, when we were playing cards, you said that life just keeps getting better. Do you remember that?"

I search my memories, the alcohol and the games. "Faintly."

"He didn't contradict you." Lily smiles at me. "He's been a cynic since he was eight years old, and he didn't even blink, just raised his glass to cheer."

I look down at my handbag. In my pocket, I can feel my phone buzzing with a call, but I ignore it. "I see."

"I'm sorry if I've said too much," Lily says. "You do whatever you want to do, and feel free to curse him out if he needs it. All I'm saying is… he's complicated."

"So I've noticed," I say, and we both laugh dryly at that. "Thank you for the ride."

"You're welcome," she says. "I hope I'll see you again, Ivy."

I pause with a hand on the passenger door, and this one is easy to answer, with or without her brother in the picture. "I hope so too."

25

RHYS

My little sister is the one who tells me where Ivy's gone, knocking on the door to her own cottage. It swings open to her touch and she looks at me, pacing in the living room.

"I drove her to Bridgeport," Lily announces.

"You did what?"

"She asked me to, Rhys. And trust me, she needed to get out of here, judging by her mood."

I run a hand through my still-sweaty hair, guilt and anger pulsing through me in waves. She'd seen the ill-timed text from Ben fucking Rieler, and the chance to tell her myself was lost.

"I'm assuming you know why she left?" Lily asks. "She wouldn't tell me."

I mutter something, heading to the kitchen to pack up my stuff.

"What?"

"I said, I know why she left."

"But you're not going to tell me."

"No," I say, opening my suitcase with jerky movements. "I don't like myself very much at the moment, and I don't need you to join in."

"Fine." Lily uncrosses her arms and walks to the table,

where the breakfast I'd bought lies untouched. She sifts through and finds a ham and cheese sandwich. "She did say something of interest, though."

She takes a bite of the lukewarm sandwich and I focus on not blowing my lid while she chews slowly. "Tell me."

"Well," she says finally, "she said that she'd started to believe that what the two of you had was more serious than you thought. I said that I've never known Rhys to be anything other than honest," Lily continues, and the trust in her voice, in me, is a gut punch of guilt. "*But*, I also know you. And you're not really known for being affectionate."

I sink down onto one of the kitchen chairs, stretching my legs out in front of me. Burying my head in my hands.

"I wasn't honest with her."

Lily's chewing stops. "Oh."

I tell her everything, pulling no punches. The bet with Ben, the way Ivy and I met. How she found out. The finer points of our relationship I omit, but every mistake of mine is there for her judgement.

She sits down opposite me. "Well," she murmurs finally. "That doesn't look good."

"No, it doesn't."

"You should have told her."

"I should have," I agree, looking up to see her gaze serenely back at me. There's no judgement in her eyes, though, and I'd expected a considerable share of it.

"Rhys, you like her. It's obvious in the way you spoke to her yesterday, the way the two of you looked at each other."

"I think I do, yes," I murmur. It feels like a confession.

"She likes you too. Liked, perhaps, before all of this. You're going to have to grovel."

"I'm prepared to."

"And you're going to have to do it properly," Lily says, picking up her sandwich. "Because there is a reason why you didn't tell her those things, and if you want to win her back, nothing but the truth will work."

I push away from the table and head to the bedroom. Rummage around for my clothes, shoving them down.

How had she not thought this was serious? It felt like the most serious connection with a woman I'd ever had. My sister's voice drifts from the other room. "She might need a few days before she'll consider talking to you."

"I have to try."

"Good, just don't give up." She steps into the room, eyes wide and earnest. The same way she'd looked at me when she was little, when it was us against the world. When I supported her art and she supported me. She'd moved back to Paradise Shores, to face our father and start her own life here, rooted in the past but not controlled by it.

But she always was braver than me.

"Rhys?"

"Yes?"

"It's been a long time since you really *tried* at something," she says. "I remember what it looks like, and it's glorious."

Henry's words from last night flash through my mind. "If you try at something, you might fail," I say.

She reaches up on her tiptoes to kiss me on the cheek. "But you might succeed, and if I were a betting woman, I'd bet on you."

Two texts and three calls, but no response from Ivy the coming days. Not a sign of life, either, on her social media accounts. I'd downloaded the apps just to be able to see.

It's like she's tossed her cell phone in the Hudson.

My eyes stray to the giant pile of paperbacks stacked along the wall of my New York apartment. Books I haven't read. Books I've yet to read. Books I've started and stopped. And manuscripts, endless manuscripts I'm sorting through to sign to the company.

It's been a long time since you've really tried at something.

I dial the number to Ivy's modeling agency, going for broke.

"Star Models, this is Maria."

"Rhys Marchand," I say. "I recently worked with Ivy Hart, one of your models. I need to drop off some material."

"Ah," the voice returns. "Ivy."

"Yes. Do you have her address on file?"

"Well, she's no longer with the agency."

"What?"

"She's no longer with the agency," the woman repeats.

"Do you have any—"

"I can't give out information on former employees," she continues. "Sorry. Have a good day, Mr. Marchand."

I stare at the phone in my hand for longer than I like to admit. Had they dropped her? What happened? Rieler Travels hasn't determined which marketing campaign will be used yet, not with the launch party weeks away.

I try to lose myself in work, but even that is fruitless, because there's only one person in those pictures.

Silhouetted by a waterfall in Bali.

Smiling under the Eiffel Tower.

Twirling on a street in St. Barts.

I get it now, seeing all these pictures. There's not an ounce of distaste left in me about the marketing concept, because I get it. Ivy is the gateway to all these places. She's enjoying them all, a wide smile on her lips and wonder in her eyes, and through her, they come to life.

I pause at the pictures from the trattoria in Rome. Ivy's looking at Paolo like she's in love with him. My hand grows tight around the edge of my laptop. The irrational envy is still present, watching that expression on her face directed at someone who's not me.

Because I want it to be at me. Always, at me.

The pictures I'd taken of Ivy in Bali are gone. The ones we'd taken for our own pleasure, where the air had been humid and time had stood still. Only her and me and the light dancing across her naked skin.

They're all gone.

I flick through and see the images she'd seen, looking at them from her perspective. The models or women who'd requested I shoot them nude. For their portfolios, or simply for the pleasure of having portraits. For immortalizing a moment in time.

From Ivy's point of view…

I think of the look in her eyes when we were in Kenya, where she'd first told me she'd never been with a man before. The tentative trust that had burned like embers, and how I'd watched it grow into a flame.

Had it been blown out entirely?

I push my computer away in disgust. To think those images, the ones from a different time, might have made Ivy feel less in any way makes me sick.

She'd always been the one who was painfully authentic.

I dip my head in my hands and sit, aching and furious at myself, on my couch. Furious for not being more honest. For not saying the things I'd felt.

The itinerary. She'd always wanted to follow it. I'd barely looked at it, but wasn't there…? My hands tremble with adrenaline as I pull out the crumpled sheet of paper from my bag. Her address is there, listed at the top, for when the car picked her up to the airport.

I'm out the door and calling for a cab within minutes. There's an overwhelming chance that she won't answer. Won't want to talk to me. But perhaps it's time I start taking real risks in life.

The midtown apartment building is nothing special, but as I stop outside the door to the lobby, it feels like everything. We know so little of each other's real lives.

I send her another text. *I'm outside your apartment. Please talk to me.*

And then I wait. Ten minutes. Twenty. Leaning against the

cold brick, my eyes closed, arms crossed over my chest. People come and go, but it's never her. Not until I've nearly given up hope, not until my legs ache from standing still.

She steps out of the front door to her building. Her hair is a golden braid down her back, her skin free from makeup. She wraps her arms around her body.

"Hi."

I push off from the wall, taking a step closer. "Hi, Ives. Thanks for coming out."

She nods, looking past me to the busy street beyond. My whole body feels taut, like a drawn violin string. If only I knew the notes to play. "Still jet-lagged?"

"A bit," she says. "It's getting better."

"It's been quiet, not being around you for the last week."

"I thought I spoke too much," she says, but without any real conviction. "Grated on your cynicism."

"It could use being grated on," I admit. "You're not with the agency anymore?"

She looks down at her hands, twisting them in her grasp. Like the rest of her skin, they're tan from our days in Bali. A real tan, this time.

"I quit."

"Good."

Her lips twist into a sardonic smile. "It wasn't because I've suddenly started hating modeling."

"Of course not."

"It's just... They never liked that I tried combining work and my studies, and I don't want to work for an agency that holds dropping me over my head like that."

"Not to mention the pressure to grow your social media."

She nods, her gaze flicking past me to the street again. The air is uncomfortable between us.

Things unspoken.

"I'm proud of you for quitting."

Her gaze returns to mine. Surprise burns there, together with a deep-seated mistrust that shames me.

"Ivy, I—"

She shakes her head, cutting me off. "Please thank your sister for driving me to the train station. I didn't mean to take up part of her Sunday."

"She didn't mind." The cold hand of fear grips my insides, that she won't want to hear me out. That the open, trusting look in her eyes is lost forever to me.

"She's nice. Your entire family is, Rhys."

"They are. Thank you."

She nods, looking past me. "I told your father that your photography is amazing. Perhaps it'll help."

She'd stood up for me. The knowledge sharpens the pain in my chest at her distance. I don't want to say the words.

I don't want to hear her say them.

But I start the conversation anyway. "Let me explain what you saw on my computer, Ivy."

"Do we have to?" she whispers. "It won't change what they proved."

"They didn't prove anything. Only that I've worked on and off as a photographer for a decade, and that has included professional models, some of whom asked me to photograph them nude. But there is no other meaning to them, Ivy."

Something breaks inside me when her eyes line with silver, as she refuses to look at me.

"Ivy, trust me on that."

"I feel so foolish," she whispers. "About the whole thing. Like I've been playing out an alternate reality in my mind, and all of a sudden it broke."

Pain grips its claws in my chest. "You haven't been foolish, Ives. Not the least."

But she just nods. "The things we've done... I'd never done them before. And to realize they meant so little to you? I was part of a bet. Thrown in for good measure as a joke between two guys."

"The things we did meant a lot to me."

She runs fingers underneath her eyes, turning them heavenward. Her shoulders curve inwards. "Perhaps not nothing, then. But not the same as to me. The women I saw... have you slept with them?"

I won't lie to her, not ever again. "A couple, yes."

Her breath turns shaky. "Right. And you never promised me anything, either. I'm the one who was stupid enough to expect them anyway."

"Please," I tell her, "expect things from me. I want the chance to live up to them."

She looks down at her feet, her throat swallowing. "We had fun, at least."

"Being with you was never just about having *fun*. It was never something I took lightly. And it wasn't planned by Ben."

"He said he chose me because I'm your type."

"He doesn't know my fucking type. We see each other every now and then, and I once had a blonde girlfriend. He extrapolated. Incorrectly, too."

"So what is your type?"

"You," I say. "Just you."

Her mouth curls into a self-deprecating smile. "He chose me because I annoyed you at a party in the Hamptons."

"He's an idiot."

She closes her eyes, like she can't face me. Like it's easier to pull away.

I understand the impulse. For so long, I've thrown myself into what's new and risky and easy, instead of what's challenging. Running into new battles instead of staying and fighting the ones I'm in.

But not again.

"Ivy, do you know the real reason why I didn't tell you about the bet right away? Why I couldn't bring myself to it?" I take a deep breath, and then I tell her the truth, no bullshit. "Because it shamed me. It only took me a couple of days to realize you were nothing like what I'd described you as at that party. I made those remarks to shut the other men up, but

I didn't think twice about how they'd sound to you. And then you dove in after your friend... right away, no hesitation."

Summer days spent in Paradise Shores flit through my mind, the days my brothers and I had been taught how to rescue people from the water. "And you were so honest, Ivy, in all of your reactions to the places we saw. So earnest and excited and you *trusted* me."

She looks down at her hands, but I keep going. "Hey, I'm saying that as a good thing. I haven't had people be that open with me, you might say, for longer than I can remember. There's always a motive or an end goal."

Ivy worries her lower lip, her eyes narrowed. "Perhaps you surround yourself with the wrong people."

"Yeah, I'm starting to realize that too. And when I thought of how I'd behaved at that party, and the inane fucking bet with Ben... it looked small and petty in comparison to you, to your goodness and humor. I didn't tell you because I was scared."

Her eyes flash on mine. "You were scared? That's the big reveal?"

"Yes." I reach out to steady myself against the brick wall. "You told my sister that you didn't think we were on the same page, regarding us. You and me. But Ivy, this feels like the most serious thing I've experienced. I don't want to stop being around you. Not now, and not ever."

She shakes her head, uncertainty sketched on her features. The features that had so often been open and honest and determined and curious.

"Rhys... I don't know how to do this," she says. "How to trust, how to be together with someone. I've never done any of it before. Even if I forgive you, how would we do it?"

"I'm not an expert, either," I admit. But nothing has ever felt like being with her. No one has made me question everything I know and still made me feel more certain than ever before.

"What would we do, then?"

"We'll make it up as we go along," I suggest, crooking my smile the way I know she likes. "Isn't that how life works? It'll be an adventure, at least, traveling that road with you."

Ivy takes another deep breath, stepping back toward the door. "I'll need time, Rhys. I need to think."

"Of course. Take as long as you want. But if you're wondering something, please ask me. Let me explain it. I promise you'll hear nothing but truth from me from here on out."

"Okay," she breathes.

"Okay?"

She wipes at her eyes. "Okay, I'll think about it. It's the best I can do."

"I'll take it."

"Regardless, I suppose I'll see you at the launch party, to discover which of your campaigns ended up being chosen." She shakes her head, a wry smile on her lips. "I swear, Rhys, I don't know if I'm hoping you lose or win."

The launch party is weeks from now. But I don't let the disappointment I feel show. "I'll see you then," I tell her. "Just promise me you'll call me if you get caught in your own thoughts. I don't live far away."

"I promise," she says, the door shutting behind her.

26

IVY

The doorbell rings just as I'm applying lipstick, sending a line of dark red skittering down my chin.

Penny chuckles behind me and bounces up off the couch. "Do you need me to get that?"

"Yes, please."

Wiping at my face, I follow her to the front door. I'm not expecting anyone, nor any deliveries, and we only have half an hour left until we need to leave for the launch of Rieler Travels' new marketing campaign.

Whichever one it might be.

"For Ivy Hart," a delivery guy says, yellow cap pulled low on his head.

"I didn't order anything."

That doesn't stop him from lifting a large, bubble-wrapped square into my hallway.

"No need to sign. Have a good day."

He disappears down the hallway with brisk steps, a man on a mission, and doesn't respond to my shouted *thanks!*

Penny shuts the door behind him. "What's this?"

"I have no idea."

We start tearing at the packaging, peeling off the coverings like we're unmasking a treasure. "Frames?" Penny asks. "These are frames. What… Oh."

My hand stills when I see who stares back.

It's me.

A framed, black-and-white portrait of me, one I hadn't seen before. I'm dancing on the square in St. Barts, the red dress dark now, but billowing around my legs as I spin. My hair is a curtain around me, but the smile on my face is visible.

It's grainy, not so much as to throw off the image, but enough to give it character.

"Ivy…," my sister whispers. "This is gorgeous."

I swallow. "Help me get the packaging off the rest of them."

Four framed photographs in total, all black and white and large. And all of me.

Penny runs her hand over an etched plaque at the bottom of one. "They're named," she murmurs. "Ivy, they all have names!"

I drop to my knees in the hallway to see that she's right. The portrait of me dancing in St. Barts is called *Joy.*

The one of me in Rome, putting on dark lipstick with the eternal city as a backdrop, the Tiber flowing behind me, is called *Strength.* And I suppose the challenging look in my eyes as I stare directly into the camera is exactly that. Strong.

The third has me in Paris. Standing in my blazer and skirt, talking to one of the sellers of books that line the Seine. A wide smile is on my face as I listen to the man. The photograph is called *Kindness.*

"Sartre," I murmur. "He was explaining who Jean-Paul Sartre was."

"These are so cool. Did the agency send them to you?"

My gaze travels to the fourth and final one. Me, waist-deep in the swimming hole in Bali. In black and white, the shapes stand out in stark contrast. The waterfall a stilled roar behind me. My eyes are closed and my arms outstretched, a smile on my lips.

Curiosity, this one is titled.

"No," I say quietly. "The agency didn't send these."

"Then who? The travel company? Oh, look, Ivy. There's a card." She hands me an envelope, three letters scrawled in sharp, capital letters on the front. *Ivy*.

I pull out the card inside.

Ivy,
You took my breath away in every single one of these shots. This is how I see you. Strong and kind, curious and joyful. Traveling with you was the best adventure I've ever had. If I lose this bet today, I will still feel like I've won, for having experienced it. If you'll have me, I'll by your side for future adventures too.

Looking forward to seeing you today,
Rhys

"You're smiling," Penny murmurs. "Is it from him? The photographer?"

I hand her the note in silence, my smile growing as she squeals. "Oh my God. This is... wow. Now we know, then. He will definitely be there today."

I nod, sinking down into my couch. Nerves flutter through my stomach at the mention. "He will, yes."

I look back at the photographs. No one had ever captured me that well. Captured *me*, not who I was posing as. Penny knows everything. I told her all of it, from St. Barts to Paradise Shores.

"What are you thinking?" she asks, sitting down beside me.

My throat feels dry. "I've never been in a proper relationship before. As much as I want to try, I'm not sure how it'll turn out. And I don't know if... What if I get hurt again?"

Her gaze softens. "You'll never know how a relationship will turn out before you have it."

"How did you do it? With Jason? You've been together for years."

Her smile widens, even if it remains soft. My little sister, who's bravery personified. "It's scary. Opening yourself up that way. You'll have arguments, disagreements, things that annoy one another. But instead of that ending the relationship, they make it grow stronger. It's..." She shakes her head and moves closer, reaching out to clasp my hand in hers. "Ivy, I know you've never been in a relationship before. And you're hardworking and proper and have a ton of integrity. I get why letting someone in goes against the grain, but it's so, so worth it when you do."

I wrap my fingers around hers. "That was a great answer."

"Thank you." Her smile widens. "Have you decided if you're going to give him another chance or not?"

We've discussed this at length for the past weeks, every angle, every possibility. Pouring out my heart to her and hearing her rail about Rhys had been cathartic, just as her quiet musings about his clear interest had been.

In the end, there's only one answer, and it had been Rhys who'd prompted me to it. Who'd given me permission to be spontaneous and brave.

"Yes."

Her smile widens. "I'm glad. And if he does something to hurt you again..."

"He'll have to reckon with you."

"That's right," she says. "But relationships really are an adventure, like he said. Do you feel ready to travel some new terrain?"

I squeeze her hand. "I do."

———

"You're fidgeting," Penny tells me.

"I am not," I murmur back, my hand sliding down the beads in my dress to rest at my side, the elevator slow in rising to the top.

"What kind of travel agency rents a rooftop bar for the launch of a marketing campaign?"

"One with too much money," I say. "One that caters to a luxury clientele." And one that doesn't care for guests who dislike heights.

We step out onto a terrace, the late summer air warm and the night just beginning to darken. The skyscrapers surrounding us make for a backdrop of glittering lights and towering giants. Reminding me we're far from the ground. But as long as I stay away from the edge, I should be fine.

"Look," Penny says, nodding to a giant projector screen in the corner. Images and videos roll over it, of locations worldwide. I recognize the turquoise waters of St. Barts, the savannah in Kenya.

"I can't believe they're leaving it so late to announce which campaign was chosen," I tell her, smoothing a tendril of hair back. The wind immediately whips it out again, and I give up, because it's a losing battle.

"Suspense," Penny says. "Oh! Let's grab something to drink..."

"Let's grab something to eat first."

She rolls her eyes at me but reaches for a tiny sandwich, resting on a cocktail napkin. "You're a bore," she tells me.

I grip her arm and give her a light push, not letting go. She wavers on her borrowed heels. "I know your weaknesses," I tell her, smiling. "Don't get tough."

"Traveling changed you. My sister used to be nice."

"I'm still nice," I say, scanning the crowd. Looking for people I recognize, one in particular, and he's usually a head above others... No sight of him. The nerves drum beneath my skin like a second heartbeat. Nerves make for the most potent of all drinks.

I take a sip of my drink and watch as more and more guests filter in, more than a few giving me lingering looks. It's so second nature by now that it barely fazes me, nor Penny, but it's always more frequent when I'm in heels and makeup. *It'll fade*, I want to tell them.

Ben Rieler steps up on stage, a mic in hand and in a tailored suit, smiling at the milling guests. I half-listen as he welcomes guests, craning my neck to look around the crowd.

Ben's voice filters back in. "The result has been two campaigns of astonishing quality. They're differing perspectives, capturing each of our locations with unique eyes… They reflect the differences in travelers that Rieler seeks to attract."

Was that a dark head? A man, similar in color… *Turn around, turn around*… and he does and my heart leaps, but it's not Rhys. It's Henry, with Faye radiant and pregnant at his side. So he'd invited his family to this, too.

A deep voice speaks at my side, familiar and aching. "Hello, Ivy."

I keep my eyes on Ben and the images being projected, too scared to turn my head. "Rhys."

His words are amused. "Ben had a difficult decision to make."

"Seems like it."

"So he avoided making one at all."

I open my mouth to ask, but just then, Ben steps aside on the stage and the crowd's hush turns into an expectant murmur. The screen shifts into the logo of Rieler Travel, and as it dissolves, a drone video of the hotel in Bali plays. Music, slow and hypnotic, sounds over the images.

It switches to me on the Jeep in Kenya, laughing at the camera, at one of Rhys's jokes. Another smooth transition to a glossy image of a dark-haired woman posing on a lounge chair by a pool. Interspliced with me, lying on the sand in St. Barts with the setting sun.

"They used both?" I whisper.

"Yes," Rhys murmurs. "To show how they cater to two different kinds of travelers. I think ours is meant to represent the more adventure-seeking one."

My lips curve as I see the same thing he does. The footage from our trip is colored differently. It's me swimming toward the waterfall in Bali, it's me walking along the edge of a dock in Sydney.

The other? It's the dark-haired model on hotel beds, in pools, sampling elegant desserts and enjoying the spa facilities.

As angry as I'd been at the idea of them making a bet over this, two men with too much money and pride for their own good, there's no denying this video is brilliant.

"It's amazing."

There's a smile in his voice. "I'll admit, it turned out well."

My sister turns to me and Rhys with wide eyes when the campaign ends.

"You truly went to all those places? That was beautiful."

"We did, yeah. This is Rhys Marchand, who traveled with me."

Penny grins, reaching out a hand. "Oh, I know. It's a pleasure to meet you."

"Likewise," he says. "The similarity is obvious, so I don't have to ask who you are. Penny, right?"

"That's right," she confirms. "And I'd love to stay and chat, but there is a waiter with tiny sliders somewhere around here that I have to chase."

She disappears through the crowd and I roll my eyes, smiling. "Subtle."

"Very." Rhys's gaze snags with mine, mine with his, and it's like the other guests fade away, just us and New York around us. There are questions in his eyes, mixed with tentative hope.

The air feels thick with possibility.

"Thank you for the photographs. They were delivered this morning."

His lips curve. "My pleasure. They're my favorites, those four."

"They're beautiful," I murmur. "Your portion of the video was, too."

"Of course it was," he says quietly. "I had you."

My breath catches in my throat, and I can't look away from the strength of his gaze. He had lied, yes. But I'd allowed myself to hang on to that as an excuse, an opportunity to flee from the unknown.

"I've been thinking about us."

He inclines his head, a dark curl falling over his forehead. "So have I, Ives. And before you say anything, I want to give you something." He pulls something out of his coat pocket, my eyes snagging on his hand, remembering the touch of it on my skin.

"Here you are!" a voice calls out. "My two stars!"

I clear my throat, refocusing on Ben's grinning face. He has a champagne glass in one hand, smiling at the both of us.

"Oh, don't look like that," he says to Rhys, whose face is impassive. Annoyed at being interrupted, I'm guessing. "You won."

"Co-won," Rhys corrects.

"Yes, well, yours is the more artistic of the two, even if I hate to admit it." He gives me a smirk. "It'll be a pleasure, Ivy, to watch you in all the travel catalogues to come."

My smile feels brittle, aimed at the man who gave me the campaign of a lifetime as a prank. "I'm glad."

"She was—"

But Rhys is interrupted by the arrival of a few other people. A photographer, here to immortalize the event, and the dark-haired model I'd seen in the pictures. My opponent, I suppose. "One final picture?" Ben asks. "To celebrate the launch."

"Sure," I say, extending my hand to the other model. "I'm Ivy."

"Sarah."

"Your pictures look beautiful."

She gives me a shy smile. "Thank you. I thought yours, though… they were art."

"I had a great photographer."

Ben motions for us to join him by the edge of the terrace, where the sprawl of New York beckons thirty-five floors below. Each step is an act of willpower, forcing myself closer and closer to the edge.

Is that railing really high enough?

"Come," Ben repeats, Sarah to his right. I take my spot on his left side and look straight at the camera. The death drop behind me feels like a monster, creeping up to attack.

I pose, but my hand is clammy around the champagne flute. The seconds feel like years.

Rhys is standing beside the photographer with a scowl on his face. His hands are buried in his pockets, the top button of his shirt unbuttoned. I focus on the tan skin there.

"There," the photographer says, lowering the camera. Ben thanks Sarah and me, but I can't hear them above the beating of my heart.

And then Rhys is there, his arm closing around my waist as he pulls me away from the edge. I follow him across the roof and into the stairwell, where walls keep the abyss at bay.

"A rooftop," I mutter. "It had to be another rooftop."

"Are you okay?" His fingers tip my chin back, my face lifting to his.

"Yes. Just…" I shake my head. "I have to keep away from the edge."

"I remember."

My palms land on his chest, hard beneath his shirt. "Nobody has confused me like you have," I accuse him. "Nobody has made me as angry, or as irritated. Nobody has made me laugh as much, either."

His thumb slides along my jaw. "You've confused me too. Every box I wanted to put you in, you've defied."

"Rhys, I know you consider life an adventure and people

something to savor, but I can't handle it if *we* are like that. It's not in me to be casual."

"I don't want anything casual with you," he replies. "And for the record, you made it difficult to stay cool and casual."

"So did you. Impossible, even."

His hand closes over my wrist, fitting with my palm flat to his chest. Right over his heart, where I can feel the pounding beneath his skin. "You're trusting and earnest and innocent. Sarcastic and smart. An optimist to your core, Ivy. You take your coffee with too much sugar and your tea with too much milk, but I couldn't care less." He rests his forehead against mine, the inky blackness of his hair spilling over mine. "And I *always* care about that."

My hands creep up to his neck, to the warm skin waiting for me. "I liked you even when I didn't like you very much."

He's so close that I can't see his smile, but I can feel it, as if it's an extension of me. "I know," he says. "The feeling was mutual. Seeing that Italian model kiss your neck in Rome damn near killed me."

"I hoped you'd be jealous of that."

A wicked spark in his eyes. "You surprise me, too, at every turn. I hope you never stop doing that."

I wet my lips. "Are we really going to try this?"

"Being something, you and me?"

"Yes."

"I think we should. We'll probably argue half the time, about what movie to watch, what book to read, about whether or not peanuts should be salted... but I'm okay with that."

"I'm okay with that too." My hand slides into his hair, it's silky thickness caressing my skin. "I don't think you'd want it any other way."

His lips close over mine, and I respond in kind, the two of us reuniting like we're closing a deal—agreeing on our future, on us, on this.

What he is and what I am fits together so well, in so many

ways, that even the areas where we don't match up feel right. I surrender to the delicious simplicity of his touch and wonder if love will always feel like this, like falling, scary and exhilarating in equal measure.

Because love means you have to trust. You have to open up. And you have to allow someone else in, with the power to hurt you, and have faith they don't.

Rhys's eyes are open when he lifts his head. "Why are we still at this party?"

I laugh, feeling light, like a balloon ready to float up to the ceiling. "Because we earned it. We won."

"Co-won."

"No," I say, lacing my fingers through his. "We won."

He's wearing that slanted smile that's so uniquely his. "This is how it starts, isn't it? I'm forced to change my attitude, one peppy comment at a time."

"I'm not going to stop challenging you."

"Good." He reaches into his pocket, withdrawing a USB stick. "And to think I had an entire speech prepared. I've never begged in my life, Ivy, but I was prepared to beg for your forgiveness."

"What's this?"

"The pictures you deleted from my computer? The ones from Bali?"

The nude pictures. "I remember."

"Well, they'd already been backed up to my hard drive. Automatic save and all that. I transferred them all to this USB. I didn't peek, and there are no other copies." He puts the memory stick in my hand, closing my fingers around them. "Yours to do exactly what you want with."

My hand tightens around the memory stick, a flood of emotions threatening to drown me. Perhaps Rhys sees that, because he presses a kiss to my temple, his hand curving around my waist. "I'm on your side, Ives. No one else's."

"Okay."

"And I'll never lie to you again. I want to be so honest it tears me apart."

I can't help but laugh at that, looking up at him. "We're back to violent metaphors?"

"Seems like it," he murmurs, bending his lips to my ear. "As much as I want to get out of here, I think we've misplaced our siblings somewhere."

Grinning, I slide the memory stick into my handbag and take his hand in mine. He grips mine back firmly, pushing the door open with his free hand. "After you."

27

RHYS

"Did you grab this from my apartment?" I ask, holding up the old paperback.

Ivy untangles her legs from the blanket, reaching for the pre-loved book. "Yes, and I'm enjoying it so far."

"You'll hate it when you get to—"

"Don't you dare," she says, holding up a finger to my lips. "Not again."

I grin beneath her finger. "I really thought you'd read the other one before."

"Yes, well, I hadn't."

"I'll be quiet this time," I promise, sinking down on the couch beside her. She tucks a leg over mine and opens the book again, finding her spot easily. She dog-ears books, and I don't. One of the many things we'd discussed over the last two months. One of a hundred debates, many started just for the heck of it. More than one had ended passionately.

I reach for my own manuscript, a novel one of my editors had sent along to me. *Think this one could be big,* she'd written. And so far I'm inclined to agree.

My hand traces lazy circles on Ivy's leg as we read. Spending weekends like this has become increasingly common, something of a ritual. Wake up late and languorously in bed. Argue about which piece of the morning newspaper we read. Argue over how we take our coffee.

And then read until the sun is high in the sky.

This weekend is different, being back in Paradise Shores, but our routine still holds true.

"I got my first new shoot," Ivy says, flipping over a page. "Did I tell you?"

I put the manuscript down. "No, you didn't."

"Checked my email earlier, and it was there, waiting for me. I'm booked for a toothpaste ad." To punctuate her words, she shoots me a wide, white-toothed smile.

"Ivy, that's awesome." The new agency she's recently signed with is far smaller than Star Models, but they respect her studies and let her have a say in what she works on.

"You don't have to lie," she teases. "I know it's commercial."

"Hey, toothpaste needs to be sold. It's a public good. In fact, the more people you can encourage to buy it, the better."

She laughs. "Yes, I'm doing people a favor."

I fit my hand to the crook of her waist, my favorite place to grip. "Congrats, Ivy."

"Thank you."

"I want to shoot you one of these days, by the way."

Her grin flashes again. "Don't say that when we're in public."

"Funny."

"You shoot me all the time?"

"Not enough. Can't believe I'm saying this either, but I'd love to shoot you for a big campaign again. Something of our choosing, this time."

"We can shoot later today, if you want." The light filtering in through the curtains of Lily's seaside cottage gilds her blonde hair, natural and tousled, and dances across the freckles on her nose.

"I'd like to photograph you on the sailing boat." I slide my hand higher, running fingers over her cheek. "The pictures from a few days ago came out really well."

I'd used my old Canon, with natural grainy texture and a higher contrast ratio. She'd sat in my apartment, on the windowsill, and I'd caught her and New York beyond. Her eyes drift closed as my fingers move to tangle through her hair, loose and wild. "I haven't told you what I've done with the pictures you took of me in Bali."

"No, you haven't."

"I didn't delete them."

My fingers still. "No?"

"The USB is in the safety deposit box in my apartment. I looked through all the pictures the other day, after you dropped me off at home."

"What did you think?"

She tosses the book on the sofa table and swings her legs off my lap. The blanket slips from her body as she dances into the space between the two armchairs. The silken fabric of the slip she'd slept in flows like water over her lithe form.

"And we're going to do it again, one day."

I raise an eyebrow. "Really?"

"Yes."

A few clicks on her phone and soft music fills the space. She spins slowly, in front of me, her eyes closing. Every line of her body swaying in tune to the music.

Still watching her, I reach for my old Canon, lying on the sofa table.

A soft smile settles on Ivy's face as she dances, arms stretched wide and above her head, twirling on the linen rug. It's easy to see the dancer she could have been.

The model she is.

And the woman she's becoming.

I take a few pictures of her moving, the calm settling through my body. There's something about capturing the world on film that has always made sense to me.

"What are we doing today?" she asks, hips flowing from

side to side in tune with the music. The easy smile on her face doesn't falter. "Besides dinner with Parker, Lily and Hayden?"

"Anything we like." I put my camera down, motioning for her to come closer. She does, hips still swaying, and laughs when I catch her around the waist. Her legs settle on either side of me. "Have I told you recently how much I like you?"

Her eyes glitter. "Yes, but you're welcome to tell me again."

I press my lips to the smooth skin of her neck. Dressed in nothing but the silk slip, there's plenty of it on display. "I like you," I murmur, moving down her collarbone. Teasing the spaghetti strap down her smooth shoulder.

"I like you too," she breathes, her fingers settling in my hair.

"A great deal, actually." My hands tighten on her hips, keeping her in place. Meeting her earnest, beautiful gaze with my own. "I might even be in love with you."

A soft smile breaks across her dear face. "You love me?"

"I'm afraid so," I admit, catching her lips with mine. The kisses we exchange go on forever, soft and slow and so sweet they make my chest ache.

"I love you too," Ivy whispers. And I know I'll never see a more beautiful sight than that, her eyes shining with emotion. Emotion she's not afraid of me seeing, a trust that I've managed to rebuild. It's the greatest gift I've ever been given.

She laughs when I stand with her in my arms, all the way to the bedroom, where the sound turns breathless and hot.

It's a long time until we speak again, and when we do, the silk slip she wore is discarded on the floor. She's draped across my chest, my fingers trailing her spine.

"Ivy," I murmur.

"Yes?"

"I was thinking of speaking to my father today."

She looks up at me. "Really?"

"Yes."

"How come?"

I consider that. It's a good question. "Somewhere over the past months, my anger has... I don't know. Not disappeared, perhaps, but shifted. It doesn't do me any good. He is what he is. I am what I am. Talking to him doesn't mean I give in, or that his pride is bigger than mine." I shrug, running a hand through her hair again. "You were the one who said a planned rebellion was an oxymoron."

She smiles, slightly abashed. "I did say that."

"And you were right."

"Do you want me to be there? I will, if you want me to."

I press a kiss to her temple. "Yes. Thank you."

This time, I can't see her smile, but I feel it against my skin. It's a wondrous thing, to be in love with your best friend, and to have her love you back.

We drive to my parents' house in the old Mustang I'd bought over a decade earlier, when I'd still been a teenager with my head deep in Bukowski and parties and entitlement. It feels aged now, but appropriately so.

The giant house is as it's always been, and yet subtly different. Autumn leaves litter the lawn, a sign that the gardener hasn't been there for a few days. There's no Atlas running out to meet us, and though it's been more than a decade since the dog died, I still expect it. Memories interpose on one another to form a kaleidoscope, a mirage, years past and hence blending.

"You okay?" she murmurs, her fingers gripping mine tightly.

"Yes."

My mother is delighted with our visit. It's the first time we're back since my father's party, and she takes the opportunity to show Ivy around. More than anything, I think she's happy I'm in a relationship. She's mentioned my lack of one more than once before.

"Your father's on the back porch," she tells me.

I wonder if she knows, somehow, what I'm here for. If she

suspects, or if she's just letting me know so I can better avoid him. No matter. "Thank you," I tell her.

As she retreats with Ivy, I hear her voice as it trails off. "Of all my children, Rhys is most similar to his father. Now, my youngest, she has…"

I carry the offhand comment with me as I walk through the kitchen and out to the back porch. For so long, I'd wanted to be nothing like him. Determined to make my own path.

Like he had, once. His arguments with my grandfather are the stuff of family legend.

Dad's reading his newspapers in the same chair he's claimed for near on two decades with the ocean as his only companion. The button-down is rumpled, boat shoes on his feet. Face settled into a familiar scowl.

I lean across the porch railing beside his seat, eyes focused on the ocean beyond. "Hey, Dad."

It takes him a few moments. The sound of a newspaper behind neatly folded and set down on the table.

"Rhys," he says.

I nod toward the waves. "It's calm out."

"It is, yes."

"I think I'll take the boat out later."

A cleared throat. "You should. Take that girl of yours with you, too."

"I plan on it."

He rises from his seat and comes to stand beside me on the porch. A few inches shorter than me, but wider across the chest. We're silent as we both watch the waves beat against the shoreline.

"Remember when I taught you to sail?" he asks. His voice is low, cautious. An echo of mine.

"Henry taught me to sail."

His laughter is genuine. "Ah, but who taught Henry?"

My lips curve despite myself. He might always have been an asshole, but then, he's always owned it.

"Your mother bought your latest book. The one with all the photographs, that your publishing company released."

It's an unexpected comment. I nod, glancing over at him. He's still looking at the ocean. "What did you think?"

"It's good. I don't have an eye for that sort of thing, but…" He nods. "It was good."

It's more than I expected. Reluctant, faint praise, but praise nonetheless, and there's not a sneer in sight. Perhaps he had been anxious for this conversation, too. For us to talk without intermediaries.

"I'm thinking of making Lily an offer for the beach cottage."

He turns to me fully then, and there's true surprise in his dark eyes. "You are?"

"Figured I should have a place out here of my own."

Dad nods, deep in thought. "Well, she'll give you a good deal for it."

"She better."

We share a laugh, short and perfunctory, and the first in more years than I can count. He gives me one last, long look, appraising. Then he shrugs, a reluctant smile on his face. "Well," he says. "Perhaps I should meet this girl of yours again, Rhys. Seems like she's had a bit of an influence on you."

EPILOGUE
IVY

A year later

"They looked happy."

"They looked like they needed a solid week of sleep." Rhys shrugs out of his jacket, hanging it on the peg in the hallway.

I make a beeline past him for the kitchen. "Do you want tea?"

"Not tonight, thanks."

I turn on the electric kettle and reach for my box of herbal teas. "Let's just say they looked good *and* like they needed a week of sleep," I compromise. "I feel bad for all of them, Hazel included. It must be tough not to be able to sleep through the night."

Rhys comes up behind me, wrapping his arms around my waist. "Poor thing," he says of his niece. "But judging from the glow in their eyes, she has them wrapped thoroughly around her little finger."

I lean back into his warmth. "She is the most adorable little baby."

"Almost makes you want one yourself."

"Almost?"

Rhys gives an affirmative hum, pressing his lips to my neck. "Almost," he confirms.

I smile as I pour my cup of tea. Having children is a topic we've been speaking a lot about lately, just as we do about everything. Debating and compromising and discussing. Meeting Henry and Faye's little daughter never fails to reignite the debate, although truth is, neither of us want children yet. But the idea is fun to play around with.

Rhys presses a last kiss to my neck, his hands smoothing over my hips as he releases me. "Did you pack your fitness bands?"

"No, shoot. Thanks for reminding me."

I head into the living room and past our open suitcases. The one thing I needed and I'd of course forgotten... Rhys sinks down on the couch and watches as I fold the three fitness bands, all in varying strengths.

"So neat," he teases.

"A cluttered suitcase, a cluttered mind."

He grins. "You know it won't stay that way."

"No, but I'll never give up trying." I run my hand over the workout clothes I've packed for the trip. All there, and now so are my fitness bands. My yoga mat is already rolled up tight and stowed at the bottom.

"Thanks for helping me with this, by the way," I tell him.

"You know I love shooting your workout videos."

I give him a withering look. "Yes, so you can try to make me lose focus." I'd lost track of the things he did behind the camera to make me break.

He laughs, stretching out long legs on the coffee table. "It's my favorite sport."

"I thought that was sailing." But I'm smiling as I stand, inspecting my suitcase. "And you got all your camera equipment?"

"All packed," he confirms. "Now come here."

I sit down beside him and he pulls me close, an arm

around my shoulders. He's warm through the fabric of his linen shirt and I put my palm flat on his chest, the familiar strength beneath it comforting. "I'm so excited."

There's a smile in Rhys's voice. "I'm glad."

"An entire month."

"An entire month," he repeats. "The hike will be the best part."

"I can't wait." We're set for a four day trek to Machu Picchu, hitting the Peruvian trail with two of his friends. It's just one of all the amazing things planned for our South American adventure, but it's the one I'm the most excited for. Well, the fact that Penny and Jason are joining us for the final week is pretty awesome, too.

Both of us can work while we're there. Rhys will be shooting for a prestigious new photography exhibition he's been asked to contribute to, one of only twelve photographers chosen. And while we travel, I can shoot more workout videos for my social media channels with the mountains as the backdrop.

It's a project that makes me excited to my core. The past couple of months, I've started using my social media presence as a resource to share information on health, nutrition and exercise. Using my physical therapy degree to inform and explain, focusing on wellness rather than beauty. Rhys has been my biggest supporter, and not once has he snorted or laughed when I've asked him to help me.

He wraps his other arm around me and I lift a leg over his, settling in at his side. "Is it possible to have wanderlust and travel nerves at the same time?" I ask.

"Yes. Are you feeling both?"

"Most definitely."

His hand trails down my back. "I might admit to feeling some of that myself."

I press a kiss to his shoulder. Flying still isn't his thing and I doubt it ever will be. And yet, he gets on a plane time and time again, knowing that the reward outweighs the discomfort. He'd laughed when I'd told him he was incredible for that. Inspiring, even. But it was true.

"Do you remember our first trip together?"

He smiles. "Of course I do. I'm still grateful you forgave me for the whole thing."

"The trip itself was amazing. The waterfall?"

His hand slips under my shirt to curve around my hip. "We'll go back there one day."

"I'd love that," I murmur, closing my eyes.

"We could go back to all the places we visited. Spend a week in each, at least. Explore them thoroughly." His hand tightens over my skin. "Revisit the memories."

"That sounds like a dream."

"Making dreams into reality is what I do best," he teases.

"You're joking, but I think that's definitely one of your talents," I tell him. Not only does he pursue his own without fear, but he keeps encouraging me to do the same.

To say no to modeling gigs I don't approve of, or to carve out my own unique career path. There's still much to be decided in our life. Where we'll live, instead of our current shuffle back and forth between our two apartments. What kind of life we'll lead. A quiet family life in Paradise Shores or a life on the road, seeing the world.

But I know that every step of the way I'll have Rhys, and he'll have me. Keeping me honest. Loving me and allowing me to love in return. A person to grow and evolve with, to challenge and support me. Breathing in the comforting scent of him, I know now that's the greatest adventure of them all.

THE STORY CONTINUES

The Marchand family returns in the fourth and final book in the series, following Parker Marchand.

He's running the town's yacht club and hires a new waitress, only to discover she's not new at all. It's Jamie, his sister's best friend from childhood. She's finally returned to Paradise…

Read on for the first chapter!

CHAPTER ONE
JAMIE

Paradise Shores looks the way it always has. I don't know if that makes me feel better or worse, that the town I grew up in is unchanged, when I so clearly am not. On some days it feels like a relief. On others a personal attack. Today? It's nerve-wracking.

I've been standing outside the Paradise Shores Yacht Club for ten minutes. My bike is locked. I have my bag. And I can't make my feet move.

The yacht club is an emblem for the town, an institution. My friends and I used to buy their famous lobster rolls and eat them on the docks in the marina, beneath the hot summer sun. The building looks unchanged from the outside. The smooth wooden slats of its roof are the same. So are the steps up to the front door. The giant anchor resting in the flowerbed.

One day of working here and the news will be out. *Jamie's back in town after a decade away.*

I desperately hope no one will care.

But I already know that's not true. My best friend moved back to Paradise a few years ago, and I haven't told her I've followed suit. Only my mom knows I'm back, and that's because I'm staying with her.

Showing up at her doorstep had been *mildly* embarrassing. But not, perhaps, as embarrassing as this. I have a job.

As a waitress at the yacht club.

I take a deep breath. And then another one. I'd been lucky to see the posting, to get this job. So I swallow my pride and walk up the steps. The yacht club has a new coat of paint, navy, and it sits overlooking the Paradise Shores marina. Row after row of sailboats and yachts lie anchored at the docks. The ocean rocks them all gently.

For years, I saw this view every day.

And for years, I didn't see it at all.

The yacht club is empty when I step inside. It's early, and the first round of sailing classes should already be out at sea. So I head toward the back office and see Neil, sitting at his desk. He's still in charge of the marina.

He sees me and gives a wave. "Hello, there."

"Hi. I'm Jamie Moraine? The new waitress?"

He runs a hand over his balding head. *Well, that's new.* "Of course! Welcome, welcome. We spoke on the phone. Thanks for coming in on such short notice."

"Thanks for having me," I say.

"Come, let me introduce you to Stephen. He's head of the waitstaff. He should have arrived by now…" Neil closes the door to the office and walks me through the lobby, past tasteful nautical decor. There are gold-framed paintings of boats at sea on the walls and in a corner is a giant statue made out of boating rope.

The place looks much better than I remember. Fresh coat of cream paint on the wainscoting and a deep blue on the walls.

"All settled in to Paradise?" Neil asks.

He had been a sailing instructor when I was young, and then head of the marina. Not surprised he doesn't remember me. I was never one for sailing.

"Yes, thanks."

The man named Stephen is wiping down a set of menus,

splayed out on a wooden table. "You're Jamie?" he asks without looking up. He might be in his forties, tall and gangly, with a mustache.

"Yes," I say, feeling underdressed. His pristine waiter's uniform doesn't fit with my sundress.

"Good, you're right on time." He hands me the rag. "Continue wiping these down while I get you your uniform."

He disappears through the staff door.

Neil snorts by my side. "He's good folk, once you get to know him."

I start wiping down the laminated menus. "I'm sure he is."

"The place looks good, doesn't it? What do you think?"

"Yes, it does," I say.

"The new boss renovated it in the off-season. The kitchen has all brand-new appliances, looks like a damn spaceship in there. These are new hardwood floors, too."

"It looks good," I say, and I mean it. Gone is the old wallpaper, yellowed after previous decades with indoor smoking allowed.

Spending the summers waitressing at the yacht club had been a rite of passage when I was a teenager. The cool girls from Paradise High did it, while the cool guys would teach sailing lessons down on the docks.

My best friend and I had stayed far away from the marina those summers.

"Well, Stephen'll take good care of you," Neil says.

And I have to give it to them, Stephen does. He tells me to tuck my shirt into my pencil skirt and makes me recite the specials on the board. It wouldn't be rocket science to a new waitress, and I've done this on and off for years.

But I understand just why he gave me such a thorough introduction during lunch. I've just served a family of six, the youngest child in that wonderful babbling age, when he stops me.

"They'll be here at four," he says in sotto voce.

"They?"

"The owner and the new chefs he's interviewing."

Now it makes sense. "Is he here a lot?"

Stephen nods. "And he always has opinions."

I bet he does, I think. The world would be a lot nicer if people stopped having so many.

The rest of the lunch service is calm. I do what I've always done, take orders and deliver food. Some ask me if I'm new, and I answer yes. I don't make much small talk.

I need the tips, but I don't have the energy.

Two young waitresses work beside me. It's clearly their summer job, and they like to whisper amongst themselves by the window, close to the heat lamp. They look like my best friend and I did at the age. Bright and happy and sharing every last thing that happens, like they're living one shared life instead of two.

It's a miracle that I don't run into anyone I know. Not an old elementary school teacher or an old classmate, and not the girl *I'd* once shared every last thing with. Lily Marchand and I haven't spoken in years, and it's entirely my fault.

It's a reunion I dread.

As the lunch service draws to a close, I watch Stephen set up a table in the corner with extra care. It doesn't take a genius to figure out it's where the owner will interview new chefs… and they'll be able to oversee the waitstaff at the same time. Isn't that just lovely?

I have one table left to wait before my shift ends. Three middle-aged men on their second round of beer, all talking louder than necessary. I've just cleared away their plates—club sandwiches, extra mayo—when Stephen stops me.

"They're here," he says with a subtle nod to the corner.

"The owner?"

"Yes. He's interviewing the first potential new chef now."

I peer around the corner at the two men shaking hands. I can't make out either of them at this distance.

So I take another lap around the room, eyes shifting over

the few guests that remain. Lunch has always been the yacht club's most popular time. People across Paradise Shores come by, often to eat before heading out on their boats. We're in May still, but come June and July, this place will be packed.

"Sweetheart!" someone calls. "Get us another round of beers, will you?"

Me?

I turn to the table with the extra mayo men. The guy who's spoken has gray at the temples, a crooked grin on his face. His eyes travel over my uniform and pause at my chest, right where the white shirt fits a bit too snug.

Anger rolls over me, tempered by a fear I hate. A fear I can't shake. So I zero in on the empty glasses at the table, speaking to them rather than the men. "Coming right up," I say, leaning past him to grab them.

A clammy hand curves around my bare thigh and slides up, under my skirt.

"Good girl," the man says. "You new around here?"

I take two steps back and away from the grip.

My heart pounds in my ears.

"Welcome to town," he says, like he didn't just touch me, and his smile widens.

I'm frozen to the spot, shame heating up my skin.

A man steps past me and puts a firm hand on the creep's shoulder. "John," he says. "I'm going to insist that you settle your bill and leave. Right away."

The voice is familiar. I stare at the short, dark blond hair that curls over the tan neck, the broad back beneath a linen shirt. If I'd been frozen before, I'm boiling now. Embarrassment crawls its way up my cheeks.

"Marchand," the creep says. "How's it going?"

"Now, John."

He sighs and gets to his feet. "Sorry, fellas," he says. "I guess someone's in the mood to play bad cop."

"Settle your bill with Stephen," Parker says, because it has to be him. "And John? I don't want to see you here again."

John's eyes narrow. "You can't be serious."

"Dead serious," Parker says. I can't stop looking at him. It's Lily's older brother.

He has to be the new owner.

The other two men mumble something and rise from their seats, eyes downcast. The three make their way over to where Stephen is waiting.

John gives Parker one last glare. It's the sort of look that promises a strongly worded email in a few hours. *Coming to an inbox near you…*

Parker stares back at him without the grin I'd always associated with him. He'd been Paradise Shores' greatest sailor, Lily's older brother, one of the shining Marchand siblings.

I haven't seen him since I'd been twenty-two. He'd been a college athlete, with sun-bleached hair that fell over his forehead and a sorority girlfriend.

Now he must be thirty-four.

Parker doesn't turn to me until John is out of the restaurant. "I'm sorry. That should never have happened, but I can promise you that he won't bother you again."

He looks at me, eyes steady. Voice sincere. Tanned from the sun and grown, hardened, in a way he wasn't the last time I'd seen him.

He doesn't recognize me.

I don't know if the crushing feeling in my chest is relief or regret.

"If you'd like to file a report I will help you every step of the way." Parker ducks his head slightly and gives me a smile. It's polite and conspiratorial and something thumps painfully in my chest. "How does that sound? Let me give you the rest of the day off, too."

I shake my head. "No, I'm okay."

He pauses. Eyes pass over my face and down to where my nameplate rests. Stephen had made it with a little laminating machine and presented it to me with a flourish. *Jamie.*

Deep blue eyes return to me. He has new wrinkles at the corners from sun and sea. "Jamie? As in, Jamie Moraine?"

I nod. "Yes. Hi, Parker."

"Hell, it's been years! I didn't know you were back in town?"

My hands shake at my sides. He's going to tell Lily, I think. And Jesus, I *work* for him. Mortification makes my voice thin. "I just got here. Sorry, I shouldn't keep you."

"That's all right," he says, his smile turning into a frown when I start to back away. "So you work here?"

I give a few nods. "Yes, and I should get back to work. Good luck with your interviews."

He looks after me, a frown between his eyebrows. "Jamie," he says. But I'm already hurrying toward the kitchen.

I knew I wouldn't be able to escape the questions in Paradise Shores. Wouldn't be able to escape the past, the confrontations. If Parker knows, it's only a matter of time before Lily will too.

I avoid the table in the corner for the rest of my shift, but I can feel the weight of his gaze more than once. I finish up the last tasks. I fill up salt in the shakers on the table and wipe down the menus again.

And by the time my shift is done, the table in the corner is empty. Parker is gone.

"Thanks for today!" I tell Stephen and change in the staff room. Biking home in a skirt won't be possible. I sling my bag over my shoulder and step out through the back entrance, into the late-afternoon sun.

I can't wait to get home, to close my eyes and breathe. To count down the days until the paycheck arrives.

But there's someone waiting for me in the parking lot. There, leaning against his dusty Jeep, is Parker Marchand. And he's looking right at me.

OTHER BOOKS BY OLIVIA
LISTED IN READING ORDER

New York Billionaires Series

Think Outside the Boss
Tristan and Freddie

Saved by the Boss
Anthony and Summer

Say Yes to the Boss
Victor and Cecilia

A Ticking Time Boss
Carter and Audrey

Seattle Billionaires Series

Billion Dollar Enemy
Cole and Skye

Billion Dollar Beast
Nick and Blair

Billion Dollar Catch
Ethan and Bella

Billion Dollar Fiancé
Liam and Maddie

Brothers of Paradise Series

Rogue
Lily and Hayden

Ice Cold Boss
Faye and Henry

Red Hot Rebel
Ivy and Rhys

Small Town Hero
Jamie and Parker

Standalones

Arrogant Boss
Julian and Emily

Look But Don't Touch
Grant and Ada

The Billionaire Scrooge Next Door
Adam and Holly

ABOUT OLIVIA

Olivia loves billionaire heroes despite never having met one in person. Taking matters into her own hands, she creates them on the page instead. Stern, charming, cold or brooding, so far she's never met a (fictional) billionaire she didn't like.

Her favorite things include wide-shouldered heroes, late-night conversations, too-expensive wine and romances that lift you up.

Smart and sexy romance—those are her lead themes!

Join her newsletter for updates and bonus content.
www.oliviahayle.com.
Connect with Olivia

- facebook.com/authoroliviahayle
- instagram.com/oliviahayle
- goodreads.com/oliviahayle
- amazon.com/author/oliviahayle
- bookbub.com/profile/olivia-hayle

www.ingramcontent.com/pod-product-compliance
Ingram Content Group UK Ltd.
Pitfield, Milton Keynes, MK11 3LW, UK
UKHW041412020125
3930UKWH00037B/341

9 789198 793673